VANISHED IN PARADISE

PARADISE SERIES

BOOK 20

DEBORAH BROWN

VANISHED IN PARADISE
All Rights Reserved
Copyright © 2020 Deborah Brown

ISBN: 978-1-7334807-1-0

Cover: Natasha Brown

PRINTED IN THE UNITED STATES OF AMERICA

VANISHED IN PARADISE

Chapter One

Three loud knocks disturbed the silence of the sun-washed morning streaming through the open patio doors.

I looked up from where I sat on the couch, my cats, Jazz and Snow, asleep on my feet. The loud noise hadn't disturbed their nap, as neither opened an eye.

A cop knock at its best. And on my door. It wasn't my best friend, Fab, as she'd have picked the lock, knowing after a quick count of the cars that I was home alone. Besides, she had an early appointment to install a security system and would be gone for most of the day.

I got up and walked into the kitchen, pausing momentarily in front of the junk drawer and giving a brief thought to opening it and removing my Berretta. Deciding it was probably a workman and a firearm wasn't friendly, even if it wasn't pointed at someone's face, I opened the door. "How the heck did you get past the security gate and my fence?"

Casio Famosa stood on my doorstep, a stupid grin on his face. The Miami detective moved his overly large and muscled frame forward in an attempt to hug me. I stepped back. "Lucked out at the front gate and came in when the gardener drove out. Your fence — lockpick." He chuckled, holding it up before pocketing it. "I know you're familiar with how they work."

"I suppose, good manners and all, that I should invite you in." I continued to stand in the middle of the doorway.

"Maybe next time. I don't have time for niceties." Casio tugged on my hand, yanking me out the door and into the driveway.

My flip-flops barely touched the ground. "I fall and I'm shooting you."

Casio came to an abrupt halt and made sure I had both feet on the ground before he let go. "You know those IOUs you've strewn about like cheap confetti?"

"I take exception to your description," I said huffily. "I do no such thing."

Amongst my family and friends, we traded favors in the form of IOUs, which came with the understanding that there would be no whining when they were redeemed.

"Anyway, I have a few, and I'm here to cash them in." He whistled.

I rubbed the side of my head, wincing from the shrill sound. "Another reason to shoot you — if I go deaf."

"I'm also reminding you of your own words — not exact but close enough — that they come with a no-grumbling clause. I wouldn't want you to forget and feel bad." He smiled cheekily.

The doors of his SUV flew open, and four children piled out. My uneducated guess was that they ranged in age from pre-teen to kindergarten.

"Kids, this is the nice lady I told you about." He waved expansively to them and turned to me briefly. "I'm on a very important case, one that I've been working for a long time—a really big one. It means ridding the streets of drug-dealing vermin and making them safe for your children and mine." He crossed to the driver's door, jerked it open, took a large manila envelope off the dash, and thrust it at me.

"The problem with this conversation is that you know what you're talking about and I have no clue." I pointed to the kids. "Why are they unloading suitcases?"

"I'll only be gone a couple of days, week max, and before you know it, I'll be back to pick them up."

I felt like a deer caught in the headlights. "I don't know anything about kids," I said in a bit of a panic. "Cats, yes. Not kids."

"That works. Just treat them like two-footed furry things."

The oldest kid caught my attention. Leaning against the bumper, he had the same smirk on his face that I'd often seen on his father's. "Your son." I pointed. "Alejandro, I believe. Given that he had me arrested for kidnapping and hauled off to jail, aren't you the slightest bit worried I might leave him on the roadside to play in traffic?"

"Two reasons: you shouldn't hold a grudge, because that's unbecoming and old news, and he was a kid and still is." Casio turned to his son and bellowed, "Alex, an apology, please."

"I promised my dad not to have you arrested on bogus charges again. Or anyone else." He added the latter grudgingly, not looking happy.

I waited for a curtsy or something after that performance and got a tight-lipped expression. "Great apology," I mumbled.

As the three boys and one girl stood waiting patiently, you couldn't miss the resemblance to their father. They were lined up oldest to youngest, suitcases in hand, staring expectantly as though being dropped off at a stranger's house was normal.

"I can't do this," I said in a near-panic, realizing the man was serious. "I'm not qualified. What about your family? I heard somewhere that you have a bushelful of relates."

Fab and I had done work for his twin brother, smarmy Brick Famosa, in the past. The only difference, looks wise, was that Brick had a thick head of dark hair and Casio was shiny bald.

Casio tugged on the sleeve of my t-shirt, turning me away from the kids and lowering his voice. "I chose you to help because I know you're the best person to help me keep my promise to my dying wife." He took notice of my stricken expression and explained, "She died of cancer a year ago, and I swore that I wouldn't fuck them up. Besides, you can count on Alex to help with the others. He's the smartest of the bunch; takes after his old man." He beamed with pride. "If this wasn't such a big case... A couple of days to get these criminals locked up, and I'll be back. I told my kids that you're a longtime family friend, which is kind of the truth, and that you'll be a hell of a lot more fun than any of my kin, who already think I suck as a father. One went so far as to suggest that I give up my parental rights." That visibly angered him. "I did try Disney World, but they don't have a camping program." He winked.

"I don't want to be mean, and I do keep my promises, but staying with me is not a good idea. I'm sure your wife wouldn't approve of this cockamamie idea."

"That's where you're wrong. Celia came to me in a dream and suggested you," he said with a cagey smile.

"You're so full of it," I said. "Celia and I never even met."

"Please. I trust you with my kids and know that I won't have to worry." Casio grabbed my face in his hand, his brown eyes boring into mine. "You'd be doing your civic duty."

I didn't remember nodding, but I must have, as he patted me on the back.

"You're the best." Casio ran over to his kids and hugged and kissed each one, and then they did a group hug. "Be good. I'll be back in a couple of days." He got in his SUV, rolled down the window, and waved as he roared down the street.

I watched as he disappeared, thinking he'd turn around and come back, but the brake lights didn't even flicker. I turned to the kids, and we exchanged stares, none of us seemingly knowing what to do next.

"I'm Madison," I said, realizing there'd been no introductions. "I want to disclose up front that I have no kid experience and chances are high that I'll make mistakes. I apologize in advance." I struggled for an encouraging smile.

The youngest, the little girl, dropped her suitcase and ran over, arms out. I bent down and caught her in a hug. "My daddy tells us the same thing, and he does okay." She gave me a big kiss on the cheek. "I'm Liliana; everyone calls me Lili. My brothers are Cisco and Diego." The identical twins waved, not the least bit fazed by being dropped off. Alex stood next to them with his arms crossed, his expression cocky, waiting for me to… I wasn't sure.

I appreciated Lil's confidence but didn't share it.

Chapter Two

I herded the foursome into the house and offered cold drinks—water anyway, with or without fruit. They crowded into the living room, the three boys looking around, clearly not impressed. Lili spotted the cats, plopped down beside them on the couch, and combed their fur with her fingers.

"Where are we sleeping?" twin one or two asked. "We didn't bring our sleeping bags."

I smiled lamely.

Alex snorted. "That's because we've never camped."

The other twin piped up. "You're supposed to be fun. Because Disney World is closed."

Alex laughed at me. He must have known before leaving the house that his siblings had been conned, but he obviously hadn't outed his dad.

"If you'd give me a few minutes to conjure up some fun, I'm sure I can come up with something." I tried not to be snappish, but it was hard to think up some entertainment while staring at their disappointed faces.

I looked around the beach hideaway that my

husband, Creole, had renovated from top to bottom, knocking out all the walls and turning it into a large, open living space. It had a large bathroom, but still only one, and our little house was never meant for six people. I gasped out loud, which had the boys looking at me expectantly. I faked a smile. When Creole got home and found out we were suddenly responsible for four kids… I didn't even want to imagine his response.

I grabbed my phone off the coffee table and went into the kitchen, sliding onto a stool at the island and called Macklin Lane, aka Mac, the manager of the beach rental property I owned. I took a deep breath, waiting for her to answer. When she did, I skipped the niceties. "Is cottage one available?" I asked, my harried tone coming across the line.

"What's going on?"

I took that as a yes; otherwise, I'd have gotten a lengthy description of the current inhabitants as she ran down the oddities of whoever occupied the unit. "It's off the market until I give the okay." I struggled to remember the exact layout. "I'll need a rollaway in one of the bedrooms and one in the living room." I ignored her question; she'd never believe the truth. Or maybe she would and then subject me to a litany of questions. "I'll be there in a half-hour." I hung up. "We're changing locations so we have more room," I told the kids as I went into the closet and packed an overnight bag, throwing in things for Creole… if he didn't leave me.

"Okay, let's get in the car." I shepherded them outside and opened the liftgate of my Hummer, leaving Alex to load the suitcases as I ran back in the house for beach towels and a few other linens. I didn't have much of a selection, as I had barely replaced anything after my house caught fire. Although it didn't burn to the ground, I'd lost the entire contents. I locked up the house and ran back to my SUV, impressed to find that they'd all gotten in, fastened their seatbelts, and were occupied on their phones. "Did you bring bathing suits?" I got a chorus of yeses in response. Good, because the pool and beach were on the top of my fun list.

I drove out of the "compound," as it had been affectionately named after Fab and Didier moved into the manse at the other end of the street. As a wedding gift, her papa, Caspian, had bought the rest of the block. He'd put up security fencing and secured the entrance, which worked unless someone driving in or out let another person in. Another item for my list of things to do—tell Fab to put a bug in the gardener's and pool dude's ears to stop letting people in. My mind going a mile a minute, I called Mac back.

"If it isn't Mrs. Friendly," she grouched.

"Have I told you lately that you're the best employee ever?" I struggled to sound sweet and not harassed. "Trust me, friend, it will become crystal clear once I get there. Maybe not without a bit of explanation, and then…" Da-da-da in my tone. "I need someone to run errands. If you're not interested, can you sign up Rude?"

Gertrude Banner and her someday-husband, Cootie Shine, had moved to The Cottages when they were booted out of the mangroves for squatting. I'd hired them to work on another project, and when that didn't work out, I suggested that they move to The Cottages. Rude had signed on as Events Coordinator, and her gigs had rapidly become a favorite with guests and others in the neighborhood. Cootie had also become a favorite once it was discovered he was an adept handyman and didn't charge a limb.

"You know me; whatever it is, I can get it handled," Mac said, and we hung up.

I could feel Alex's eyes on me. He sat in the passenger seat, the rest relegated to the back. I glanced over. "What?"

"Where are we going?" he demanded, replicating one of his father's more irritating tones.

"I own a beachfront property not far from here. The waterfront unit was open, and you'll find there's more room there. Not a lot, but no one has to sleep on the floor. And there will be entertainment." At his raised eyebrow, I added, "Water toys, and there's a basketball court."

"We don't play basketball."

I thought, *Fine, don't play*, but kept that to

myself. "What about school?" I asked.

"We've got two weeks of homework assignments in our bags that need to be handed in when we get back."

Two weeks? I stopped myself from squealing. "How about…" I stalled. "School in the morning, outside by the pool, and in the afternoon, I come up with some A-rated activity?" Okay, that was possibly overhyping my abilities, and judging by the smirk on Alex's face, he agreed with my unspoken thought. "You know we're all doing our part for our country. Okay, that's overselling it, but I'm hoping you'll be somewhat cooperative and ensure I don't fall on my face. Or do I need to remind you that you owe me?" Yeesh, I sounded like his father.

"Yeah, yeah, got it. I already promised my dad I wouldn't be a dick kid."

I flinched, recovering when I saw his huge smile.

Thanks to green lights and light traffic, it wasn't long before I turned off the highway, around a corner, and into the driveway of the ten-unit u-shaped property I owned. I bypassed the office and parked to one side of the cottage we'd be occupying for the next several days… and hopefully not weeks. Mac and Rude came out of the office and were halfway down the driveway when the kids all piled out. The two women stopped and stared.

Now that the two middle-aged women had

become hot friends, they tended to dress alike, although the outfits looked different on the voluptuous Mac and stick-thin Rude. Today was workout gear and light-up tennis shoes.

I wondered what activity was scheduled for the day. I'd been afraid to ask what Rude had come up with after I'd had to pull Mac aside and ask that she put an end to both goat and nude yoga. That didn't go over well with her.

"Don't think I don't know what you're doing," Mac huffed. *"You want me to be the killjoy and tell Rude. I don't know why you can't hold your shorts until the cops get called. Then we mop up and move on."*

"The nudity and defecating animals are too much for me," I whined, getting no sympathy, only a scowl.

"You have the keys?" I yelled down the driveway. Mac nodded. "You're in time to help us carry everything inside."

"No kids allowed," Mac said, "per the owner."

My phone rang, and I recognized the ringtone and hung back as Mac and Rude led the parade, Rude talking a mile a minute. "Hi, hon," I said.

"I thought we'd go out to dinner," Creole said.

"Something's come up, and I need to you to come by The Cottages so I can explain."

"Someone die?" he asked.

"Thankfully, no cop action today." I laughed hesitantly, weighing whether to blurt everything out and squirming at the thought.

"Are you sure you're okay?"

"It's been a long day, and I could use a hug."

"I'll be there soon."

The kids were hungry. After a vote, it was decided that Mac would make a hamburger run. Rude got with Alex and made a grocery list for snacks and breakfast.

"Pizza for dinner?" I asked, and all hands shot in the air. "Get in your bathing suits. When lunch gets here, we'll eat it out by the pool, then go swimming." They were all happy with that idea. I left Rude with the kids and went to bang on Crum's door.

"You're the rudest knocker," the retired professor grouched when he opened the door, white hair sticking on end.

He had on a pair of normal-looking shorts that weren't skin-tight, which was a pleasant surprise. "I have a convoluted plan to pitch you. But right now, I need a lifeguard for four children."

"Children?" He grumbled under his breath and looked around. "What's in it for me?"

"Not the kindness of your heart, apparently." He mumbled something. "I plan on pitching an all-encompassing deal that will please your larcenous heart. I'm not making individual deals that I have to keep track of. Are you in?"

"Sure, why not? I don't have anything better to do today."

"You need to clear your calendar for at least a week. No trotting around in your tighty-whities or that speedo thing I've seen you wear. Your current attire will work." I eyed the bedraggled shorts, which on closer inspection didn't fit at all, as evidenced by the two safety pins at the waist.

Looking at him, you'd never guess that he retired from an acclaimed private college in California and came highly recommended. I'd verified his employment myself, and the woman on the phone had been effusive in her praise of the man.

"I need you now. It includes lunch, and meals for the rest of the week will be part of our agreement."

"Uh-huh." Not believing me, Crum shot me a hard stare, which I returned. "I need to get a bathing suit on." He shut the door.

I called Mac over and had her add to the order. We generally over-ordered for everything, and I figured she would on her own but didn't want to chance it. I waved and made my way over to the cottage to change.

The kids had claimed one of the bedrooms and changed into their bathing suits. Alex had brought in the beach towels, and each kid had grabbed one. I hurried to put on my bathing suit and led the kids over to the pool area.

Relieved to see that Crum owned a suitable bathing suit, I introduced the kids to the man, and he took over, firing questions, demanding to know if they could swim, and insisting on a demonstration. They shrugged off his abrasiveness and jumped in the pool to do what he asked without complaint.

After the first awkwardness, the day got better. The kids were having a good time, and when lunch arrived, they climbed out of the pool to eat. Crum engaged them in several games of poker before they jumped back in. It surprised me that they all knew how to play cards, including Lili.

I dragged a chair to the pool's edge and sat down, motioning for Mac to join me. Rude thought that included her, and I didn't say anything, figuring I'd need her help and why repeat myself? I told them what had happened and swore them to secrecy. Then ran my plan for Crum by Mac. She approved, and I told her she was in charge of keeping an eye on the professor.

My phone rang, and I looked at the screen, smiling at Creole's picture. "Where are you?" he asked.

"I'm at the pool. Wait where you're at, and I'll come and meet you." I jumped up and, before heading to the gate, paused to tell Mac, "Be right back." I'd barely got the gate open when Creole was standing in front of me and swooping in for a kiss.

It took me a minute to realize that the kids, who'd taken another break from the water and were again playing cards with Crum, had gotten suddenly quiet.

"I have something to tell you," I said. "We

should go somewhere else." I put my hand on his chest, encouraging him to back up.

"No running," Mac yelled.

I turned, and Lili was coming at me full-speed, crying. I held out my arms and caught her up. "Diego told me I was ugly and stole my cards."

I didn't know one twin from the other. Since they were sitting together, I glared at them equally. "Rule number one: no making your sister cry."

"That's a stupid rule," one of them said.

"Too bad." I hugged Lili.

Creole reached over and brushed her tears away. "Brothers are a pain, and you'll just have to learn how to manipulate them. I'm certain my wife can give you a tip or two. She has a brother, and I've heard stories."

Lili laughed. "Are you friends with my daddy?" She held her arms out to Creole, and he didn't hesitate to take her.

"Who's your daddy?" Creole looked around.

"Casio Famosa," I said.

He again scanned the pool area, this time checking the corners and any place a person could drop out of sight. There was only one place — the tiki bar — and the area was empty.

"Daddy's not here," Lili told him. "He's saving the world. But he promised to be back soon."

"And those are your brothers?" Creole asked, and she nodded. He waved to them, laughing and moving Lili to his shoulders.

"Please don't divorce me," I said pitifully.

He laughed again. "Once this is all sorted out and I get the details, you're going to school to learn how to say no."

It was widely known that I had a hard time telling people no, but truly, I'd gotten better. If it hadn't been for the IOUs and the four sets of eyes staring at me, I might've figured out a way to say forget it and mean it.

Creole walked Lilli back over to where her brothers sat and smoothed the waters between the siblings. Soon, they were all laughing again. He turned to me, said, "Fill me in," and walked me over to the bar, where we slid onto stools.

I told him about Casio's visit, pleading my case about how I'd been caught off guard. When I finished, he laughed. "That's so mean." I pouted.

"This should be an interesting few days."

"You're not leaving me?"

"Heck no." He swept me up into a kiss.

Creole turned out to be the hit of the evening. He changed into swim trunks and orchestrated the activities—pool games, pizza, and more horseplay—until the kids walked back to the cottage, asleep on their feet.

Chapter Three

The next morning, I'd just finished my coffee when Fab kicked open the gate to the pool and stormed through it like a wild wind. The sexy French woman's blue eyes had me in their sights as she marched over. "I'm out of the loop for one day." She held up her finger. "One day. And you move. Here?"

The gate banged against itself and slammed shut, making me jump. I looked up from my laptop as Fab threw herself into the chair next to mine. So much for getting my life completely organized for the next week. "What?"

"Don't even deny it. Creole told me. And another thing—he wouldn't tell me where you moved to, and I had to track you down."

I'd joked with Creole, when he left to go to the jobsite, that he could be the one to tell Fab about Casio's visit and that we'd be staying at The Cottages for probably a week. He'd laughed but agreed. Now, I was thinking that was a bad idea. "Sorry," I said when she growled. "I have no clue what he told you, but I'm thinking it was probably not a lie but misleading." Or he'd lied, if he'd told her we moved.

"He informed me that the two of you packed up because you needed more room. If that's true, why here? Your house in danger of sliding off the foundation and into the water?"

"I'd like a larger house so I could entertain my family without being crowded, but being here has nothing to do with that," I said.

Fab humphed. She jumped up and dragged over another chair so she could put her feet up. She'd calmed down and looked around the pool area, her eyes falling on the large round table with the open thatched umbrella. "What's with the kids? And who'd leave their children with Crum?"

I kicked her leg. "Ssh." Then I told her everything that had happened the previous day, not leaving out a single detail. Before I was finished, she'd kicked back in shock, staring between me and the kids.

"If I'd been here—"

I cut her off. "You'd have done what, exactly?"

"Helped you unload their suitcases," Fab said after a long sigh.

I stood. "Come on, I'll introduce you."

"Didn't the oldest have you arrested? I'm steering clear of him." Fab gave Alex the evil eye. Thankfully, he wasn't paying attention.

"One of those jobs that should've gone to you. So, you owe me, and I'm collecting." I laughed at her frown, waiting for her to say, *I don't remember*, when I knew she did. "One more thing…" I stepped in front of her, forcing her to stop. "No scaring the kids. They're well-behaved, so you won't have provocation."

"What if Casio doesn't come—"

"Don't say it. Because that would mean…" He'd be back because he'd promised. I turned and walked over to Crum and the kids. "Good morning, Professor." I smiled at him, then introduced Fab to the kids.

"We're getting all our school work done today," Alex said. "The prof said it's all drivel and busy work and there's more interesting stuff to learn."

I'd worked it out with Crum to homeschool the kids. I'd thought I'd have to do some major arm-twisting, but to my surprise, he readily agreed. The idea clearly appealed to him. He liked it even better that he could hold class at the pool.

I shot him a one-eyed stare. "This afternoon, we're going to the beach."

Yays all around, so that met with approval.

Fab and I walked away with a wave. I kicked off my flip-flops and sat on the edge of the pool, sticking my feet in the water. Fab slipped out of her sandals and sat next to me. "Am I going to have to find a new partner?"

"I'll be available once I get the kids' week planned," I said.

"Why doesn't it surprise me that you're in planning mode?"

"I'm thinking I'll be available starting tomorrow. They'll spend mornings with Crum, and I'll have an activity planned for each afternoon."

"So, you're going to be like a working parent that isn't really a parent?" Fab squinted at me.

"Pretty much."

The pool gate opened, and Mac came in and joined us poolside. "I've got some good gossip. Having you here saves me a phone call."

"Please tell me that no tenant or guest has wandered into the street drunk," I said. "You need to put the word out that everyone could at least try to be on their best behavior."

The rule was to rent to guests only, no regular tenants, but a few had slipped in or were snuck in, and I didn't boot anyone unless the cops showed up.

"The apartment building next door is for sale. That tidbit is on the hush, and I haven't found out why. The current owner, Horace Blaine, got himself a second wife young enough to be his granddaughter, and it's rumored that she's behind the sale," Mac said, clearly proud of finding out the information.

"Didn't the original Mrs. Blaine die, like, a month ago?" I asked.

"The new one swooped in, whisked him off to Las Vegas, and they came back wedded. The bliss part remains to be seen. No more Horace for him; he's now Ace, although sometimes he forgets. Anyway, the old man introduced me and Rude, and the wifey gave me one of these." Mac gave me a snooty head-to-toe once-over. "Turned up her nose and wiggled away. Ace had a stupid smile on his face, so you know what he's getting plenty of."

"He will as long as the new missus gets what she wants," Fab said. "I know the type. I haven't met her, but I bet she fits the mold to a tee."

"Sorry to see Ace go because he doesn't rent to criminals; the crazies can't be helped. There *is* pee-er guy, but his stream can't reach my property, so I haven't made a big deal about it," I said. He'd lived in the building next door for a few years and had peed out the window that whole time; something about saving water.

"It's not like you can see his appendage if you're standing in the driveway." Mac laughed uproariously.

"Red flag," Fab said. "Why doesn't this Ace character want anyone to know the property's for sale? I'd think the more interested buyers, the higher the offer."

"That part is being whispered about, and I haven't been able to nail it down," Mac said.

"But you know something? More gossip?" I asked. Mac nodded. "Now that you've issued that disclaimer, what is it?"

"I got all this from Maisie Drake, in the little pink house across the street. She was devastated when Ace ran off and got married. She'd had her big brown eyes set on him, although she hasn't admitted it. Then the new missus put an end to the friendship."

"Do you think you can move this along before we fall asleep?" Fab grouched.

Mac shot her a dirty look. "If you were friendlier, you'd know this stuff."

"No fighting. There are kids present," I said.

"In case you've forgotten where you were in your story, we'd like to hear the gossip part," Fab said.

"Neither of you are good examples." I laughed.

"The unsubstantiated gossip is that the new missus is the orchestrator of the deal and her bestie, Trigger, is the buyer," Mac said in a smug tone.

"The drug dealer?" Fab gasped.

"That's the one," Mac said.

"Over my dead body," I said. "Which would probably happen anyway if that man thinks he's going to turn the neighboring property into a drug drive-thru. No. Way."

"Don't say dead anything too loudly," Fab said. "Trigger's got quite the rep amongst the criminal crowd."

"Nothing's been proven," Mac said.

"That's because no one lives long enough to tell what they know," Fab countered.

"So, you're telling me that Ace's new wife is in league with a drug dealer?" I asked.

Mac nodded. "Maybe."

"I don't like Ace's odds of a nice long life," Fab said.

"I'll have Xander investigate her," I told Mac. "Anything you find out, call me right away."

"I've been working on it," Mac said. "Ace and I exchanged hellos before the marriage, but the only one in the neighborhood he was friends with was Maisie, and now that's ended."

"How often does Ace come around, and when was he here last?" I asked.

"Tomorrow is his regular day. He always shows up in the morning, makes the rounds, and leaves," Mac said. "The wife comes along and never lets him out of her sight."

"You got a plan already?" Fab asked me in disgust.

"I've been making them one after the other in the last twenty-four hours, so now they're coming faster." I smirked at her. "This one's going to take all three of us. Mac, you're going to lure Ace away on some pretext so I can have a friendly chat. You, my friend…" I pointed to Fab. "You're going to keep the snooty missus busy. You're certain to be up to her high standards."

"I'm in," Mac said excitedly. "About time I was part of a sting."

"The only way this gets exciting is if guns show up, and that's not going to happen," I said.

"You're going to have to make it fast, in case the missus gets suspicious," Fab said. "What are you going to do, threaten him?"

"That depends on Ace. Corroboration of this gossip before tomorrow morning would be helpful." I pointed to Mac. "With or without it, I'm going to do my homework and make him a fair offer on the property. I'll let him know the problems he'll have closing on the property with a criminal as the buyer and hint that the law could come snooping around. That sounds mean, but too bad. Trigger gets a foothold in this neighborhood, and it's only a matter of time before the law-abiding residents move out."

"When Trigger gets wind of your part in all this?" Fab drew a line across her neck. "And he will. Then what?"

"Maybe he'll go away nicely." I shook my head, knowing that was unlikely. "Probably not, but I can get some scary muscle to convince him to move along and out of town."

"I haven't heard Trigger's name associated with any legal sources of income," Fab said.

"Same here," I said. "Mostly drugs, guns, prostitution."

"My advice is to keep your name off the deal," Fab said. "If Ace is in negotiations with Trigger, no matter what you offer, he's probably not going to accept it."

"Then I'll need to stay one step ahead, starting with finding out who's closing the deal. A reputable title company isn't going to close a cash deal when the money shows up in a brown bag. They'll definitely back off if they think the transaction is under scrutiny by the law." I looked at Mac. "You need to stay on top of the gossip and call me with anything new."

"Tomorrow, when we're done with our meet and greet with the neighbors, I've got a job. It's here in the Keys," Fab said.

"You got the kids booked on the alligator bus trip?" I asked Mac.

"I took a vote first thing this morning, and they're all in." Mac fist-pumped. "In fact, they're excited. I put the word out, since we had a few empty seats, and the bus filled right up. Crum and I are going, and of course, Rude, who'll make the drive to Homestead more interesting by pointing out stuff that doesn't exist. Cootie's driving—turns out he had the appropriate licensing. We're all legal-like, so that should make you happy."

"I was going to ask about the bus and kept forgetting. It's got seatbelts?"

"When Spoon tricked it out, he had the seats recovered and seatbelts installed, so yes. Now, it needs a paint job." Mac raised her eyes to me. "We need to agree on a color."

My stepfather, Jimmy Spoon, ran an auto body shop, which came in handy for getting top-quality repairs without getting screwed on the price. Mac had made a deal on a short bus for The Cottages, and between her and Rude, they brainstormed fun trips for the guests. Room permitting, stragglers from the neighborhood were invited. Tomorrow's trip was to an alligator farm in the Everglades, up in Homestead.

"I don't know why you're asking my opinion-permission-whatever on the color, since you didn't to buy the bus." At Mac's disgruntled look, I added, "Don't get me wrong; I'm happy about the purchase. So, we've got tomorrow covered then?"

"No worries. It's going to be fun, and there will be plenty of supervision."

"One more little issue before we disband this fun group," I said. "I need to come up with something healthy-ish for lunch. Ixnay on hamburgers and pizza, since we did that yesterday. I don't want them going home hopped up on junk food."

"You should call Didier," Fab said.

"That's a great idea," I said, my tone saying it really wasn't. "Call your husband. He can come over and make kale shakes, and the kids will hate me after they're done throwing up."

Mac made a barfing noise and laughed.

"I'm going to tell him what you said," Fab said, pleased with the idea.

Chapter Four

The next morning, Fab and I were waiting in the office for Mac, who was foot-cruising the neighborhood for the latest news and keeping a lookout for the first sighting of Ace. When that happened, she'd text me. Fab had blown through our favorite coffee haunt and brought me a cup of my preferred brew, which I hadn't indulged in in a couple of days.

"What did Creole say about you strong-arming the neighbor not to sell to a drug dealer?" Fab asked.

"He'd be all in... if he knew. That's the thing about listening to four kids chat about their day, getting them fed and off to bed, and then up the next day, dressed, and out the door—there's not a lot of time for Q&A. I got out of the 'what are you doing today' interrogation without even a 'be safe,' since he was feeling a bit harried himself. He put himself in charge of breakfast, and I got raised brows when I suggested cereal."

"You laugh now." Fab wagged her finger at me. "He's not going to be happy when he finds out that Didier's got our itinerary for the day and he has no clue."

"I'll call and update him when we're headed out on your job."

Mac threw open the door and, out of breath, said, "Time to get a move on. The Blaines are coming up the block; they stopped to talk to one of the neighbors."

Fab and I jumped up and hip-bumped to see who could get to the door first.

"You need to keep the missus busy for at least ten minutes," I said to Fab. "That'll give me enough time to impress upon Ace how much I don't want a drug dealer moving into the neighborhood. It doesn't even matter that he wouldn't actually occupy an apartment; I can easily imagine the trouble he would rent to."

Fab blew out an exasperated breath. "What the heck am I going to talk about?"

"Pretend she's part of the glitzy-glam crowd you used to hang out with in South Beach and gossip about other people. Doesn't matter that you don't know them; just remember to have the same response that she does, and she'll think you're fated to be besties. That is, until she meets me and I threaten to shoot her for intruding into my friend territory."

"Stop dawdling." Mac motioned frantically. "I'll split the two up and send them in different directions. You," her eyes narrowed and homed in on Fab, "create another diversion and pronto. I can't do everything," she said with a trace of a smirk.

Fab glared, as if to say, *Who are you to hop into the director's chair?*

"We work as a team and hope for the best." I followed the two, who were playing who'd blink first.

The distraction went off easier than I'd imagined. Mac began a rant about weeds on the side of the building. Aside from it being none of our business, since it wasn't on my property, that strip had been paved from front to back for years; no wonder Ace appeared confused. Turned out the missus had a first name, and it was Karen. Fab got the woman laughing and easily led her away.

"Don't mind her." I smiled lamely and inserted myself between Mac and Ace. "It's been a while, Mr. Blaine. I'm Madison from next door." Knowing the clock was ticking, I hurried on. "I understand that your building's for sale, and I've got an interested buyer for you. Cash close. I hope you'll entertain the offer with the good of the neighborhood in mind."

"I've already got an offer, dearie," he said, and attempted to step around me.

I blocked him. "The word is that it's Trigger, the drug dealer."

Ace's expression registered surprise—that I knew who the buyer was or that I'd outed the potential buyer as a drug dealer, I wasn't sure which—but he didn't dispute what I'd said. He appeared to be at a loss for what to say.

"You've been a longtime resident of this area," I said. "As you know, it's undergone a significant transformation, and property values are on the rise. A drug dealer opening up shop—and that's what Trigger would do, since he's up to his neck in all things illegal—would turn all that around. It would screw up everyone's property values, and most likely, the neighborhood would deteriorate. I'm certain your first wife would be appalled, since she's the one who helped you build your portfolio."

"That's none of your damn stinkin' business," Ace spit out.

"I'm sorry to come on so heavy-handed, but it appears I don't have the luxury of wait-and-see," I said in an apologetic tone. "I'm telling you now that I can get you a legitimate cash offer for your property, and I'm talking full value, not a fire sale. I'm also not talking laundered money, and if you get involved in a business transaction with the likes of Trigger, that's what you'll be accepting. It'll be downright dirty. You can't spend the money from jail. Prosecutors look down their noses on ignorance as a defense. Plus, you know Trigger, or his reputation anyway, and we both know he hasn't made a legitimate dime in his life."

Ace bristled. "Are you threatening me?"

"I guess you missed the phrase *legitimate* business deal. If you move forward on this contract with Trigger, you're going to have to deal with crooks all the way around, as no legitimate title company is going to accept a bag of cash to close the transaction."

"You don't understand," Ace said in a whiney tone. "Trigger's turned his life around. My wife told me so. They're friends, and that's where the offer came from."

His wife and Trigger—friends. I tried not to grimace. Ace needed to watch his back. "I'm telling you that there's nothing legit about the man. You don't believe me, I can put you in touch with a couple of detectives that can disabuse you of the notion."

"You must be wrong." Ace sighed out a ragged breath.

"Doesn't it bother you that your new wife has a relationship-slash-friendship with this Trigger fellow? How long have you been married? And now she's bringing you this oh-so-great deal." I looked down the block and saw that Fab still had Karen distracted.

"I don't like what you're insinuating, young lady."

"I know what I'm talking about where Trigger's concerned. As for the new Mrs. Blaine, if you weren't thinking with your—" At his raised eyebrows, I caught myself. "If you give this some thought, you'll know that a legal, legitimate offer would be the best way to go."

Ace sputtered at me.

"Just know that if you go through with this

deal, law enforcement will be on your doorstep in a hot minute, so don't spend the money." I didn't know that for certain, but I'd raise hell until someone investigated just to shut me up.

"What's going on over here?" Karen yelled. She'd finally noticed that her husband's attention had wandered elsewhere and now stomped in our direction.

"If you're ever in need of help of any kind, Mac is always around, either here or at her house across the street. Don't hesitate to call on her," I said hurriedly.

Karen threw her arm around her husband but not in time to hear anything we'd said. She looked between us, expecting an explanation, and didn't get one.

"It was nice talking to you," I said to Ace. "Don't be a stranger."

Ace didn't say a word; instead, he grabbed his wife's hand and marched back to his car, not bothering with his usual morning rounds of his property. Karen shot questions at him, which he ignored.

Mac—who, true to form, had stayed in hearing distance—strolled over to stand next to me. "Fab went around the bend and over the hill and will meet you back at The Cottages. She didn't think it was good to be seen with you."

"That woman knows more secret paths than even the people whose properties they run across or around." I shook my head.

"I feel sorry for Ace," Mac said as we headed back to the office. "He's caught between good sense and little Ace. Another thing: when Karen worms the conversation out of him, she'll be back. I'm going to put out the alert, since we now have kids to look out for."

I promised myself I was going to get better at this kid thing. In the meantime… "Do we have an open cottage?"

"As a matter of fact…" Mac said, and waved to the one that bordered the barbeque area and had an unobstructed view of most of the street.

I pulled my phone out of my pocket and called my go-to guy—after my husband, who was going to flip at how long he'd lingered in the dark. "Need a favor," I said when Spoon answered.

Mac opened the office door, and I followed her in and sat in a chair across from her desk. The couch was taken by Fab, who was kneeling and peeking between the blinds. She threw herself down, put her feet up on the back of the couch, and raised her brows, wanting to know who was on the phone.

"Just call me favor-doer dude." Spoon growled out a laugh. He was a man who'd taken a badass reputation, shined it up, and was now a pillar of the community. Now that Mother had given him the green light to say yes to my requests, he didn't hesitate.

"I like that. Can I put you on speaker so I

don't have to repeat every word and be accused of forgetting, blah, blah, you get the gist? I'm with Fab and Mac."

"Go ahead."

I hit the speaker button. "Here's the deal." I told him about Aces' plan to sell.

"That's all we need—Trigger and his ilk hanging around," Spoon growled.

"What I need—" There was a scratch at the door, interrupting the call.

Mac got up, rounded the desk, and opened the door. Fifty pounds of fur aptly named Furrball jetted through the door, leaped on the desk, and stretched out. If Mac had any ideas about getting work done, she'd have to come up with a relocation plan. He meowed when she sat back down. She opened her drawer, took out cat treats, and sprinkled them in front of his face; craning his neck was the only effort he had to make in wolfing them down.

"Where was I before being interrupted by a cat?" I asked, which made Spoon laugh. "I need one of your guys to come and stay for a few days, keep an eye on the property and enforce the No Trespassing sign that we need to put up. He'll need to have bad-assery skills, be good with children and cats… the latter both dead and alive."

I looked up to the top of the bookcase, where Kitty lay on the top shelf, still dead and stuffed and in her permanent place. Her owner, Miss

January, was probably drunk, though maybe not, since liquor store deliveries didn't happen until midday. She was one of two original tenants that had come with the property. Her doctors kept swearing that the end was near, and she kept laughing at them, lighting up another cig, and pouring herself a shot of vodka.

"I didn't think you rented to kids," Spoon said.

"That's right." I tapped my forehead and winked at Fab. "You don't know the latest and neither does Mother or Brad. Since you never get to impart the latest family gossip, I'm thinking it's about time."

Mac looked horrified.

Fab laughed.

"I heard that," Spoon grouched.

I told him about Casio's visit.

"Four?" Spoon said in a tone of disbelief. "Your mother and brother aren't going to believe me, and the latter isn't going to be happy to be the last to know."

"I'm getting into this kid thing. Since I've handed you hot gossip to pass around, I'm thinking," I said, and Fab groaned. "The kids are still going to the alligator farm this afternoon?" I looked to Mac for confirmation that the trip was still on, and she nodded. "Are you listening, Spooner?" He grunted, which I took as a yes. "If they don't get eaten, they're going to need dinner. I'm thinking tasty and healthy, so while you're inviting the rest of the family to swim and eat here at The Cottages, could you maybe come up with something yummy? Mother's going to think you're more perfect than she already does."

The line sounded like it went dead. I looked at the screen. Still connected. I blew into it really loudly.

"That's damn annoying," Spoon grouched. "Do that again, and I'm hanging up. You need to give a guy a minute to catch his breath after everything you just dumped in my lap. I'm thinking about how to get out of all this favor stuff and not come off as a dick."

Fab spoke up, loud enough that he could hear, "Good luck with that."

"Your mother will love planning the dinner once she gets over the shock of the kid story. I'll bring the bodyguard with me, so he has a chance to check in and mingle." Spoon laughed. "This ought to be an interesting evening. Have you ever thought of holding a family dinner where everyone nods and smiles until it's time to run out the door?"

I laughed. "That sounds like a bore."

We hung up, and I put my phone back in my pocket. "Okay, I'm at your disposal," I said to Fab.

"The kids?" Fab questioned.

"Got some fun planned, and they're tripled up on supervision," I said. "The kids asked Crum to go on the alligator excursion, and he was in. Not a snotty word because, although he wouldn't admit it, he's having fun with his little crew."

"Once I heard Crum had decided to go on the trip, I decided to stay here, in light of recent events," Mac said. "I think someone needs to keep an eye on the property, since you're provoking the neighbors."

"When do I get to find out what transpired between you and Ace?" Fab asked.

Mac snatched up her phone. "I taped it. I'll forward it to you." She grinned at her own cleverness.

"Didn't you stomp on my privacy rights with that one?" I asked.

"You should be thanking me. You'd never remember the whole conversation, and the parts that got a bit contentious are too good to screw up in the retelling," Mac said without looking up from her phone.

"What worries me is that our chat didn't end with any variation of *I'll call you*, *I'm interested in your deal*, or anything. Ace just walked off. More like stomped off," I said. "Wish I had the name of the title company he plans on using."

"It wouldn't surprise me if it was an out-of-town office," Fab said.

I stood. "*Anything*," I said to Mac, "let me know." I reached to comb my fingers through Furrball's fur. "I'm going to go get my cats; I miss them. That cottage isn't full to the brim, so what's two more?"

"Too late. I stopped to feed them last night and relocated them to my house, where they're doing just fine. They did send their regards, and I forgot to tell you." Fab smirked.

"They say anything else?"

"Yeah, the treats are better at my house."

I laughed. "Don't get attached."

Chapter Five

"When do I get to hear the details of this job of yours?" I asked as Fab drove south down the Overseas Highway. "I'm about to call Creole and do an info dump. Irritate him all at once, then blame you for as much as I can."

"I stopped blaming you. That doesn't work for me anymore… or I should say never did." Fab grimaced. "Had to try, though."

"Let me guess: another Gunz job." When he hired us to be the "fixers" of his family issues, I never thought he'd keep us as busy as he did. I wrinkled my nose. He did his best to keep his boatload of relations on a tight leash, but they had a tendency to break free and run wild.

"Gunz's nephew or cousin. You know how he is; he's never specific. I think it's because he takes their word that they're related. Young guy, Garrett Scott, lived in an apartment building just south of here until recently, when it burned down. Management is blaming him and threatening to sue for damages."

"Totaled?" I frowned. Fab shrugged, which I took to mean she didn't know. "Why not let insurance deal with it?"

"There's some issue with their coverage. Gunz says they weren't forthcoming when he tried to question them."

"They probably let it lapse. Very stupid, but you can't convince people of that." I shook my head. "They get their property paid off and don't want to carry insurance any longer, and somehow, they work it out in their own minds that that's a good idea. No one can convince them that it's totally lame."

"It was declared arson—accelerant was used and a lighter was found at the scene. The fire started in Garrett's unit."

"This Garrett guy in jail?" I asked.

"Not yet. Probably because he almost burned to death, as he was in bed when the flames leapt up, the fire alarm screaming. He barely made it out the bedroom window, and without someone tugging on his arms to help pull him out, he would've fried."

I sucked in a breath and made a face. "That's not the way I'd want to go. My powers of deduction say that the cops don't think he was planning to set his own self on fire, hence the reason for no arrest. They haven't found anyone else, and we got hired to find the culprit. How did I do?"

Fab snorted. "Gunz isn't convinced that the cops have cleared him entirely, as he's been called in for questioning a couple of times. Stupid man was going to go in by himself until his mother called Gunz, who in turn called Garrett and yelled some sense into him, then sent him to a lawyer."

"One thing I'll say for Gunz: he takes care of his relations. Plus mark in his column. Although I'm surprised he signed up to be king to the lot of them." A title one of his other relatives had bestowed upon him behind his back.

Fab turned off on a side street and drove slowly, checking out each house and the one other apartment building, until we got to the burned-out shell, which was half-standing.

"It used to be a ten-unit building," Fab said.

"Six of the units look totaled, and as for the others, it's hard to tell. I'm fairly certain this can't be fixed. It needs to be torn down and rebuilt, and without insurance that's costly."

Fab continued down the block and turned around.

"If this is all Garrett could afford rent-wise…" I gazed around at the rest of the so-so neighborhood. "What good does it do to sue someone who can't pay?"

"If Garrett's innocent, Gunz doesn't want some big judgment hanging over his head, even if it isn't collectible. Or worse yet, for him to end up in jail." She pulled up in front of the burned-out building and parked. We both stared out the windshield.

"He lived in the end unit." Fab pointed to the right.

"I'd suggest a good look around, but neither of us are fire inspectors."

"Gunz had in mind that we'd walk the neighborhood, ask a few questions, and see if anyone knows anything."

"Premonition coming on…" I rubbed my forehead.

Fab's hand swung out, and I leaned back. "I hate when you do that."

"You're interrupting the flow. This is where Gunz suggested that you insist that I come along, knowing I'm the one with the gift of BS and you're the sexy, slinky one."

"We all have our strengths."

"Yes, we do, and I'd like to borrow yours once in a while."

"You got a plan?" Fab asked.

"No, but I'm going with one of our favorite game plans. We'll wing it. I'll do the talking. You snoop through their underwear drawers if we get inside, which I'm telling you now I'm averse to, and fair warning, I won't be following you."

We got out of the SUV and continued to stare at the building, as though it would start talking. Fab took out her phone and snapped pics. "You forgot to call Creole," she reminded me.

"I'm racking up the crappy wife points today, and I've done it more than once lately."

"I've got an idea or two for how you can wipe them out all at once," Fab said with a smirk.

"No, thanks." I rolled my eyes. "Swinging off

the chandelier and then doing what comes next, which would be breaking my neck, doesn't appeal to me."

Fab laughed.

We started up the street and stopped at the first three houses. No one answered, although someone was home at every one. They'd come to the door, loiter at the peephole, and disappear. My favorite was the one that turned the television up louder.

"They think we're selling something or whatever, and they're not interested," I said. I turned and caught sight of an older woman digging in her flowerbed. "This way." I tugged on Fab's sleeve. "Let's go find out what this woman knows. We got any bribe money to work with?"

"Gunz never complains about expenses, as long as they produce something."

I led the way across the street. The woman saw us coming and sat back on her garden mat, pulling off her gloves. I waved as I walked up her driveway and over the paver stones.

"Whatever you're peddling, I'm not interested," she said. "Saw you going door to door. No one opens up in this neighborhood. Nothing good ever comes of it. You got me because I had to do some weeding, but I'm cleaning up and going back in now."

I flashed a big smile. "I'm looking for a friend I haven't seen for a while. Last address I had was

the burned-out building across the street."
Thinking quick, I said, "Mary… Williams,"
rejecting Smith and Jones and hoping the fact
that I paused went unnoticed.

"Don't remember that name, and I've lived
here a lot of years. Guess it's true that I don't
know everyone." She eyed me up and down and
craned her neck to get a look at Fab, who stood
behind me.

More of my phony smiling. "How did the fire
start?"

Whatever tiny bit of friendliness she'd shown
disappeared, and she squinted at me. "This is
also a neighborhood that minds its own
business."

"You averse to making a few bucks in
exchange for answering a couple of questions?" I
stared back and put my hand behind my back,
rubbing my fingers together. Fab slapped money
in my hand. I glanced at the hundred-dollar bill
and held it up. "Would this buy anything? Or
should we try our luck with the next neighbor?"

"No one has to know?" the woman asked. I
shook my head. She held out her hand.

"Any clue how the fire started? We're asking
for a friend."

She nodded and thankfully didn't question
my previous "friend" story. "There's talk that it
was that nice young man, Garrett. Then the talk
moved on to his girlfriend, Carly, who was sweet
as could be. After the fire, she went crazy." She

shook her head with a grimace. "Hasn't seemed right in the head since."

"All the tenants move away?" Fab asked from behind me.

"Three of them are sharing the turquoise house down at the end of the block, next to the highway. Bet that's noisy." She made a face. "Carly moved to the other end of the block, into that one-room house next to the empty field. That's it. The rest packed up what was salvageable and lit out of here. Can't say I blame them any. The folks that lived in ones with only smoke damage were planning to stay until the building was red-tagged."

Fab knocked me in the low back, translated: *Time to go.*

"Appreciate your help." I waved and turned, following Fab back to the car. After closing the door, I asked, "You thinking the same thing as me?"

"Crazy girl's house, here we come." Fab backed out of the driveway.

"Sounds like the fire had a lasting effect on her. I say we watch our backs."

Fab drove down the street and easily found the house, the size of a postage stamp and surrounded by weeds.

"This place could be sort of cute with a paint job and some repairs. Why let the termites eat it?" I asked in disgust. "I talked to that last woman; it's your turn. I'm not feeling it for this place. I'd rather hit the road for something cold to drink. Get a margarita to go and take it… I guess not home, and with kids, I can't show up sauced."

"You know what, if I were Casio, I'd have chosen you, too."

"The nice compliment isn't going to get you out of being the frontwoman," I said. "I have your back, and that's the best I've got."

Fab pulled into the driveway, parked in the weeds, and we got out. I followed her so she wouldn't get any ideas about me doing the schmoozing. She knocked on the door.

A woman inside yelled, "It's open."

Fab and I exchanged a look. She pushed the door wide open but didn't step inside. The scent of mildew rolled out and right up our noses.

A disheveled twenty-something, long brown hair hanging in her face, sat in an easy chair, a ten-watt bulb barely illuminating her face. She was sobbing her heart out, a handgun in her hand. She sent the cylinder spinning, pointed it at the wall, and pulled the trigger. Nothing.

"That's a dangerous game," Fab said in a placating tone. "Carly?"

The woman nodded. "What do you want?" She bunched her shirt in her fingers and blew her nose on it.

Fab looked at me. I shrugged.

"We've got a few questions about the fire that happened down the street," Fab said. "We understand that you lived in the unit, along with Garrett Scott."

"I answered all the cops' questions. What I could remember." Carly laughed, a high-pitched, unnerving sound. "Such a trying time," she added with a dramatic flourish, pointing the gun at her forehead. Then turned the weapon toward the wall and pulled the trigger again.

Fab took a step and kicked it out of her hand, sending it flying to the floor.

"What the hell did you do that for?" She stood, grabbed her purse off a nearby table, and pulled out a box of ammo. "I'm going hunting," she said to herself.

"Hunting for what?" I asked.

Carly smiled smugly and drifted off for a few seconds, then took notice of her surroundings again with a jerk. "This and that," she answered vaguely.

"Maybe we can help," Fab said.

"Yeah, maybe." She pondered that for a moment. "You got an address for Garrett? Went by the hospital, but he'd already been released." Her mouth was a grim line. "I thought for sure he'd die," she said, more to herself than us. "I saw him once after, but we argued. It was all a misunderstanding."

I jerked on the back of Fab's top.

"Hey girl," came a shout from the open doorway. A skinny blond female leaned against the frame. "Found some change; let's go get a beer." Her bloodshot eyes checked us over.

Carly turned to her friend. "I've got a couple of cigarettes rationed from yesterday. Any more questions?" she asked us, then turned back to her friend. "They've got questions about Garrett."

"Who'd have thought he could slither his fat ass through the bedroom window?" the blonde said. "Good thing it wasn't nailed shut." She laughed, sounding less unhinged than her friend.

Garrett's girlfriend shoved her feet into a pair of well-worn tennis shoes and slung her purse over her shoulder. "It's party time." She slipped past us and out the door. "Close the door," she yelled over shoulder. "Keeps the roaches out."

The two took off down the street without a backward glance. I caught up to Fab after closing the door, and the two of us stood next to the SUV and watched them go.

"What the heck just happened?" Fab asked.

"Not sure. I think that whatever went down between Garrett and Carly, he's better off not leaving a forwarding."

"You stand guard. If those two turn around, call me."

Before I could try to stop her, Fab backtracked and disappeared inside the house. I kept an eye on the retreating backs of the two women. They slung their arms around one another and leaned in, as though holding each other upright. I wondered where they'd go once they got to the highway, since it was an empty stretch in both directions. Maybe there was a neighborhood bar that I'd missed. If they had no clue where they were going, it hadn't deterred them so far.

I was ready to shout, "Hurry up," when Fab reappeared, closing the door behind her.

"The dust is thick in there." Fab turned up her nose. "Interesting find, though." She brushed her clothes off and practically ran to the driver's side.

I didn't have to threaten physical retribution to find out what happened because as soon as I closed the door, Fab started talking. She'd come out of the house with her phone in her hand, which meant she'd taken pictures. Of course.

"There was a cardboard box on the counter in the kitchen. Inside was a package of lighters and a couple of big cans of lighter fluid."

"Isn't that how the apartment fire started?" I asked.

Fab nodded. "I left her gun on the floor. Who doesn't pick up their firearm and put it away when they're done shooting up the living room?"

"A woman who's barely got a foothold in reality," I said. "She spent more time talking to herself than us. I think she only occasionally noticed the two of us standing there."

Fab started the engine and crawled down the street, speeding up once the duo got to the corner and jaywalked across the busy highway. "This isn't an easy town to get around in when you don't have transportation. Even a bike would be better than walking." Fab sat at the corner as the two continued down the highway.

"I'm afraid to ask what you're doing."

The two turned, facing traffic, and stuck out their thumbs.

"Hitching a ride. That's a great idea," I said in disgust.

It didn't take long before a beat-up pickup truck pulled over. The women approached, and after a minute, Carly got in and the truck shot down the street. Her friend stuck her thumb back out.

Fab cut across the highway and pulled over just ahead of the woman, who came running. I rolled down the window and leaned back.

The woman shoved her head inside and blinked in recognition. "Twenty bucks. Two of you—forty."

"Hop in." Fab unlocked the back door. The woman slid inside. "Fifty if you answer some questions."

"That's it? Don't gotta do anything else?"

"Just questions." Fab made a face. "I'll also drop you off wherever you want to go."

"Dealie-o." She giggled and held out her knuckles for a bump, which we ignored.

"One more thing," Fab told her sternly. "It's got to be the truth or you get nothing. I'd rather you say you don't know then make something up and waste our time."

"Yeah, gotcha."

"Who started the fire in Garrett Scott's

apartment?" Fab demanded in a stern tone.

"I, uh..."

Fab held up the fifty and waved it out of her reach.

"I don't know anything. Let me out," the blonde demanded.

Fab pulled into a turnout and turned to the woman. "Would another fifty jog your memory?"

"A hundred?" She licked her lips.

"Tell me what I want to know. Just so you know, this is a limited-time offer, as I don't have all day. So, you have one minute to make up your mind." Fab tapped her watch.

The woman debated with herself in an indecipherable tone. After a minute, she said, "It's all Garrett's fault. It wasn't planned. It just happened. Hell, it's not like he died."

"I'm more interested in the details of how the fire started, not rationalizations," Fab snapped.

"Carly came home early. She was going to surprise Garrett with his favorite foot-long. The surprise was on her, or I should say shock? She caught him in bed with two other women. They were so busy, they didn't notice that she stood in the bedroom doorway watching. Maybe if one of them had... Carly backed out and went to the gas station, bought her a zippo and a can of lighter fluid, and went back. She soaked the front door and entry and lit it on fire. Then hightailed it out of there."

"How is it she escaped the notice of the cops?" I asked.

"Went across the street to the vacant house, sat on the porch, and watched as the building went up in flames and the tenants ran from the fire. She says all she remembers about the questioning is that she gibbered on about Garrett being dead, and after a couple of minutes of that, she got transported to the hospital. She overheard the nurse talking about a psych hold and lit out of there. She was mad when she found out Garrett had already been released."

"Anyone die?" I asked Fab, who shook her head.

The blonde shook her head, too. "Carly thought that she and Garrett would be getting back together, but he dodged her calls. Then she arranged to meet up with him as a surprise, and the fact that it was her that set the fire came out while they were talking. They got into a fistfight and beat each other a good one. Carly's still got a couple of bruises. Garrett took off, and that was the last she's seen of him. She knew about the shit shack at the end of the block and that it was empty, so she moved in, since she didn't have anywhere else to go. Owner doesn't have a clue that she's living there. Thought it was a clever idea, since she knows how to poach utilities."

It's all fun and games until you get caught and go to jail.

"What are Carly's plans for the future?" Fab asked.

"She bought that gun and ammo off Ernie on the next block over, and she practices every chance she gets."

"Which means what exactly?" I asked.

"Carly's got a plan to kill Garrett, but I know her pretty well. She'll get bored with all the planning and move on to something else. It's all good."

"Where do you want to go?" Fab asked.

"Drop me at Ernie's Tackle. He serves beer in the back. I'd appreciate it if you don't tell Carly that I ratted her out. She'd understand about me taking the money, but it would end our friendship and I don't have any others." She cleared her throat. "I'd like smaller bills, if you have it. I come prancing in with a C-note, and that'll attract unwanted attention."

I jerked the cash out of Fab's fingers, fished around in my purse, and made change, handing it back to her. Fab pulled into Ernie's parking lot and let the woman out. She waved and walked inside.

Fab and I stared at one another for a long minute; then she cut back out to the highway, u-turned, and headed home.

"My advice…" I said. "Dump this whole messy situation in Gunz's lap and let him deal with it. I don't hold out any hope that Carly's going to get over wanting to kill Garrett. There's always the cops, except they're going to want more than our word. We can't even give them the girlfriend's name, since neither of us asked what it was." I fished my phone out of my pocket. "Where are you?" I asked when Creole answered.

"The office. You okay?"

"You can check me out for yourself. I'm going to have Fab drop me off. I'll see you soon."

Chapter Six

Fab pulled into the reserved parking at The Boardwalk and turned off the engine. "I'm coming in because I'm certain you're going to discuss things I should know." She got out and closed the door before I could tell her how nervy I thought she was.

The biggest family project to date was The Boardwalk, which consisted of shopping, restaurants, and a few low-key rides for the entire family. It had rapidly become a destination spot. Creole, Didier, and Brad ran the day-to-day operations without any interference from the rest of us, the silent investors.

Apparently afraid I might physically restrain her somehow, Fab raced up the stairs. I followed at a more leisurely pace. She held the door to the offices open and smirked as I passed her into the reception area. Creole made an imposing figure, standing in the middle of the room; he held his arms out, and I walked into them and got a hard hug. As I went up on my tiptoes and grazed my lips against his, Fab disappeared down the hall and into the large office the guys shared.

"How was your day?" Creole kissed me long and hard.

"Gunz job. Need I say more? A cousin relative person needs to lie low, or blow town, in my professional opinion."

"Heeey," Fab yelled at the top of her lungs, or close. "We can't hear what you're saying from back here."

"Fabiana," Didier hissed.

"What? It's true," she told her husband.

Creole laughed and took ahold of my hand, and we walked down the hall and into the office. Instead of breaking the space into three small offices, they'd opened it up to make one large one. In addition to three desks, there was a sitting area with chairs facing the double doors that opened onto a view of the grounds.

"Hey, bro." I walked over to Brad's desk and leaned over to lay a kiss on his cheek.

My brother hadn't lost his "boy next door" appeal, but had added serious muscle after his crazy ex decided he was the only man for her. His sandy brown hair was tousled, and his blue eyes twinkled at me.

I turned and princess-waved to Didier, who laughed. The dark-haired, smoking-hot ex-model caught many a female eye but couldn't be bothered with any woman other than his wife.

"Seriously happy I'm here and get to find out firsthand what the two of you have been up to." Brad grinned. "Hopefully, you've got something good, which I can brag to everyone at dinner that I wasn't the last to know about."

"I hope you're not disappointed." I made a face at him and sat next to Creole on the couch. I looked at Fab. "Since Gunz is your client, you do the honors."

Didier groaned.

"You'll be happy to know that no shots were fired," Fab said, and then amended, "Not by us, anyway."

"You need to teach me that ninja kick thing you do," I said as my leg shot out.

"What the hell?" Didier spit out.

"*Hell*, Frenchie? You know that, by your own proclamation, no bad words are allowed," I said.

The guys laughed. Didier's deep-blue eyes bored through me as he shot me a "behave" stare.

Fab launched into relaying how everything went down and, surprisingly, didn't add any extra drama to the retelling, not that it needed any.

"What does Gunz want you to do?" Didier asked.

"It was Madison's suggestion to dump everything back in his lap and let him take care of it however he wants," Fab shared with a smile. "I mulled our options over on the drive back, and we don't have any that don't involve the cops. And everything else I came up with was illegal. One thing is certain, and that's that the girlfriend needs some mental health care, and my guess is she won't go willingly."

"I thought this was where you were going to announce that you're going to be a stay-at-home mom now that you've acquired four kids," Brad said to me with a smirk. "It's hard to believe how it all went down, but since you were in the middle, I believed every word."

"We're doing a good job," I said to Creole.

"They're great kids," Creole said.

"Let's not get sidetracked," Fab said. "It's Madison's turn to tell you about the ambush she orchestrated."

"Errr," I squealed, then asked Creole, "Do I have skid marks from the pricey sports car that just rolled over me?"

"No, and it's a damn good thing." He sent Fab a ferocious stare, then laughed.

"My morning… Before I get started," I looked at Brad, "no repeating any of this to Mother. Cross your heart? Or leave."

"No way. You got my promise as long as you're not in danger," Brad assured.

I told them about my meeting with Horace "Ace" Blaine, and his plan to sell the apartment building next door to The Cottages to a drug dealer.

"Sounds like you have a buyer in mind," Creole said.

"I want the building," I said.

Brad's hand slammed down on his desk.

"That's a bad idea. You already have one problem after another with The Cottages, and the apartment building will be more of the same."

"Maybe it's something we can interest our investor group in," Didier said.

"Probably not, since Mother holds the same attitude that Brad does." I turned to him. "I'm not selling my inheritance from Aunt Elizabeth, and besides, I've proven I can handle the issues that come up." I was en route to Florida to stay with my aunt when, before I could get the suitcases in the car, she died. Little did I know, at the reading of the will, that she was bequeathing me a new life, one that I loved and wasn't going to give up.

"Get on the phone to your attorney and have him set up a corporation, then hire someone with moxie to be your front person and make the deal on your terms," Creole said.

"You're going to screw a drug dealer, and you think that won't go badly?" Brad sniffed. Clearly, he thought it was the worst idea he'd ever heard.

"Better yet, buy the property under a trust," Didier said. "That would keep the names secret, or at least require a heck of a lot more digging."

"You told the owner you could bring a cash deal, quick close; that's going to take a chunk of change," Brad said.

"I have some cash." I glared back at him. "I also have a big line of credit at the bank. Once I buy it, I can refinance."

"I'll sign on as a silent partner and money won't be an issue," Creole said.

"I think you owning the building is better than anyone else owning it," Fab said. "I volunteer my eviction services, starting with the guy that pees out the window." She grinned at me.

"I remember him." Brad shook his head.

Didier didn't know what we were talking about, so Fab relayed the story, much to his disgust.

"Since it looks like you're determined to do this," Brad said. "Make sure you've got your paperwork in order. A good lawyer will know how to protect you. You don't want anything coming back on you."

"I don't understand why Trigger's allowed to operate in our small town," I said. "Surely, the cops have noticed his illegal activities, and you'd think they'd want him gone."

"He's on the police radar, all right," Creole said. "Some of these criminals are slipperier than others, and it takes time to build a case. I can assure you that there are cops working on it as we speak."

"What are you going to do if this Ace guy doesn't cave to your not-so-subtle blackmail?" Brad asked.

"I have no idea."

"You step back and send in your front person right away. Let him or her do all the negotiating," Didier said.

"We could dress Toady up so he'd make a decent impression, or at least look like someone who has the money, and you know he's not afraid of anyone," Fab said. That was true. And thus far, the one-toothed reptile had never turned down a job.

Brad stood. "I've got to go pick up Mila at school. She's excited about having dinner at the pool tonight. I'm hoping your tenants will be locked away in their cottages."

"Your daughter's taking after her Auntie Madison and has great weirdo rapport. Much to your disgust, I'm sure." I smiled at his groan. "See you later, bro."

Brad left with a wave.

"I'm booking you tomorrow afternoon," Fab said. "I've got a cat case."

I knew she was full of it, but would call her on it later. "The kids are scheduled to go out with a dog walker tomorrow afternoon. They're going to learn a trade. Not that they'll need one, but they might own a dog one day, and they'll need to know what to do."

"You talked someone into taking on four kids and who knows how many dogs?" Didier squinted.

I laughed at his disbelief. "It's called cash. I'm paying the woman. The kids like the idea, so there." I made a face at him.

"My wife is doing a good job keeping these kids busy and out of trouble." Creole hugged me to his side. "It's good practice for when we have our eleven."

"Oh yeah, the football team." I rolled my eyes. "Just know that I'm going to let Fab lead and I'll follow. See how far we get."

Fab laughed. "We'll get right on it." She winked at Didier.

Chapter Seven

The morning went smoothly. To my relief, it had all been peaceful since the kids arrived, and I wanted it to stay that way. I grabbed my laptop and phone and followed the kids out to the pool for school. Whatever spell Crum had them under, they were all eager to spend the morning with him. Before setting up my office at the tiki bar, I took a drink order and texted it to Fab. She didn't answer, but I knew she wouldn't show up empty-handed, as she wouldn't want to fall to the bottom of the kids' favorites list.

"What do you have for me?" I asked Mac as I slipped onto a stool.

"More gossip. As you know, it's not always the whole truth, but generally there's a grain." Mac glowed at being the bearer of the news of late.

I cocked my head, *get on with it,* implied.

"Pink house lady claims that Ace's wife harangued him all the way back to the car yesterday, demanding to know what you wanted. Karen was screaming at the top of her lungs when the car door closed and Ace screeched it up the street." Mac looked pleased with herself. "If you're known to be the buyer, you're in for a pot of trouble. I thought about it last night, and there's no easy answer. Trigger would be bad for the neighborhood. The thought of him hanging around at any time makes my skin crawl."

"You're going to meet the buyer today. And you're sworn to secrecy."

"I never talk about your business, not even when your mother comes around trying to weasel information out of me. I know she wants something big when she shows up with food."

I laughed. "My mother thinks food can fix anything. She did such a great job last night with all the food and non-stop fun for the kids. It was nice to sit back and watch all of them laughing and having fun. Mother took it well when a couple of the guests joined us."

"The only thing missing was some family drama." Mac smirked.

"It was a first that we were all well-behaved; mostly, that applies to me."

The kids yelled hi and waved.

I looked up and saw Fab coming in the pool gate, Dodger behind her holding two beverage trays.

Dodger — six feet of skinny with a growly expression — was the guard Spoon had sent over to stop any trouble before it got started. He was supposed to be on night duty, but Spoon had changed it to round-the-clock. Adults took one look and stepped back, but the kids thought he was the greatest after he jumped in the pool with them last night and ramped up the antics.

Karen stormed through the gate behind him, her blond ponytail swinging from side to side. She had the advantage over Dodger, as his hands were filled with cups of hot coffee and cold drinks. He growled, setting down the trays on the nearest table, and turned on her. She wasn't the least bit deterred by his menacing glare, instead shooting him a drop-dead look and skirting around him, headed straight for me.

"You listen to me…" she hissed.

I slid off my stool. "You listen. You make a scene in front of the kids, and I'll personally drag you out of here by your hair."

Dodger didn't waste any time coming up behind her. He looked ready to wring her neck, but rethought that plan and instead camped on her heels. "If you don't heed the warning, I'll do the dragging and then call the cops and have you arrested for trespassing. Since you were warned nicely and chose to ignore it."

"You and I…" Karen gestured between me and her and then at the pool gate. "Now."

I followed her around the pool, Fab joining me. I turned to her and half-laughed. "Karen could've waited until we drank our coffee."

Fab was not amused, her face filled with anger.

"Don't shoot her," I whispered. "Ass-kicking is fair game, though."

Not even a flicker of a smile.

Karen kicked the gate open, stomped into the parking lot, and turned. "This discussion doesn't include the two of them." She flung her hand out dismissively.

It was then that I noticed Dodger, who was hanging back, but could easily intervene if necessary. "That's not your decision to make," I said. "Why don't you spit out whatever it is that's got you so agitated? Make it quick."

"You stay away from my husband," Karen seethed, shaking her finger in my face.

I brushed it away. "Do that again, and I'll snap it off."

"You stay out of our business. The sale of the building is a done deal, and if you interfere again, you'll regret it." Her brown eyes burned a hole in me.

"You listen up, sweetie," I ground out. "No one threatens me, and certainly not some money-grubbing Barbie doll with drug dealers for friends. You need to do your homework before you toss around threats—start with my step-father, Jimmy Spoon." That didn't mean anything to her now, but it would if she followed my advice. Even Trigger wouldn't want to go head-to-head with Spoon.

"Trigger has turned his life around and is an upstanding citizen," Karen mewled.

Dodger snorted so loud, we all turned and stared.

"You're deluded," I told the woman.

"You come back here," Fab said with a menacing stare and pulled her gun, "you'll be shot."

"Screw with the deal at your own peril," Karen bit out.

"I already passed along the information that the property was for sale, and I'm out of it. So no worries about me talking to your husband again, and if he attempts a conversation, I'll tell him to get a written note from you. Happy?" I flashed an insincere smile.

"You bitch." Karen turned and stomped back toward the street. Halfway there, she noticed Dodger following her and practically ran to the sidewalk.

"Wow. That was a scene." I looked at Fab.

She hadn't taken her eyes off the woman's hurried exit. "How old do you think Karen is?"

"Thirty-ish, and before you ask, Ace is in his seventies."

Fab shifted to watch Karen's retreat back to her car. "Circumstances being what they are, it's an easy leap to think that she married the old guy for his building. Wonder what her cut is for making it happen?"

"Karen's trouble all the way around, and she's made that clear, so we need to watch our backs. The last thing I want is any trouble going down while the kids are here, which should only be a few more days."

"I like that you have the extra security. Didier and I could move in for a few days." Fab deserved an award for making that offer without screwing up her nose.

"You're going to leave your beachfront mansion for a cottage? You really are a good friend." I reached out to hug her.

She stepped back. "Don't get carried away." She kicked open the pool gate. "You better drink your coffee before the whipped cream melts."

We slid onto stools at the bar. It wasn't long before Dodger was back with Toady at his side. A new, cleaned-up version. Fab had clearly had a hand in his makeover. The silk shorts and tropical shirt were a huge improvement over his usual wife-beater and stained jeans. High-end cowboys boots made from some unfortunate reptile finished off his eccentric, money-to-burn look.

"I hope Karen didn't see him," I said as Dodger opened the pool gate.

"I told Toady to make it look like he had no association with this property, and that, if he was going to come and go, he needed to sneak around. I saw him come around the side of the building, so he's learned that shortcut." Fab grinned at me.

Toady yelled to the professor, waved to the kids, and made his way over. "Morning, ladies."

He bowed and smiled, his gold (and only) tooth front and center. "Don't think Dodger is slacking; we go way back." He preened for Fab.

Dodger settled in a chair next to the gate; no one would be getting past him.

Fab looked Toady over from head to toe and gave him a thumbs up.

"Nice watch," I said, eyeing the Rolex.

Toady barked a laugh. "Got it from Ernie for twenty bucks. Gave me a discount because I've bought his knock-offs before."

"Did you get the diamond that's big enough to put out an eye from him?" I pointed to his finger, noticing at the same time that he had a matching one in his right earlobe.

Toady nodded with a grin and twirled around. "Do I look the part of a dude who can write a million-dollar check?"

"You look good." It was a huge step up from his usual attire. He pulled off the look I was hoping for, dressed for the part as my new frontman.

Toady slid onto a stool.

I pushed a piece of paper at him. "Here's everything that Xander was able to find out about Horace Blaine, AKA Ace. It includes background and contact information."

Xander was our Information Specialist and had recently graduated from college. He wasn't eager to go to work for someone else and was in the process of building up a client base while trying to decide what he was going to do next.

"You're going to have to arrange the meeting yourself," Fab said. "Be careful of the wife. If she finds out, she'll do what she has to to stop the deal. The less she knows, the better, until the paperwork is signed."

"Just so you know, Karen just left after tossing out threats that I'd regret it if I interfered in any way," I said.

Toady nodded. "Your lawyer working on the paperwork?"

"My CPA. I called Mr. Whitman this morning and ran the idea past him, and he's on board and expediting the paperwork." I pushed a folder at him. "I worked up a report. Here are the numbers for what the property's worth and what I'm willing to offer. The name of the title company is also noted."

Toady opened and perused the report. "I did some checking of my own on this Trigger character and gathered together some little-known facts that I plan to use in the negotiations, which will hopefully speed things along. His last business partner was found face down in the street of a sleepy residential neighborhood with a bullet hole in his back. No suspects. The case is still open."

I grimaced. "You need to be careful. If you decide at any time that you've changed your mind, I'll understand."

"Don't you worry about me, girlie." He

tugged on a strand of my wayward red hair. "No one scares the puke out of old Toads; it's the other way around."

"You need backup, I'm in," Fab said.

"That pretty-boy husband of yours would kill me for sure." Toady laughed. "It's nice being worried over, but no need." He stood. "Time for me to get to work. I'll be in touch." He gave a short wave, stopped to say a few words to Dodger, and disappeared back the way he came.

Fab and I stuck around until the kids had lunch and the neighbor lady showed up to pick up her charges for the dog-walking excursion. Crum gruffly informed the group, "I'm going," which brought me peace of mind.

"I'm adding to your duties," I said to Dodger as the group hit the pool gate. "Keep an eye on the kids; their safety comes first."

"Got it covered." He got up and joined the group, which included five dogs of assorted breeds.

Chapter Eight

I climbed into the SUV and turned to Fab. "I know the cat case was a big huge lie, so what's really up?"

"Sometimes it's amusing to see how long I can keep you guessing." Fab backed out of the driveway and hit the highway going north.

"If we're headed to Miami, I'm getting out now. I don't have the energy for the trip today."

"Homestead."

I turned my head and rolled my eyes. I didn't want to go there either, but at least the trip would be considerably shorter. "I'm still waiting to hear some details about this job."

"I got a call from a new client. A woman, Asha Webster. She wants help locating someone from her past. That's all the details I got out of her."

"Why not hand this job over to Xander? He could ferret out this guy, even if he was camped out under a rock. Then... you take all the credit."

"She insisted that we meet. She babbled on about wanting to make sure that we were the 'right fit,' whatever that means. I expected her to hang up after I quoted my price and demanded payment up front. Instead, she gave me her credit card number, it went through, and here we are."

"I hate to throw a bit of reality into your sorely lacking enthusiasm for this new client, but considering some of your previous ones, we're not meeting her in a dark alley, are we?"

"Sarcasm is unbecoming," Fab said.

"I've heard that said and don't believe it." I chuckled at the look of disgust she shot me.

"The client wanted a face-to-face meeting, and I didn't want her coming to the office," she said, as though stating the obvious pained her. "We're meeting at a coffee house. Happy now?"

I'd rather have been on the beach, but it wouldn't do any good to complain about that now.

Fab had pre-programmed the GPS and cruised up the highway, finding the location and parking in front. "I'd guess that's Asha Webster; she fits the description she gave me." Fab pointed to the lone woman sitting at an outside table under a large umbrella.

"If she asks..." I mentally rolled my eyes, as her clients seldom questioned who I was and why I'd been included in the meeting. "I'm your bodyguard. Sounds badass." I got out and shut the door on her laughter.

We walked over to the table, and I was surprised to see a twentyish pixie-faced young woman, with big brown eyes and a mop of brown curls, staring up at us. "Ms. Merceau?"

Fab nodded and pulled out a chair.

I sat with a direct view of the client.

"As I said over the phone, I want to locate a childhood friend." Asha's eyes darted around, a cagey smile on her face. "My father has recently passed, and I know my friend would want to be informed of the news. Our families were close once, but we lost touch. Now that I've received my inheritance, I can afford to have him found." She downed half of her iced tea.

So far, this had been a waste of time, but I didn't voice the sentiment.

"I wanted to meet," Asha preened. "Because I'm hoping that this is something we can work on together."

"As I told you on the phone, locating this man will be done via a computer search," Fab said, sounding exasperated.

"I'd hoped that once you located him, you could accompany me so I can break the news. I don't drive," Asha said matter-of-factly.

"Must be hard to get around," I said, eyeing the bicycle leaning against a nearby post.

She ignored me, saying to Fab, "I'd like it to be just the two of us."

I spoke up again. "Sorry about that. Ms. Merceau doesn't leave home without her bodyguard. That would be me."

Fab flashed me the *Be nice* stare.

I responded with my own stare: *No.*

"I'm sure we can figure out something. I could

be your guard." Asha giggled. "That would be fun."

"Once… Mr. Blanchard, isn't it?" Fab said. Asha nodded. "Is found, I'm sure he'll be eager to see you after he hears the news. If he doesn't live too far away, he might agree to come here."

"I'd rather surprise him." Asha smiled.

My crazy-people antenna shot in the air. Something was off with the woman, but I couldn't put my finger on it. The fact that she couldn't sit still was a giant red flag.

"We should put off this discussion until Blanchard's located, and then we can work out the details," Fab said in a patient tone. "I'll get started once you email the information I told you I'd need."

"Let me buy you a cup of coffee or something cold," Asha offered.

"Next time maybe." Fab glanced at her watch and stood. "I have another appointment. I look forward to hearing from you."

Asha wasn't happy that the meeting wasn't ending however she'd had it planned out in her mind. "I'll be in touch," she said reluctantly.

I followed Fab back to the car, and once both doors were closed, I said, "This meeting was a complete waste of time."

"Did you happen to notice that she was twitchy and manic?" Fab asked.

"Yep." That was a good description of what I'd witnessed.

"I don't know why I can't get normal people to call." Fab slammed her hand on the steering wheel and backed out of the parking space.

I flipped down the visor to see where Asha went. I was disappointed that she continued to sit at the table and stare as Fab hit the closest exit.

"Put 'normal' in your next ad and see what you get." I laughed at her dirty look. "My opinion is that before you deliver any information to her concerning the whereabouts of someone else, you run a check on her. Based on my experience, I'd ask Xander to run a mental health report if that's possible."

"You're so... so suspicious."

"I do my best to dispense good advice, and you ignore it," I said in a faux huff. "If you search back in that pretty head of yours, I'm certain that you'll remember I've been right a few times."

Fab's lips quirking was the only sign that she was even listening.

Chapter Nine

Creole and I decided that once the kids started school with the professor, we could meet Fab and Didier at the Bakery Café. We managed to arrive at the same time, grabbed parking spaces in the front, and claimed our usual table on the sidewalk, which was prime for people-watching.

Fab and I exchanged a smirk as we waited for the guys to begin asking us a multitude of questions now that we'd finished breakfast and were enjoying a last cup of coffee.

Didier asked Fab, "What's this client want?"

"The interrogation begins," I joked and got glares from both men. "I meant to say, our regular meeting begins, where you two catch up on the latest." They both shook their heads.

"I got a call last night from a client from the old days," Fab said.

I thought I'd groaned inwardly, but it must have slipped out since all eyes shot to me.

After glaring at me for a moment, Fab said, "Mr. Conrad would like me to make a delivery to his son, who happens to be away at college."

"Away? As in across town? Out of the state?" I asked, definite eye roll in my tone.

The guys were content to sit back in their chairs, smirks on their faces as the facts came to light. Well, maybe.

"Mr. Conrad's office is in Miami, so now that you've been forewarned, no complaining about the drive. On the upside, the university is just a few miles away from his office."

I stopped myself from making a snarky comment about traffic and instead said, "You're in luck." That came off too sweetly, as all eyebrows went up. "I want to stop by Brick's office and see if he's heard from Casio. He's overdue, and I'm a bit worried."

Creole pulled me into a hug. "These cases don't always go as planned. Casio's a seasoned detective and knows how to get himself out of a tight situation. If I bet on such things, my money would be on him."

I smiled up at him. Creole had just reminded me that morning that it was too early to start worrying. I looked back at Fab. "I've come up with an alternate plan. If the kids are going to stay, we need to move to your house because we're cramped in the cottage."

"I don't know why you didn't think of that at the beginning," Fab snapped.

"We've got plenty of room," Didier said.

"Everything happened so fast when they arrived, and you were nowhere around. I didn't have the nerve to call you and say, 'Hey, you have room for six?'" I gasped. "Did you see Fab roll her eyes at me?"

The guys laughed.

My phone rang, and I fished it out of my pocket and held it up. Toady. "You have news for me?" I asked.

"Got you a signed contract. Took some schmoozing, one millionaire to another, and after I hit the highlights of the kind of man Ace would be dealing with in Trigger, I think he was relieved to sell to me. He did tell me he wished he'd never gotten involved, that he didn't want to sell but now saw no other way out. This offer might not have stood a chance, no matter what I said, except Trigger offered twice the amount the property was worth and expected the extra kicked back."

"That would've sent me running," I said. "Can you do me a favor and drop the contract at my CPA's office? He's got a guy in the next office over that specializes in real estate and is handling everything."

"You got it."

I hung up and relayed the conversation.

"So, Trigger wanted Ace to commit a felony during the transaction. The old guy had to know that it would land him in jail if the authorities found out," Didier said.

"What happens when Ace sees you at the closing?" Fab asked.

"Congrats." Creole stuck his hand out, then pulled me in and kissed me. "Madison can sign her part ahead of time. All Ace will see is the name of the buyer, and in this case, it's a corporation. As for Ace, he goes to the title office at his convenience, signs, money is wired, and it's over."

"You going to keep the current tenants?" Didier asked. I nodded. "The building needs a little work. I volunteer our company; I can get you a good deal."

"That's a great offer, but since it's vital to keep the buyer a secret, I'd want to use a crew that has no ties to us, and we also need to be upfront with them about the possible danger."

Creole's phone dinged, and he looked down at the screen. "We've got a meeting to get to." He stood and pulled my chair back. "One of you needs to call after you finish with Fab's client and again after Brick. He's going to be surprised to see you two."

"It's been a while, thankfully." Didier stood and helped Fab to her feet. "If I have a vote, I'm hoping that you don't start taking jobs from him again."

"I second that," I said.

"Surprises me to say this, but I'd rather work for Gunz," Fab said. "With Brick, we got ambushed on the job almost every time. With Gunz, if a job goes off the rails, he insists that we think about our safety first and then steps in and handles it. It was never that way with Brick."

Didier pulled Fab into a hug and whispered in

her ear. She went up on her toes and kissed him.

Creole hooked his arm around me and walked me over to the Hummer. Opening the door, he swooped in for a kiss. "Don't forget to call."

"I'll be the designated caller today." I kissed him again.

Fab and I waved as she backed out and headed to the main street. Thanks to light traffic, she made good time getting to Miami. Hating parking garages, she found a parking spot on a nearby side street.

I got out and smoothed down my skirt. "Do your best to make sure this job is legal; it makes it an easier sell to the husbands." I joined her on the sidewalk. "This wouldn't be your first client who thinks it's okay for you to commit a felony as long as it keeps their name untarnished."

"Think positive." Fab flashed a cheeky smile.

It was a short walk, and we rode the elevator up to the penthouse. The sign in the waiting room said, "Conrad and Associates." Fab announced herself to the receptionist, who waved us to a chair and got on the phone.

"I take it we're here to see the top dog. What's Mr. Conrad's gig?" I whispered.

"You need to behave. Ed Conrad is in Public Relations and an image consultant."

"I'll be sure to remember my manners, or try anyway. So, someone high profile gets into trouble, and they hire him to smooth the waters?" I asked.

A middle-aged woman came down the hall and walked over to Fab. "Ms. Merceau, if you'll follow me."

We both stood, and the woman gave me a once-over.

"I'm her partner." My tone said, *and I'm coming*. It didn't escape my notice that she didn't introduce herself.

The woman motioned for us to follow and led us down a long corridor to an office at the end. She knocked, opened the door, and ushered us inside, then stepped out and closed the door.

"It's been a long time, Fabiana," Mr. Conrad said in a gushing tone. He waved toward the chairs in front of his desk. The sixty-something, grey-haired man, overly tanned and rocking a custom-made suit, ignored me, which wasn't the first time that had happened.

"Nice to see you again," Fab said in a deceptively friendly tone.

"This is a simple delivery to my son, Scott." Mr. Conrad swiveled around in his chair and grabbed a briefcase off the credenza, setting it in front of Fab. "Here's the address." He thrust a piece of paper at her.

I looked over her shoulder at the address, which said Dania Beach. I knew that wasn't too far up the highway and also knew that it wasn't close to the university he'd mentioned in the call.

"Scott will be home the rest of the day and awaiting the delivery," Mr. Conrad said.

Fab stood, and I followed, smacking her in the back when she picked up the briefcase without a word.

"What are we delivering?" I asked.

After a moment's hesitation—long enough for Conrad to glare at me and give me the stink eye—he said, "My son left a couple of things behind when he went back to school and needs them ASAP."

"I'll call as soon as I've completed the job." Fab turned and walked out of the office.

I caught Mr. Conrad's smirk before I followed and hustled to catch up to her. "This is another of your cases that's too good to be believed. Conrad's going to pay your rate when he could hire a delivery service for far less and it would already have been delivered."

Tight-lipped, Fab continued to the reception area, sat in one of the chairs, and tried the locks. No surprise, they didn't open. She took her lockpick, which she always had ready, out of her pocket and opened the briefcase. Cash. Stacks of it. She slammed the lid shut, stood, and marched back to his office, ignoring the receptionist, who'd been watching eagle-eyed and stuttered for her to stop as she headed down the hall.

I hurried to keep up, not about to miss a minute. I couldn't wait to hear his explanation.

Fab barged into his office without a knock, interrupting his phone call. She slammed the briefcase down on his desk, flipped the locks and lifted the lid, and turned it to face him. "You deliver it." She turned and left the office.

I waved and followed.

"That's the last of my old clients," Fab announced as we rode down in the elevator. "I get another call, and I'll be informing them I'm out of business." She jerked on my elbow when we hit the sidewalk, turning me in a different direction than we'd come. Another of her infamous shortcuts. "I'll find clients closer to the Cove or only work for Gunz."

"I wanted to clap when you dropped the briefcase on his desk, but you left too quickly."

"What do you suppose that was about?" Fab asked.

"I'd like to have heard his explanation — not that he'd have given us a truthful one. My guess is that we weren't going to find his son at that address. I'm proud of you for turning down the job."

Chapter Ten

Fab cut across town, rocketed into the parking lot of Famosa Motors, and parked off to the side of the roll-up door. "Does Brick know you're stopping by?"

"It's a surprise." I grimaced.

We got out and walked into the middle of the showroom. The receptionist, who was new and on the phone, didn't notice us. We cut around the elevator and headed up the stairs to the second floor.

Brick Famosa, who was sitting behind his desk, looked up from a pile of paperwork as we crossed the threshold, a surprised expression crossing his face. He swiveled his considerable bulk around in his chair — not an ounce of fat on him, and judging by the trophies, he was still boxing.

"Have a seat." He waved his hand. Following her old habit from when she worked for him, Fab sat on the ledge, which had an unparalleled view of the busy street and car lot below. "If you stopped by for the snack bowl, I threw everything in the trash. Decided if it wasn't healthy, I didn't need to be eating it."

I'd taken a chair in front of his desk. "I wanted to know if you've heard from Casio."

Brick looked surprised at my question. "I forget that you two know one another. To answer your question, no. Mind if I ask why?"

"I'm taking care of his kids while he's on a case, and he's late getting back."

"That's par for the course. He always underestimates." Brick laughed, not concerned in the slightest. "You were probably his last resort for someone to take those brats."

I bristled and tried to calm down. "They're great kids, and we've been having a good time."

"Sure you have." Brick snorted. "That's why you're here. Before you ask, I'm not volunteering to take them."

"I'm not asking. This probably surprises you, but I'm a little worried about Casio." I regretted coming here and wanted to leave. "If you hear from your brother, have him call me. You can also reassure him the kids are doing great."

"Yeah, sure I will." Brick turned his attention to Fab. "I've missed you, girl."

"Are you done?" Fab asked, and I nodded. "Would you give me a few minutes with Brick?" She held out the car keys, and I took them and walked out.

I went down, got in the car, and took my phone out. I started to call the old chief of police of Miami for any information on Casio before I remembered that I'd forgotten to get his new number. I missed having that connection. I knew he'd gotten a new job, but no forwarding was rude, and I'd tell him so when I saw him next.

I called Creole. "Hey, babes. You want to put me on speaker?"

He yelled for Didier. "You both in one piece?"

"Yes, we are."

"I'm here," Didier said.

I apologized for the one call instead of two, then told them about Conrad and how proud I was of Fab. I grouched that Brick hadn't heard from Casio and about his lack of interest when I'd thought they were so close. "Wanted to call the Chief, but I don't have the new number."

"Almost forgot…" Creole laughed.

"I'm happy to hear that you forgot something, since I do it all the time, so we're even."

"The Chief called and wants to meet for dinner at Jake's tomorrow night. Wants to cash in a favor or six," Creole said.

"Any clue what?" I rubbed my head, warding off a headache and trying not to anticipate what the Chief wanted.

"As irksome as I find it, and you know I do, my old boss talks more to you than he ever did to me."

I heard Didier laugh.

"I'll call Cook and have him make something special," I said. "Wait. We have four kids. What about them?"

"Do what you've been doing and put it up to a

vote—give them the choice of coming along or staying at The Cottages," Creole said.

Fab opened the door and slid behind the wheel.

"Creole and Didier are on speaker." I held out the phone.

"I wanted a few moments with Brick to tell him that I made up the baby story because my working relationship with him was playing havoc with my marriage," Fab told us all. "And that I needed to distance myself and didn't know how to just blurt it out, mindful of his feelings and all, and so I lied. He was decent about it and said he hoped we could remain friends."

"As long as that doesn't mean you'll work for him again," Didier said.

"I sidetracked all discussion of that and changed the subject."

"Are you two headed home?" Didier asked.

Fab started the engine. "Shouldn't take us long." She hung up and handed my phone back.

"I'm surprised that Brick didn't want you to come back to work for him," I said.

"He started to mention it, or so I thought, and I talked up Toady and how he handles everything I throw at him. Also told him that, in light of past events, Didier was more protective than ever. That didn't stray too far from the truth."

Fab cruised back to town and took one of her shortcuts, going the back way to The Cottages.

"Look at that." She hit the steering wheel. At the stop sign up ahead, two young guys were wrestling a man out from behind the wheel of a vintage convertible BMW Roadster. The sixty-something was giving the two twenty-somethings a hell of a fight, trading punches. Apparently frustrated that the older man wasn't going down without a fight, one pulled a gun.

"I don't think so," Fab growled. She threw open the driver's door, whipped out her gun, and shot the one with the gun in the arm. He yelped and dropped it. The other reached into his pants, and Fab yelled, "I wouldn't if I were you." She turned her aim on him.

He picked the gun up off the ground and helped his friend to his feet, shoving him into the Toyota Corolla parked in front of the BMW. The engine roared to life.

"Not going to happen." Fab leapt up on the running board and put a bullet in one of the back tires.

The car swerved and came to rest wrapped around a mailbox. The two guys got out and started running.

"Bet the car's stolen," I said to myself, since Fab was now running to the owner of the BMW. I got out and followed.

"Nice shot," the old guy said. "I used to carry and stopped. I got to where I wanted to shoot every stupid person on the street." He clapped her on the shoulder. "Thanks, girlie."

"Someone needs to call the cops," I said. "Or..." I looked up and down the street. "Since no one appears to have taken notice, let it be a surprise." I knew this was a quiet neighborhood for the most part—you'd think a gunshot and crash would attract some attention.

"Your call," Fab said to the man.

"I don't have any use for the police, but if this were to come back and hit the fan, we all might be in a bit of trouble," he said.

To my surprise, Fab pulled a business card out of her pocket and handed it to the man. They exchanged a few words I couldn't hear; then the man waved, got back in his roadster, and drove away.

Fab and I turned and got back in the SUV.

"I'm fairly certain that driving away isn't the best decision," Fab said.

"You might want to think about covering your tracks regarding your handgun. What went down wasn't illegal—or I don't think so anyway—but now that we've left the scene..."

"You're good with names," Fab said, ignoring my advice. "The man's name is Zell. There can't be too many guys in town with that name, if we ever need to track him down."

"You surprise me. I was still trying to register what I was seeing, and you were out of the car, keeping Zell from getting shot. I barely had my foot out the door. If he were depending on me, he'd be dead and his car would be gone."

"Great car. Didn't deserve to end up in the hands of thieves who'd probably be stupid enough to strip it."

"Let's hope that guy gets medical attention and it doesn't get infected. I don't want to think about the ramifications of him croaking." I whooshed out a big sigh. "It wouldn't surprise me if those two had rap sheets and were wanted for other crimes. Painful shoulder or not, they'll be back, lying in wait for another collector auto."

"If they make the mistake of attempting to jack the Hummer, they'll have a surprise waiting for them." Fab laughed devilishly.

"Don't get any blood in the car."

Chapter Eleven

I needed to get to Jake's ahead of the dinner meeting with the Chief. I'd wondered more than once what the man wanted. I knew it wouldn't be illegal, but a little hint might have been nice. Fab was there when I put the vote to the kids as to what they wanted to do for dinner. Alex threw out eating by the pool and swimming afterwards, and that was decided on unanimously. Crum, who'd also been listening, volunteered to orchestrate the evening. He threw out barbecued hot dogs and beans, and the kids clapped at that suggestion. Fab made a puking motion behind his back, and I gave her the stink eye. It surprised me that the kids hadn't tired of bossy Crum, but instead seemed to idolize him.

"What time?" Fab demanded.

"What?" I knew what she wanted, but took a smidgen of amusement in making her ask.

Fab squinted at me. "Whatever favor the Chief wants, you're going to need backup, and that's me. It's more efficient if I get the details up front and not sloppy seconds."

"I object to your characterization." I laughed at her. "Would you and Didier like to join us at six-thirty?"

"Didier's going to think I invited myself; there's no need for you to confirm it for him."

"Tell him after the fact. What's he going to do? Drag you out of there? He's tried that in the past and it hasn't worked."

* * *

It wasn't often I got to drive my own car. I pulled into the parking lot of Jake's, which sat at the back of the lot, and slowed as I passed the lighthouse. Fab claimed ownership, as it had been payment for a job. I'd never been able to get out of her who'd paid for the trucking cost. Since it sat on my property, I contested her claim. She now rented it out to Gunz as office space, for when he had a client to impress. I'd put a bench and some potted flowers in the front and let it be known that anyone was welcome to stop and take pictures.

The only other business sharing the block was Junker's, an old gas station that had been turned into a garden antique store. Junker bought in volume and sold mostly to other dealers.

I pulled around the back and parked. As I cruised through the kitchen door, I waved to Cook. This was his private domain, and he ran it without any interference, staffing it with family members. I stopped in front of him. "Do you have something yummy planned for our guest?" He nodded. "Do I get a hint?"

"One would almost think you don't trust me." He squinted at me, but failed to cover the amusement at the corners of his lips.

"How do I put this nicely? I don't. Just so we're clear, if you grill up some house pet to perfection, I'll shoot you." I returned his squint.

I gave him credit for trying, but he burst out laughing. "You're no fun."

"I'm also going to demand that you taste test it in front of all of us." I winked at him and waved, then cut down the hallway to the bar.

Kelpie, our pink-haired bartender, looked up at my approach. She waved and yelled, "Hey, Bossaroo." She shook her torso, and the multi-colored bells on her tank top lit up. Then she stepped back and showed off that she'd paired the top with a miniscule skirt, the lights she had hanging down the front flashing continuously.

Before I could place a drink order, two women in the corner caught my attention. They were bumping and fighting with one another on the nonexistent dance floor in front of the jukebox, yelling curses re: their parentage at one another. All the men at the bar had turned on their stools and watched with rapt amusement. A couple of tables were filled, and they had their eyes peeled as well. One woman took a swing at the other, and drunk mumbling followed.

"I know this is the kind of entertainment you live for," I said to Kelpie. "But not tonight. Get rid of those two before law enforcement shows up."

"I might get hurt," Kelpie whined.

I rolled my eyes. "I'll fill in for you. You need to hurry, though, in case I get an order for a mixed drink, get it wrong, and the person chokes. Then we'll have to close for the night."

The yelling between the two women had ratcheted up.

"You're no fun." Kelpie brushed by me.

"Heard that before," I grumped and slid behind the bar. "Beer, anyone?" I asked with faux cheerfulness. Not one of the patrons acknowledged me.

I stood on my tiptoes and watched as Kelpie stamped over to the two women in a huff and yelled, "Take it outside."

One took a swing at Kelpie.

Oops. Bad idea.

Kelpie caught her fist, jerked her arm behind her back and, judging from the yelp that came out of the woman, tightened her hold, escorted her out the front door in short order. She came back inside, standing in the doorway, and yelled to the other woman, "You got five seconds."

The woman grabbed their purses and actually ran out.

Everyone in the bar clapped. Kelpie curtsied, a big smile on her face, less irked than she was a minute ago.

I walked out from behind the bar, and as she passed me, I said, "You rocked breaking up that bar fight, so no more complaining. You took on two women and came away without a scratch."

"I take back all the mean thoughts I just had about you."

"Gee, thanks." I moved to the end of the bar. "Our usual bar order when everyone hits the door. I'll take a pitcher of margaritas." I waited until she pushed a drink at me, then took it, walked over to the patio door, and turned the "Keep Out" sign around. I continued out on the deck and flipped on the overheard string lights and ceiling fans, pushing together a couple of tables to accommodate everyone. I kicked back in a chair, toasted myself, and laughed.

The door opened, and Creole came out. "You getting your drunk on already?"

"Maybe a little." I winked at him. "Did you ditch our friends?" I tried to look around him. "I expected you'd come together."

"They stopped at the bar to get drinks, and Kelpie roped them into listening to the story of a bar brawl she single-handedly broke up."

"Brawl. Great. It's good for business, or so I'm told." I winked at him.

"So I've heard, and you know I don't like it," Creole growled but without a lot of heat.

"I could serve you up as entertainment. Strip you down, wrap a little bar towel around your waist — the women would flock in."

"I'd hate the job."

I grabbed the front of his shirt, brought his face to mine, and kissed him.

The door opened again, and the Chief poked his head out, pushing it open. "Look what I found." He stood back, and Fab came out, a smirk on her face.

Didier groaned. "Please tell me we're not showing up uninvited again."

"I knew you'd be here," I reassured Didier, shooting Fab a slight grin as I motioned them to have a seat.

The last one through the door was a man I hadn't seen before — well over six feet, broad-chested, his sun-bleached hair tousled. He moved so smoothly, I was surprised to see he had a prosthetic leg.

"Everyone, this is Bouff," the Chief introduced. To the man, he said, "These are the folks I told you about." He pointed me out. "Madison owns this joint."

The door opened again, and Kelpie came through, tray in hand, a huge grin on her face. She was in heaven with a room full of hot-looking men. She served everyone, saving the Chief for last.

"How you been doing, hon? Missed you around here." She bent over, the Chief's nose almost stuck between her double G's. Judging by the grin on his face, he wasn't the least put out by the extra attention. She straightened. "You need anything, whistle." She demonstrated.

I made a face but refrained from rubbing my ears.

The Chief winked as she backed through the door, giving him a short wave.

The door opened again, and one of the kitchen workers came out, set down a platter of appetizers, and left.

"If I had a restaurant, I'd hire Henry away from you," the Chief said. Henry, AKA Cook. Only two people were allowed to call him that, and I wasn't the other one.

There were a few minutes of silence as the food was devoured. I watched Bouff across the table and wondered how he fit into the favor.

It was as if Kelpie had a camera out here and an eye peeled for when the drinks needed refilling. She came through the door and refreshed the drinks with as much flourish as the first time and left, closing the door behind her.

"Why did you call this meeting?" Fab demanded of the Chief, shooting me a smirk when he wasn't looking.

"Fabiana," Didier growled. He whispered something to her that made her cheeks turn pink.

"I was thinking the same thing," I said. "What's in that pretty head of yours?"

The Chief shook his head. "I think I'll drag it out and start with my good news first."

Fab nudged me with her foot, and I knew we were in agreement that we'd like him to skip to why he called this meeting.

"As you know, I retired from the Miami Police Department. I was offered a partnership in a security firm down in Marathon and snapped it up. I still get to tell people what to do, and as you ladies know, that's one of my favorite things." The Chief grinned.

"Congratulations." I tipped my glass. "Does this mean I have to call you Mr. Harder, sir?"

"I still answer to Chief." He laughed.

"That's swell," Fab said.

Didier whispered something else in her ear, and she made a face at me.

"Your favor?" I asked. Like Fab, I was tired of waiting.

"I'd like you to hire Bouff on as a bartender."

I looked from the Chief to Bouff, who looked embarrassed. "Why would I want to do that?"

"You owe me," the Chief growled.

"You up for a little job interview?" I asked Bouff, who nodded. "You can't help him with the answers," I told the Chief. "What kind of a name is Bouff?" I asked.

Creole nudged me.

"Wilbur Bouffant." He stuck out his hand.

I shook my head. "I don't shake hands. It's icky."

Bouff didn't actually smile, but his lips curved up on the sides.

"So far, you haven't said more than five words. If you're going to work here, you're going to need to be outgoing, since you don't have breasts."

Bouff smoothed his hands down the front of his shirt. "I could go buy me a pair."

"Take my word for it, they don't garner big tips if they look phony from a mile away. Not to be rude."

Groans went around the table. Not Fab; she smiled.

"Your prosthetic leg will make you a target for drunks picking a fight, just because that's the kind of people we're known to attract." I smiled without a bit of apology. "I would feel bad if you got your ass kicked."

Bouff grinned. "You'd think I'd get a free pass from those kinds of a-holes, but I don't, and it wouldn't be the first time I've had to kick an ass or two."

The Chief grunted, and all eyes turned to him. "Bouff here just came in second in a marathon up in Miami over the weekend."

I took in his muscular chest and well-defined biceps. "These guys know the best places to run around here and not get hit by cars." I motioned to Didier and Creole. "Next question: you adept with a firearm? Sometimes, you need to brandish one to convince the more aggravating customers to leave, and I wouldn't want you to shoot yourself."

"This is a most unorthodox interview," Bouff said.

"He was a bomb specialist in Afghanistan," the Chief said.

I narrowed my eyes at the Chief and made a locking motion in front of my lips. "I do need a closing bartender. The last one found herself a Daddy and ran off to get married. I can't promise the same for you, but you never know." I settled back in my chair and stared at the man and then at the Chief.

There was another knock on the door, and dinner was served.

Once the dishes were cleared away and everyone's drink had been refreshed, I decided it was time to get back to the reason for the get-together.

"My answer is no to employment, and not because I don't think you'd fit in—especially if you'd agree to go shirtless; we'd be standing room only at the bar—but because you're a cop, even though neither of you were upfront about it. Some of my customers have outstanding issues with law enforcement, and I won't set them up to be arrested. I'm not talking Class A felonies—mostly drinking issues that they didn't deal with." I turned to the Chief. "Am I wrong?"

The Chief snorted. "You're so irritating."

"I've been told that particular characteristic is part of my charm." I leaned into Creole, who put his arm around me.

"I'm assuming I can trust you, since your husband was one of my men," the Chief said.

"You know I have a thing for undercover officers."

"Bouff wouldn't be here to ferret out folks that have outstanding littering citations," the Chief reassured me. "There are a couple of big cases going on right now that I've been asked to consult on. I need someone to get friendly with the locals and pick up information that could be helpful."

"Why not just be upfront?" I asked.

"And miss out on your interview technique?" The Chief shook his head.

"So, you're up on the criminal activity in the area. Do you still have contacts from your old job?" I asked.

"You're countering with a favor already?" the Chief snapped.

"Can you check and make sure that Casio is well and accounted for?" I told him about taking care of Casio's kids and that he was several days late in getting back and I hadn't heard from him.

"Casio's been known to go off the radar before, so that's nothing new," the Chief said.

It surprised me that he had a ready answer. "Damn him. He better come back still sucking air, or I'm going to be furious with him."

"Don't you worry about him; he takes chances but always covers his backside," the Chief reassured me.

I didn't believe that, but it calmed me some. "I'm going to introduce you to the manager, Doodad," I told Bouff. "He won't be happy that he had no input on this hiring decision. I'm going to tell him that you being a vet was the deciding factor." I pulled out my phone and called the office. I knew he was in there, as he rarely ever went home. When he answered, I said, "I did something high-handed and went over your head and hired a bartender. If he totally sucks, you can boot him out the door and I'll triple make it up to you."

Doodad laughed. "Where is this paragon?"

"We're out on the deck."

"I already know what I want. Favors. Everybody else stockpiles them, and I need a few of my own."

"You're on." I hung up and said to Bouff, "Sparkle and shine. This needs to work out all around."

The door flew open, and tropical storm Doodad blew in, hair in disarray as though I'd woken him up.

"Oh, hey, man." He clipped Bouff on the shoulder and looked around.

"I guess I don't have to introduce you to the new employee," I said.

"Here I was, braced for some twat. You should've told me it was Bouff." Doodad motioned to the man. "I'll show you around."

"That went well, don't you think?" I asked the table at large.

The guys laughed.

Chapter Twelve

All had been quiet and uneventful for several days. The guys had decided a while back that the four of us needed weekly meetings, and in the past, they'd been at Fab and Didier's or the Bakery Café. Now that the kids had come into our lives, the location had been changed to the pool at The Cottages. Creole and I had made a bakery run and came back with a stack of pink boxes. Fab and Didier had brought their coffee pot and stopped for juice, setting everything up on the bar. Fab waved and motioned to the table that she'd set for the four of us. The kids had commandeered their own table and were studying with Crum.

After we were seated, Fab said, "Just so we're clear," and glared at the two men, "this isn't a one-way street of us making all the disclosures." She flicked her finger between her and me. "You'll do so as well. Agreed? Good," she said without waiting for an answer.

The three of us grinned at her.

Didier raised his hand. "I'll go first. I know that you signed the paperwork on the apartment building yesterday." He looked to me for confirmation, and I nodded. "Knowing that you want to maintain your anonymity in this deal, Creole and I are thinking that we'll orchestrate the repairs behind the scenes and use Cootie as the frontman."

"I talked to him about it yesterday and told him that there was an element of danger, and the crazy man seemed excited about that aspect and eagerly went for the idea," Creole said.

"Wonder if Trigger knows that the building has been sold out from under him?" I threw out, not expecting an answer.

"I talked to Toady yesterday," Fab said. "Ace is wigged out by the new wife's involvement in the whole situation."

"Let's hope he doesn't end up dead," Creole said.

"Toady said Ace was worrying about the same thing, and he's on edge," Fab reported.

"Just great," I whooshed.

"Don't worry," Fab said. "Toady's keeping an eye on the man. Says they hit it off and nothing's going to happen to Ace. Promised him and me."

"I'll go next." I waved my hand. "The kids are great. No problem there."

"My new client from the other day… in a word, she's looney tunes." Fab sighed. "I took your advice," she said to me.

"I bet that was hard. Did you have to rest up afterwards?"

"You guys wipe the grins off your faces; it

only encourages her, and she's not funny," Fab said. "I had Xander find the so-called friend and, at the same time, run a background check on her. The last known address for the character she's looking for is Tampa. Xander can't find anything current or any phone numbers, and there's no chance I'm driving up there to check out old addresses."

"There's a job for Toady. He won't complain about the drive north," I said. "If Asha's crazy, then Blanchard needs to be warned to watch his back; what he does after that is on him. Unless he wants to be found."

"What do I do about Asha?" Fab asked.

"Tell her the guy moved to Alaska. If you tell her you can't find him at all, she may go to someone else, who'll give her the information and not care what happens," I said.

"This screams freebie, and you know how I hate that," Fab said.

"How crazy is she?" Creole asked.

"In addition to a rap sheet filled with stalker-type crimes, she's a recovering addict who recently checked out of the rehab facility she'd been living in… early," Fab said.

"You need to stall her until you can warn the guy and then, depending on what he says, at least make it harder to find him," I said.

"You need to avoid any future face-to-face meetings," Didier said. "Deal with her on the phone."

"She took a liking to your wife and wants to become her new bestie." I smiled at Fab. "What she doesn't know is that I'd shoot her first."

Fab patted my hand. "You're all the friend I can handle."

I turned to Creole. "You'll be happy to know that I'm taking a couple of days off from all the drama and hanging out with the kids. Cooking class yesterday was the last of the planned activities, and I'm thinking I'm going to be a bore when I suggest the beach and building sandcastles."

"You need to bring a bag of toys and keep them running around in circles until they drop from exhaustion," Fab said.

"That's a great idea. Then bring 'em back to the cottage, feed them, and maybe they'll go to sleep before it gets dark out." I winked at Creole.

He winked back. "Just because we're having regular meetings doesn't mean that you can stop calling between jobs to let us know you got away in one piece and with no bullets flying."

The guys had a meeting to go to, so they dropped kisses on us and left.

"You going to hang out with me? You know you'll be bored if you don't." I laughed at Fab's grimace.

Chapter Thirteen

Fab and I had claimed a table under a large umbrella on the opposite side of the pool from the kids and set up office space. While she left to retrieve something from the SUV, I flipped open my laptop. The sound of cars roaring into the driveway, followed by the slamming of doors, had me looking up. It was another minute before Mac showed up at the gate, followed by two uniformed police officers out of Miami. Behind them was an older woman dressed in a dowdy suit, who had to be dripping sweat. Another woman, dressed far more casually in a sundress, stood next to Mac, a smug look on her face.

"Open the gate," one officer ordered Mac. Once she did, he pointed for her to step to the side. "Stand back."

I stood and started forward. "What's going on?" I asked.

"Madison Westin?" the officer asked, and I nodded.

"I've got a court order to pick up the Famosa children." He held up a document.

"That's them," the woman in tropical chic

yelled, pointing to the table where the children sat.

The twins scooted over next to Crum, and Lili jumped off the bench and ran over to me. I scooped her up in a hard hug.

"I don't understand what's going on," I said. "I have power of attorney from their father." I heard the woman outside the gate snort. "Shouldn't I have received notification of a court hearing?"

"You'll need to take that up with the judge," the officer said, thrusting the paperwork at me.

Dowdy woman stepped forward and introduced herself as from social services. "You were served and failed to show."

"No, I was not." I quickly glanced at the order and saw the kids' names. I tossed it on the nearest table.

The social worker waved me away and reached for Lili, who started to scream at the top of her lungs. Without any hesitation, she grabbed the little girl out of my arms. I barely restrained myself from slugging the woman.

"You need to step back and let us handle this," the cop said. "If not, we'll have to arrest you."

The twins were now screaming that they didn't want to go anywhere.

"Couldn't we slow this transfer down and talk to the kids, explain what's going on and make it less traumatic?" I asked, "Where are they going?"

The older woman ignored my request. "They're being placed with a relative." She turned and headed toward the gate with Lili, who was sobbing.

The second cop went over and talked to the boys. The twins wrapped their arms around Crum's waist and cried.

"You know my dad wouldn't want us going with you," Alex screamed at the woman outside the gate.

"Who is that?" I asked, closing the distance between us.

"That bitch is married to Brick," Alex yelled.

So that was Maya Famosa. To my shock, she smiled, as though enjoying the kids' distress.

"I'm so sorry," I whispered to Alex. "I swear I didn't know about any court date or I'd have shown up." I turned to the social worker, who had her hand on the gate, about to disappear, and called out. "They need a little time to get their belongings packed up."

"No, they don't," Maya yelled. "It's all worthless and can be replaced. They also need to leave any electronics, as they're not allowed in my house."

I turned to Maya and implored, "Please don't do this. Casio wouldn't want you to take the kids. They're happy here."

"Do you even have half a brain?" Maya snapped. "You're not family, and this place is a dump." She looked around in disdain, her nose in the air.

"Let me talk to Alex so he can help with his siblings," I said to the cop.

"If I have to tell you one more time to stay back, you're going to jail."

The other cop stepped forward and wrenched the twins away from Crum, and the three were on their way out of the pool area not far behind Lili. Crum had attempted to calm their fears and did his best to wipe their tears with his sleeves, but he didn't have enough time to give them any kind of explanation that would make sense of what was happening.

Alex leaped forward, throwing his arms around me. "I know this isn't your fault. I'll make you the same promise that I did my dad and look after my brothers and sister."

"You're a great kid." I hugged him hard. "Your dad will be proud when he hears how you handled this situation. I promise I'm going to get hot on the phone with my lawyer about this court order."

Maya laughed. "That's an empty promise. I've got enough money to keep this out of court until the kids turn eighteen. Judging by this place, you can't afford bus fare," she sneered.

Alex gave me one last hug and ran to catch up to his siblings.

The social worker came back empty-handed and nodded to Maya, who met her. The two women exchanged a couple of words and left together. They'd only taken a few steps when Maya tripped and fell to her knees, her hands splayed out to keep her from falling on her face. Fab, who'd shown up out of nowhere, clapped her hand over her mouth, looking down at Maya. "Sorry," she said, sounding anything but, a less-than-contrite look on her face.

I reminded myself to hug Fab later.

The social worker helped Maya to her feet. She cursed at Fab and was about to launch an attack, but the other woman held her back. After a short exchange, they left.

I crumpled into the nearest chair in shock. "I failed those kids. And Casio. I swear, I was never served or I'd have shown up." I grabbed the legal papers off the table, gave them a cursory glance, and crumpled them in my hand.

Fab had flown through the gate and over to my side. She put her arm around me. "You were set up to lose," she consoled.

"They were screaming and crying, and that Maya woman didn't have an ounce of compassion. How will Lili get to sleep? She's got that dreadful recording of Casio singing off-key that she listens to every night on her phone, and she wasn't allowed to take it with her. I didn't even get to hug them all good-bye." I wasn't about to sit here and indulge in a good cry, which would accomplish nothing. I stood and walked over to Crum. "Can you organize the schoolwork? I'll make sure it gets to them so they get credit for doing it." I engaged in a stare-down with Fab, then said, "I've got an appointment and need to change clothes."

I'd taken two steps when Fab grabbed my arm. "I'm coming with you."

I went back to the cottage that Creole and I had shared with the kids. It was a different kind of quiet, knowing that they wouldn't be back. I knew without consulting a lawyer that Maya Famosa could dance me around in court and not blink about running up a gazillion dollars in attorney fees. I changed into a full skirt and t-shirt. Coming out of the bedroom, I noticed that Fab had zeroed in on my tennis shoes. We walked out to the SUV without saying a word. I opened the back, unlocked the lockbox that Creole had installed, which was hidden from view, and strapped my Glock to my thigh.

I hopped behind the wheel, and Fab did a double-take but got in without saying a word. I squealed out of the driveway and shot to the corner, making the turn and cutting off someone I hadn't seen. I turned onto the Overseas, then pulled over and parked. "You better drive if we want to get there in one piece. Seems like I'm taking my frustration out on the road." I got out and rounded the front, climbing into the passenger seat. "Famosa Motors, please," I said.

Surprisingly, Fab didn't say a word about my request, instead putting the SUV in gear and tore up the highway. She had lots of experience driving like a crazy woman, and I had no doubt that she'd get us there in one piece.

Chapter Fourteen

Fab pulled into the parking lot of Famosa Motors and parked in the front. There were two salesmen at opposite ends of the property, both busy with customers.

I slid out and said, "I don't care to be announced today." I headed toward the service department, knowing that I could circle around, double back, and end up at the steps that led to Brick's office and the receptionist, with her back to me, would be none the wiser.

Fab grabbed my arm and slowed me down. "You need to take a deep breath and calm down."

"I'm as calm as I'm going to get until I find out why what happened went down and why it had to play out the way it did," I seethed.

Just like I called it, no one took notice of the two of us entering through the side door and going up the stairs.

Brick looked up when we came through the door. "Surprised to see you two so soon." He leaned back in his chair, smirk on his face.

"Are. You. Really?" I bit out.

"What's got your skirt in a twist?"

"Wipe that stupid smirk off your face." I reminded myself to be calm, but I'd pretty much lost that battle, and my inner demon yelled *to heck with that*. "Why in the hell did your wife pull the stunt she did today and devastate Casio's kids?"

"How dare you!" He rose out of his chair.

I leaned in and said, "I dare plenty."

"Okay, you two." Fab stepped in front of me. "Take a breath, and both of you sit." She pushed on my arm, and I shrugged away and reluctantly sat down.

"You brought this all on yourself, not showing up in court," Brick said, his tone saying clearly it didn't matter if he wasn't in the right, it only mattered what he thought. "Figured you were lying about the power of attorney or you'd have shown up with one of your jerk attorneys."

"You know that I didn't know anything about the court case," I yelled. "You, your wife, or both of you set it up with some shyster attorney so I wouldn't get notification and be a no-show."

Fab walked over and closed the door.

"Whine, whine," Brick spit out. "Guess you need a reminder—you're not family. I'm not wild about having the brats under my roof, but if it makes my wife happy, done deal. So get over it."

"It's clear you don't care about the kids. Does your wife, or is this some petty way to get back at Casio? I hope he kicks your ass up to your tonsils when he gets back." I returned his glare and upped it to a new level.

"Get the hell out of here." Brick pointed to the door.

I didn't move. "Your bitch of a wife refused to take their clothes, electronics, and school work. I can have them messengered over to you tomorrow."

"Throw it all away," Brick ordered. "I don't know that you haven't placed bugging devices in the electronics, so no thanks."

"You're not that interesting," I said with a sneer, enjoying that his face got redder than it already was. "Why would you uproot the kids in such a harsh way and go against what their dad wanted? You remember Casio, the brother you've professed to be close to over the years?"

"What the hell do you care? You banging my bro?" Brick laughed, full of disgust. "Let me guess, you're in one of those three-way deals with that ugly husband of yours."

"You're such a coward. You don't have the guts to say that to Creole's face, knowing that he'd break yours, which is what I hope Casio does when he gets back."

"If the kids want to talk, they can call anytime." Fab jerked on my arm to prompt me to stand up.

"You've lost your mind, hanging around with this one," Brick boomed out. "Let me make this clear, in small words that you can understand — do not set foot on any property I own." He turned to Fab. "That includes you if she's anywhere in a fifty-mile radius." His angry eyes zoomed in my direction. "Got it, bitch?"

I drew my Glock and pulled the trigger, the bullet whizzing by his head and lodging in the middle of one of his Businessman of the Year plaques. We were both in shock. Brick recovered first and started to stand.

I shook the barrel of the gun at him. "Stand at your own risk. If there's a next shot, you won't be so lucky, as I'd be protecting myself."

"I'm calling the cops," Brick blustered but stayed seated. "Hello to jail for you."

"Go right ahead." I pointed to his phone. "I know a hell of a lot about you, and when I'm done talking to the District Attorney, I'll be the one enjoying the sunshine and you'll be the one in a jail cell." I enjoyed the look of shock on his face. "Well?" He didn't reach for his phone, which I took as evidence that he wasn't going to call… just yet anyway. "I want to be clear with you—you treat those kids better than your own. If I hear anything to contrary, I'll send someone to erase any trace that you ever existed. Got it?" I shook my gun at him again.

"Get out." Other than to yell those two words at me, he still hadn't moved.

I turned, and Fab moved in behind me, probably saving me from being shot in the back.

The door banged against the wall as I threw it open, and walked out.

"I'll meet you downstairs," Fab said.

I left the building the same way I'd come, so there wouldn't be any questions asked. I got into the Hummer and reclined the seat.

Fab returned faster than I'd figured and slid behind the wheel. "That didn't go quite like I thought. He told me not to come back unless I severed my relationship with you, and I told him that wasn't happening."

"Casio needs to come back. Now."

Chapter Fifteen

Without asking, Fab drove straight to Jake's. I waved at Bouff, who was behind the bar, getting trained by Kelpie, who appeared to be thoroughly enjoying herself. Fab placed our drink orders.

I slid the "Keep Out" sign into place on the door to the deck, closed it, and sat at our usual table, Fab across from me. "I can't get my drunk on every time I have a bad day," I said. I slipped my phone out of my pocket and called my lawyer, saying when he answered, "I know this case isn't up your alley, but maybe you could give your pro opinion anyway."

"I'm assuming this is Madison, since that's the name that came up on the screen," Tank snarked. Fab had met Tank, AKA Patrick Cannon, during a jail visitation. He said he was in lockup on a case of mistaken identity, and as it turned out, he wasn't full of himself and his story turned out to be the truth.

"Whoever said you were dumb was mistaken."

"Along with a few epithets that you're not

repeating, I'm certain." Tank laughed. "One thing about lawyers, they're always happy to venture an opinion, even when they don't know jack. As for me, I'll disclose when I'm full of it."

I told him about the morning's events.

"Your best case would be for temporary return, since the father wanted them with you and left instructions to that effect. A permanent placing in the event Casio doesn't return is a crap shoot. In both scenarios, however, the courts favor family. The case would be a slam dunk for the brother and his wife if they could prove you were derelict. Shooting the kids' uncle would be frowned upon and wouldn't work in your favor. If you'd killed him, I'd be suggesting a quick trip to the Caribbean and then for you to disappear."

The door opened, and Bouff came out and set down two pitchers of drinks. I shot him a thumbs up.

"I figured that would be the case, but I had to check," I said, trying and failing to keep the sadness out of my tone. "Send me a bill and come by Jake's for free food. Thank you for not putting me on hold."

Tank laughed, and we hung up.

Fab picked up her phone. "Ride service?" she asked.

I shot her a "who are you talking to?" look, which she ignored as she made her call.

"We're at Jake's and will be needing a ride home." After a silence on her part, she made a kissy noise—the same kind she admonished me for—and hung up.

"I'm assuming that was Didier," I said.

"I don't have the time or interest to be juggling men."

"What am I going to tell Casio when he gets back?" I asked.

"The truth. Not one scintilla of what went down today was your fault. I really do hope that he rearranges Brick's brains and shoves them up his backside."

"Fabiana Merceau." My shocked tone was lessened by my wide smile.

"I told Brick it was a dick move for him to aid and abet his wife in what went down and, more importantly, how it went down. I told him we could've delivered the kids to his house, which I figured you might not have agreed to, but he didn't know that. I only wanted to make him feel bad, but that didn't work."

I downed my drink and refilled the glass. "I'd like to ask a favor."

"I probably already know what it is, but go ahead."

"Do you think you could've been agreeable without the eye roll?"

"Heck no." Fab grinned. "How about I guess, and when I get it right, you go in and order mini tacos. Cook doesn't like to make them, so I don't want to ask and ruin my standing."

"Why wait?" I took a swig of my drink, then

stood and opened the door. "Kelpie," I bellowed, and several patrons turned to stare. "Could you tell Cooker mini tacos times two?" I held up my fingers.

Kelpie gave me a thumbs up, and I slammed the door. "Done. Now, about my favor." I took another gulp of my drink. "When Cooker storms in here, eyebrows in his hairline, I'm going to tell him Kelpie was mistaken and you placed the order."

"That's going to work because we look so much alike. I'm thinking your red hair gives it away that you're not me."

"Pesky details."

Fab rubbed her forehead with her palm.

"That was my shtick, and you stole it," I grouched.

"You don't want me to totally cut ties with Brick so I can get updates on the kids. Was that the favor?"

"If you could do that, that would be swell," I said. "I'm hoping that the adjustment is an easy one on the kids, since there's a houseful of cousins, and hopefully they have a relationship."

"I'm fairly certain that Maya Famosa orchestrated what went down, and it had everything to do with her relationship with Casio. It surprises me that Brick sat back and let it unfold. I've seen evidence in the past that he doesn't have a pair when it comes to his wife, but today took it to a new level."

"Enough about today." I let out a big sigh. "Let's have a business meeting. What's on your calendar that you've failed to mention?"

"Gunz called and wants a face-to-face." Fab sighed.

"That sounds fun," I said, an eye roll in my tone. "More relative issues? He should demand ID. No one has that many relations. What happened with the cousin or whatever whose girlfriend tried to set him on fire? I suppose catching your honey-bunny in the sack with two other girls could push you over the edge. Although arson seems extreme."

"Do you have to reduce situations to the lowest common denominator?"

"Pretty much." I gave her a toothy, insincere smile.

"The cousin relocated to parts unknown," Fab said. "As for the girlfriend, Carly, Gunz did say that he felt bad; nonetheless, he blackmailed her into getting mental health care or going to jail. So, she's in a live-in facility."

"Let's hope she wants to put her life back together and doesn't get released until such time as that happens. And the owner of the apartment building?" I asked.

"Gunz bought it. Added it to his portfolio."

"Happy ending all around."

The door opened and Cook came out, a platter over his head, and set it down in the middle of the table. The guys were behind him, beers in hand. They sat down, and both Fab and I got kisses.

"New item on the menu," Cook said. "You're always wanting mini tacos, so why not make a platter so you can choose what you want to put on them?" He grabbed plates off a side cart and set them down.

"This looks yum," I said, leaning forward and licking my lips.

The guys were starving, and we all ate without a lot of talking.

"The only thing I don't like is that there aren't any leftovers to take home." I frowned.

"We haven't had a lot of that lately with all the little mouths to feed." Creole laughed. "We need to put in another order. Do you remember what they like?"

"About that..." I stared at Fab. "You tell them."

Fab told them about the events of the day, starting with the cops arriving at The Cottages. As was typical for her, she'd found a place to observe everything that went down without being seen. When she got to the part about me shooting at Brick, she punctuated with appropriate sound effects and jerked her head back. The guys didn't believe her at first, until I nodded.

"You should've called." Creole wrapped his arms around me.

"I shouldn't have acted on impulse, but I'd

endured all the smirking I could stand," I said. "I lost my mind. It didn't make me feel better. I've been thinking about everything I would've lost if my shot had blown his brains out. This might not be over; he still might follow through on his threat to call the cops."

"If Brick makes that mistake, he'll be retracting his complaint in short order," Creole grouched. "I promise you that."

"You'd go all thug on him for me?" I leaned forward and brushed my lips over Creole's.

"You bet I would, and I'd enjoy every minute. I'd be hoping that he waffles so I'd have an excuse to beat the snot out of him."

"I'm thinking his brother's going to take care of that for you," Didier said.

"I'm going to suggest that Casio put out the word so we can all come watch," Creole said.

"We're going home," I said to him. "I'll clean out the cottage tomorrow."

"We can store the kids' stuff in containers in my garage, and when Casio gets back, we'll make sure everything's returned," Fab offered.

"That's a great idea. We'll have a reunion party and make sure they get their belongings back," I said.

Chapter Sixteen

The next morning, I left the house early and headed over to The Cottages, stopping to pick up plastic containers. I took on the job of cleaning the cottage myself, as I knew what belonged to whom and wanted it packed up correctly. With Mac's help, I loaded the containers in the back of her truck and hauled them over to Fab's. That done, Fab wanted to go to lunch, but I begged off and moped around for the next couple of days.

"It's not your fault, you know," Creole said, eyeing me over his cup. He'd gotten up and made coffee, bringing it back to bed and fluffing up the pillows for me.

"The only upside is that we've had some alone time, and that's been great. You're the best and, right from the beginning, took this situation better than most husbands would."

Creole leaned in and kissed me. "I've got some interesting gossip."

"I'm hoping you're going to share."

"Normally, I wouldn't be bothered, but when the Michaels brothers' names were mentioned, I had to admit I was all ears."

I groaned. "What are those two up to now?"

The brothers, Hank and Ted, were engaged in an age-old feud over the petty question of who'd amassed more wealth. In a one-upmanship scheme, Hank had faked his death and made it appear that Ted had done the deed. As part of the scheme, Hank had dragged me into a fake real estate deal to ensure I'd discover the so-called crime scene. It had brought the wrath of the other brother down on me—Ted figuring that I'd killed his brother and was setting him up to take the fall. He didn't care if it was the truth or not, as long as the cops stopped camping on his doorstep. I had located Hank and threatened to expose his lies if he didn't reappear and put a stop to all the murder talk.

"The warehouse that Hank had supposedly wanted to sell is actually for sale now. His agent is under orders not to advertise the listing. As always, he doesn't want his brother to get his hands on the property."

"He could've had that deal done ages ago, but it was all a con." I sniffed.

"Ted apparently isn't happy that his brother's alive, nor that he's still the subject of a whisper campaign by people wanting to blame his brother's death on him, even though he's not dead. The fact that he was under suspicion is enough that some won't shut up about it. In retaliation, he sicced the county building inspectors on Hank, and he's racking up the violations."

"How is it that the next three buildings on the street, which are owned by Ted, are in a worse state of disrepair, and that's conveniently overlooked?" I asked in disgust.

Creole nodded. "You know what I think would annoy the brothers equally? If we were to buy it."

"Are you forgetting that I brought up owning that warehouse at a family dinner and it was voted a big thumbs down?" The warehouses were located down a side street from the Boardwalk, and fixing up the eyesores would complete the renovation of the area.

"I was thinking you and me."

"I'm guessing that you have an ulterior motive—get me busy looking after our own properties and I won't have time to run all over creation with Fab," I said.

"Think about it. My ulterior motives shouldn't factor in." He grinned.

"I'll be honest, I'd like to own the property, just so I could give the finger to both brothers." His grin got even bigger. "I realize that kind of pettiness is unbecoming, but tough totems."

Creole stuck out his hand, and we shook.

"So, wife, what's on the agenda for today?"

"Gunz is requesting a sit-down, and that generally means more craziness than usual," I said. "His redeeming quality is that he doesn't set us up to be shot or go to jail."

"He's okay," Creole admitted grudgingly.

"That's not until this afternoon, so I have time for a nice long shower." I winked at him.

Creole rolled off the bed and reached out and scooped me up. "I'm not one to pass up fun time with my wife."

* * *

Creole's truck hadn't made it out of the compound when my phone rang. I swear, that woman knew everything before it even happened.

"There was a fire in the front apartment in the building next to yours," Fab announced when I answered. "Mac called you first, but your phone was turned off."

"Anyone hurt?"

"Luckily, no. I'm assuming you want to survey the damage, so I'll be picking you up soon." Fab chuckled at the same time I heard the sound of a horn out front.

"Give me a minute and try not to annoy the neighbors."

Since there were no neighbors, that would be an easy accomplishment.

I grabbed my ready tote bag and purse and hustled out the door.

Fab had already backed out the SUV. I jumped in the passenger side and asked, "Arson?"

"Mac didn't say and I didn't ask, as the fire truck had just pulled up. They arrived in minutes and put out the fire, keeping it from spreading to another unit."

"I imagine it attracted quite the crowd. Any little bit of excitement in the neighborhood brings out the lookie-loos, so I'll be hoping to blend in," I said.

"Another thing I got out of Mac is that she has a prime view of the front of the property from her porch, so I'm thinking we can kick back there."

"You ready to read my mind and tell me what I'm thinking?"

"That Trigger's found out that the building's sold and not to him, and he isn't happy." Fab eyed me. "If he's heard, and he probably has, he's even more annoyed that the whole building didn't go up in flames. You had to know that the man wasn't going to take it well when he found out."

"So, he's unstable enough that he'd risk burning down the whole block?" I grimaced. I needed to do a better job of covering my tracks so the sale didn't lead back to me.

"I think hiring Toady to be the figurehead was a good idea," Fab said.

"Unless he gets hurt. I've grown fond of the old alligator."

"I had a talk with him, and he's not the least bit worried about his grizzled hide." Fab bypassed all her favorite shortcuts and took the direct route. When we rounded the corner to The Cottages, the street was blocked by a fire truck and a couple of cop cars.

"Our favorite sheriff's deputy won't be happy when he gets wind of this. It's reminiscent of his being burned out of his last place. Maybe we'll qualify for some extra protection."

Fab laughed. "Have you forgotten Kevin doesn't like either of us?"

"We've risen in his esteem; he now tolerates us." I smirked at her.

Fab parked around the corner, and we walked over to join Mac, who waved at us from her porch.

"More bad news," Mac said once we got in hearing distance. "Ace is in the hospital. Heart attack or some such. I'm not sure how Karen expected her marriage to survive after she conspired with a drug dealer and used her husband in the process."

"It wasn't brought on by his wife or Trigger, was it?" I asked, walking up the steps, taking a seat, Fab next to me.

"Pink house lady was light on details," Mac said.

"Doesn't she have a name?" I asked.

"You two never remember them anyway, so why bother?" Mac smiled.

"Fab's fault," I said. "That bad habit of hers sometimes rubs off on me."

"Hey, I've been doing better of late." Fab leaned forward. "You got an update on the fire?" she asked Mac.

"Someone tossed a molotov cocktail through the front window of the manager's unit. Thankfully, they weren't home at the time. Their daughter is on the way down from Orlando to pick them up," Mac told us.

"Make sure that Toady gets their contact info. I'll give it to the insurance company when I file the claim," I said.

"Pink house lady is gathering donations, since they lost everything," Mac said.

"Kick in a large donation and say it's from you," I said.

Fab's took her ringing phone out of her pocket, glanced at the screen, and mouthed, *Toady.*

Great. More problems, I bet.

Fab made a few non-committal responses and started to hang up. I snapped my fingers at her and held my hand out.

"I've got another job for you, so call me later?" I asked.

"You got it, girlie." We hung up. "What did Toady want?" I asked Fab.

"Ace had a fight with his wife, who went ballistic when she found out that her bestie, Trigger, had been beaten out of the deal. She was even angrier that she didn't have a clue until after the fact," Fab said. "Karen trotted out a side that scared the devil out of Ace, and he faked a heart attack. From the hospital, he called Toady, who went and picked him up, and the old guy is going to so-call recuperate at his house for a few days. Ace wants a divorce."

"Is Toady opening his digs out in the Glades?" I wrinkled my nose.

Toady owned property out in alligator alley adjoining my brother's property. What the two men saw in the area escaped me; I wouldn't go out there unless it was life and death.

"I guess I forgot to tell you—Toady rented a place here in town," Fab said. "Grouched that it was too long a hike between the alley and the Keys, now that he's getting more jobs down this way."

"That was it?" Mac asked.

"You're nosey."

"That's not news," Mac snapped at Fab.

"Okay you two, we've got enough drama going on for the day." I trotted out my deranged smile and leveled it at them, and they laughed. Okay, so it needed more work. "Before I forget…" I turned to Mac. "*Anyone* comes around asking questions, play the part of a dumb brunette obsessed with her boobs and dance them around." I stared at her tight t-shirt, which read "The Ass Family" and showed a family of five. I tried not to laugh, but it escaped anyway.

"So, my usual." She shook her chest so the Asses danced back and forth.

"I don't want you to do *anything* that would put you in danger," I said. "You never know who's asking or whether it's for themselves or someone else."

"I got my friend, Buster, here, just in case." Mac hiked her ruffled skirt and showed off the Beretta strapped to her thigh.

"I need to name my guns," I said.

Fab groaned.

Mac leaned forward and stared at Fab. "What did you 'forget' to tell us?"

"Thank you." I smiled at Mac. I'd forgotten that Fab didn't answer her question. "Yeah, what?"

"Toady's got a car recovery job and needs us to take care of it so he can focus on Ace," Fab said. "Since he never says no to us, I could hardly do it to him. It's not that big of a deal. Dude had an early flight and left the rental parked in the hotel parking lot. I'll get in and drive it back to the car lot—one of those pay-by-the-week places."

"Didn't know that those places were in the rental business. Answer me why it is that out-of-town people aren't using a regular rental agency?"

"Guess what?" Fab raised her brows. "Didn't ask because I don't care."

"That's a shock." I lifted my skirt, showing off my Glock. "I'm dressed for fun." I kicked the banister with my tennis shoe. "Do you need anything before we split?" I asked Mac.

"Nopers. I'll be snooping around, trying to get any information I can. I'll wait until later and hit up a couple of bars; by then, the fire should be the talk and I might get something good. It's not always a pack of lies."

"That's good to know." Fab turned her nose up.

"Ignore her." I shook my finger at Mac, softening it with a smile. "Be. Careful."

I stood, gave Mac a quick wave, and followed Fab down the porch steps and up the street.

Chapter Seventeen

"I should've asked where we're going, but it's too late to get out of the car now," I said as Fab took the curve north towards Miami. I hoped that wasn't the destination.

"You'll be happy to know it's not far, just south of Homestead—Florida City."

"Then you have time to update me on crazy chick, Asha whatever."

"I wound up getting ahold of Asha's supposed old friend, Dan Blanchard, via the neighbor at his old place. Chatty woman. I channeled you, and she just talked on and on, barely taking a breath in her ramblings. Finally, just when I couldn't stand it any longer, someone thankfully knocked on the door. Before I hung up, she promised to give Dan the message."

"It pleases me that you've learned a trick or two from me." I gave her a gloating smile, certain she was struggling not to laugh, much to her disgust.

"Where was I?" She flicked her hair over her shoulder and smirked. "Dan called back in short order, more curious about what the heck I wanted than anything. Once I relayed how Asha was hot on his tail, to say he was unhappy at the news doesn't quite cover it—more like freaked out. He painted a picture of mental instability and said she'd always been that way and prone to violence when things didn't go the way she wanted. Asha had proposed to him several years back, and he turned her down. And how did she react, you're thinking? She shot him. Okay… in the arm, but still. Lucky him, she didn't know how to use a firearm."

"Let me guess, since he was grateful to still be breathing, he thought, why not give this relationship a shot?"

"Sarcasm doesn't move the conversation along."

I pouted.

"Good thing I have a good memory, since I was interrupted again. Dan—I called him Don a couple of times; he didn't seem to notice."

I laughed.

"Anyway… Dan said it irked him that the court system was more sympathetic to her and her sad life than concerned that he could've ended up dead. He packed his bags and lit out of town when she got probation with the stipulation of undergoing mental health care, which he confided that Asha'd had years of and it hadn't helped. Dan was angry and disappointed that he'd been found, since he didn't leave a forwarding and thought he'd done a good job covering his tracks."

"Shouldn't have given his landlady his new phone number then," I said.

"Lucky us that he did. I told Dan not to worry, that I was going to tell Asha he'd moved to Alaska. He laughed. I also hooked him up with Xander, who's going to help him get invisible and stay that way, since we agreed that Asha's a problem that's not going to go away."

"That's swell of you," I said.

"I have my moments. I felt kind of bad for disturbing Dan's peace of mind. I did warn him that, depending on how tenacious Asha is, she might contact another company to locate him and he should follow Xander's instructions to the letter. Then she won't find him, no matter who she sics on his tail."

"And Asha?" I asked.

"Annoying thing that she is, she calls every day. I told her I needed a few more days, as he'd moved several times, but not to worry. I'm going to give it another day, then call her back and give her the address of an empty field in Alaska. Then I'm going to block her number."

Fab pulled off the highway and followed the directions the snotty girl in the GPS unit gave her, pulling into the parking lot of a three-star hotel that had seen better days. There were only a handful of cars, which made spotting the grey Mercedes easy. Fab circled the lot and the car, double-checking the license plates.

As she started to pull up next to it, I jerked on

her arm. "Keep going," I shouted.

Fab hit the gas, then slowed. "What the heck?"

"There's a man in the driver's seat. His head's turned toward the window, and I swear there's blood on his face." I shuddered.

Fab bypassed the exit to the street and slowed. "You must be mistaken." She turned around.

"How?" I uttered. I knew she planned on going back to check it out for herself. Before I could tell her what a stupid idea it was, three police cars pulled into the parking lot and across the lanes, surrounding the parked car. A man I hadn't noticed before stood not far away, waving and pointing.

Fab zipped out the exit without so much as a glance over her shoulder.

"Is that what it takes for you to follow my advice? Law enforcement squealing onto the scene?"

"What just happened?" Fab practically shrieked.

"You've got two choices — murder or suicide. I'm thinking accident is far-fetched but maybe."

Fab shuddered, then took out her phone and made a call. "I'm putting you on speaker."

"What's going on?" Toady grumped.

Fab relayed in detail what I'd seen and what went down.

"You two okay?" he demanded. Fab reassured him. "Never had that happen. These jobs are always straight up. But you can bet I'm going to get to the bottom of it. You two need to hit the highway and not get involved in whatever went down."

"Let me know what you find out," Fab said.

"How's Ace doing?" I asked. "I owe you for not ditching him to fend for himself."

"Nonsense. I don't mind doing a good turn. More people should try it. Ace is…" He paused. "Okay is a good word, I suppose. He's convinced that the missus is more involved with the criminal than she's willing to fess up to."

"So much for hoping that Trigger would go away and we wouldn't hear another word about him," I said.

"That marriage is doomed, for several reasons. One is that it didn't escape his notice that she didn't follow the ambulance to the hospital," Toady told us. "He's not sure when or if she showed up, and that really bugs him."

"I'm sorry for all the collateral damage," I said. "Anything I can do, call."

"Keep us updated," Fab told him and threw her phone in the cup holder.

I took my phone out. "Since I've been forgetting way too much lately to update Creole and he hasn't copped a 'tude with me, I'm calling him now." When he answered, I said, "You sitting down?"

He groaned. "You in one piece and all that?"

"If Frenchy's there, you might want to hit the speaker."

"What about your brother; should I send him to the men's room?"

I could hear the laughter in Creole's voice and laughed myself. "You're going to have to get Brad to swear that he won't repeat some of what I'm about to tell you. There's one thing he can blab about—the triple homicide and shoot out."

"The what?" Creole barked. "Hey guys, some of what you're about to hear, you need to keep under wraps."

They must've agreed, because he hit the speaker.

"Just kidding on the shootout, and only one murder—maybe." I ignored the chorus of groans. "I'll start with the fire and work my way through the morning." I didn't skimp on details as I relayed everything that had gone down. "The good news is that we're headed back to the Cove."

"I'll be interested to hear what Toady's got to say once he asks a few questions," Creole said.

"You two going home?" Didier asked.

"We're hitting up the office first, as we've got a meeting with Gunz this afternoon, and then we'll be home," I said. "Whatever the job turns out to be, we can give you the details later. That way, you have the option of signing on as extra muscle."

Brad laughed in the background. "You know you can always call me if you need real brawn and an extra gun."

"That's a first," I said. "You've never offered before; you usually get roped in last-minute."

"If it sniffs of dangerous, just say no," Creole said.

"Be careful, you two," Brad said.

We hung up.

"Are we going to be on time for the meeting?" I asked.

"We're going to be early, since I didn't have to drop off the car."

"Let's hope that the security cameras didn't pick up my license tag. I'd rather not get a call from the cops later."

"If they have any kind of coverage, then they'll know we had nothing to do with whatever went down."

Chapter Eighteen

Fab sped back to the Cove and took a back road to the offices. I hadn't been back since someone dumped a dead body on the property. Some things you don't forget very easily. It served as a good reminder to always be aware of our surroundings.

She pulled up to the pair of warehouse buildings, which flunked curb appeal, and keyed in the security code. Fab and Didier had renovated one building into office space that they shared and had, thus far, ignored the other building. The gate opened, and she pulled in just far enough to keep it from scraping the bumper when it closed. We'd agreed to shoot anyone attempting to sneak in after us first and ask "what the heck" afterward. She cruised into the parking garage and parked next to Gunz's Escalade.

I noticed that the big man wasn't lurking in his car but didn't ask, as I knew that to him, it wouldn't be a breach of manners to pick the lock.

As though reading my mind, which wouldn't be the first time, Fab said, "I gave Gunz the code." She got out and closed the door on any more questions.

"I'll wager Didier doesn't know." I hiked up the thirty-plus steps to the office on the second floor. Not expecting a response, it didn't hurt my feelings when I didn't get one.

I peered over Fab's shoulder as she unlocked the door and was surprised to see Xander lounging on the couch, laptop resting against his knees. He looked up and princess-waved, which amused him, judging by his grin. Gunz had claimed a chair in front of Fab's desk and, for once, wasn't in her chair.

Fab and Didier had knocked out a few walls, and the interior was now a large, chrome-and-glass open space with his and her sides differentiated by color. Fab's was all white, but Didier managed to include a splash of several colors.

I'd claimed the alcove around the corner, primarily for its view of the water, and accessorized it beachy. That was where I dropped my bag. Then I crossed to the kitchen and grabbed a water, nudged Xander's feet to the floor, and sat down next to him. "Long time, no see. You doing okay?" Although I talked to him almost daily on the phone, utilizing his computer skills to track down information, I'd missed having him hanging around the office all the time, as he had before he went off to finish college.

"I've got something I want to pitch," Xander

said in a low tone and jerked his thumb in Gunz's direction. "I'll do it when he leaves."

"No whispering over there," Fab barked. She dropped her bag and sat behind her desk.

Gunz turned to me. "You might want to come over here, since you'll be taking lead on this job."

I knew from the smirk on Fab's face that she'd known about whatever he was about to pitch and kept the details to herself. I stood, rolled my eyes at Xander, and crossed to where Gunz sat. I dragged the chair back and sat where I could stare at him and Fab and hopefully not miss anything. "It's nice that you thought of me for a job over Fab." Not really. "But no thanks. I'll have to pass."

"You haven't heard a single, stinking detail," Gunz said in a huff. Rearranging his large bulk in the chair, he crossed his arms.

Fab laughed.

Gunz had been into the hair paint again. So much for that being a trend of the past, if it ever was, and probably it wasn't. He spread the gooey concoction on his bald head, ran a comb through it, and viola: ugly hairdo. He'd overshot the sides and didn't get the sticky stuff all washed off, so it looked like dried bird poop. Since he wasn't my friend, I'd let Fab tell him… if she noticed.

"Madison would love to hear the details," Fab said, punctuating it with a "behave" glare reminiscent of Mother. "Keep an open mind," she added, a note of reprimand in her tone.

I blew out a long, aggrieved sigh. I could swear Xander laughed, but I didn't look back.

"Anyway…" Gunz cleared his throat. "I bought an apartment building on the outskirts of town. Got a great deal, good for my investment portfolio."

"Congrats," I said without enthusiasm. I was trying to stay one step ahead of him and figure out where this conversation was going, and I was tired already.

"The building needs management to reach its full potential." His signature smarmy smile made its first appearance of the meeting.

"And you immediately thought of me?" I held back a groan, as clients found it attitudinal.

"After discussing it with Fab…"

If looks could kill, the pair of them would be slumped over dead. I waved my arm and cut him off. "Let me guess, you bought a building full of problems, and you want me to broom them out. Felons, drug addicts, and folks that are generally down on their luck, does that about sum it up?"

"You know I pay really well."

"You'd have to, as this isn't a one-woman job." I glared at Fab, conveying, *You're going with me.* "If you want it done legally, it also requires a lawyer. You want them scared to the curb, you need to do that yourself. Or…" I pointed to Fab. "She can do it. She's scarier than me."

"It has to be done by the book. I have a reputation to protect."

What? I thought. *Hoodlum?* Then had to remind myself that he'd cleaned up his rep. I heard Xander laugh again and had to look down to keep from laughing along with him. "Recognizing that you're Fab's star client..." I swear he preened. "I'll check out the neighborhood and the building. If it's something I'm remotely interested in doing, I'll work up a to-do list, along with estimated expenses. Then you can decide whether to shop around or not," I said with enough sweetness to elevate everyone's sugar levels.

"I won't—"

I waved him off, which had him grinding his teeth. "Just know that any fees quoted are subject to increase, depending on any problems that should arise."

"I'm texting you the address." His phone in his hand, Gunz must have had it ready to send as my phone dinged immediately.

"Tomorrow's the earliest that I can get by the property, and that depends on Fab's schedule," I said.

"I'm available," she said.

"Okay then," I said, my phony cheerfulness having drained out of me.

Gunz leaned over and opened his briefcase, pulling out a file. "Here's all the information I got from the previous owner." He handed it to me.

I opened it and scanned the half-dozen pages,

which were handwritten. Ace had kept his records in the same fashion, although they were more legible.

"Keep in mind that I'm not striving to be a slumlord. I'll be interested in any suggestions you have for the property."

Oh great. That was a big clue as to what I'd be walking into. "You can expect an email late tomorrow or the next day." I stood and headed back to my office, pausing to smack Xander in the back of the head and motion for him to follow me into my alcove.

He grinned and shot up and followed me.

I sat across from him at the ten-foot oblong desk that Fab had custom-made for me out of shiplap. "I hope you're not here to say, 'See ya. Not working for you anymore.'"

"I've got a couple of projects on the drawing board, one being the development of my own social media app," Xander said. "I've had a lot of freedom working for you, and I don't want to give that up. So, I'm thinking I want to work for myself, call my own shots. To that end, expanding my snooping business would keep the bills paid."

"That's good news for me," I said with an inner sigh of relief.

"What is?" Fab demanded, pulling up another chair. "I don't know why you couldn't wait for me before starting this conversation." The door slammed, signaling Gunz's exit.

"Let me sum things up for you," I said. "Xander's not ditching us as clients; in fact, he's expanding. I'm thinking we can put out the word and get him some new clients." I shook my finger at Xander. "Under no circumstances do you take on anything dangerous. If you don't have enough contacts by this time that you can call someone else to do the dirty work, then call one of us and we can refer you."

"There is one more thing. I'd like to rent the building next door," Xander blurted. "I'd be sharing it with Toady, and not sure if you know this, but he'd like to live there. The way I figure it, besides making the building pay for itself, you'd have a security guard when you're not around."

"Not the worst offer I could get." Fab winked at him. "I'll talk to Didier and get back to you."

"Show of hands. Are we done?" They both stared at me. "Okay then. I want to go home. I'm calling Creole to tell him that he needs to start coughing, feign illness, and tell the guys, 'See you tomorrow.'"

Chapter Nineteen

I'd informed Fab on the way home the day before that, after thinking over how she'd colluded with Gunz to foist this new job off on me, I wouldn't be needing her assistance when I went to check out the property.

I was happy that, when she dropped me off at my house, she said, "Pick you up at nine," and took off in my SUV.

Good thing, too, because when I told Creole about the job, he was less than happy. Grouchy, in fact. He'd said, "This isn't what I meant when I said I thought you'd be good at property management."

It took some fast talking to reassure him that I wouldn't be sticking my neck out for Gunz and this was only a drive-by to assess the situation.

I walked out of the house and closed the gate just as Fab drove up. I went around to the passenger side and slid in. The interior smelled like it had just been detailed. A clean car was something Fab insisted on, and some teenager came to her house or the office and did the work. If it were left up to me, it wouldn't be pristine, that's for certain. I entered the address into the GPS.

"I think I know where the street is," Fab said as she drove out of the compound. "So-so area in need of some renovation. The building itself is full of an odd assortment of people, according to what the previous owner told Gunz."

"Your last statement is the reason my name jumped ahead of yours," I snarked.

"Creole called this morning," Fab said in a hissy tone. "Informed me that if I left you hanging out to dry, he'd shoot me. Then hung up when I started to tell him off. I whined to Didier, and he laughed. *Laughed*."

"I'll have to plan something special for my husband."

Fab made a barfing noise.

I picked up my phone and turned to the window, trying not to laugh out loud as I texted Creole a heart and a smile.

It was a short drive through town.

I made my first note when Fab turned off the highway. "The street's paved. That's a plus," I said. "I'm going to need you to take pictures. It'll look professional if I include a couple with my report. And yes, I'll be taking all the credit."

Fab slowed as she drove down the street, and we checked out the mixture of apartment buildings, single family homes, and the one lot that had been bulldozed, leaving only a driveway pad. It was an anything-goes neighborhood — from fixed-up to needing attention. Gunz's new purchase was a two-story, washed-out grey building that had mold crawling halfway up from the foundation. A quick count verified that there were eight units. The parking spaces in the front were filled with older-model cars, a couple in such dubious shape that it would surprise me if they ran. The giant dumpster off to the side was overflowing. Fab did her usual and went to the end of the block, a dead-end, turned, and drove back, parking across from the building.

"Playing to your talents besides shooting people," I grinned at Fab, "I'm going to need you to shoot a video in addition to taking pictures."

"Do I get paid?"

"Probably not, since that would interfere with me taking all the credit." I focused on the building through the windshield and gave it a once-over. "A good power wash and a coat of paint would perk the place up." I checked out the two floors. "How's this for an impromptu plan? We go door to door and say hello for the new owner."

"I'll wait here. I only planned to come along and check the place out; thought we'd go for early lunch and do some shopping."

"You do that," I snapped and grabbed her phone out of the cup holder. "Since you won't be needing this, I'll take my own pics." I got out and crossed the street. I heard another door slam and knew Fab was behind me.

"Give me that." She grabbed her phone back. "By the time you're done fiddling around with it, it'll stop working altogether."

"There's that possibility."

"Listen to me." Fab stepped in front of me before I could step up on the curb. "The building, the block, it's creepy."

"What could go wrong?" I laughed at the "you actually asked that?" look on her face. I pulled out my phone to make notes or I'd forget.

I pasted on a smile and knocked on door number one. Not the cop knock I preferred, because I was going for friendly. No answer, and I couldn't hear anything from inside. I kept an eye peeled for movement at the curtains and stopped short of pressing my ear to the door. I moved to the next one and got the same response, although this time, someone looked out the curtains and darted back when I made eye contact. I sensed a pattern by the time I'd finished with the four units on the bottom and headed up the stairs. Either no one was home or they were and weren't answering. Fab had ditched me after the creepy talk and disappeared around the back of the building, which I didn't appreciate, but she got away before I could wrestle her to the ground. I laughed at the mental image of me knocked out cold.

The first door at the top, an old man answered and checked me out from head to toe. "What can

I do for you, little lady?"

"I'm here to let you know that there's a new owner and you'll be receiving a letter in the mail. It will give you contact information for any concerns that you have, and I assure you that each and every item will be looked into." I was happy that he'd been receptive and considered it a win that he'd answered the door and hadn't shut it in my face.

He stuck his head out and looked down the walkway and over toward the stairs. "You'll find the best time to find folks out and about is around midnight."

I pulled some cash out of my pocket, where I kept it stashed, as one never knew. "How about if you fill me in?" I held up the money.

He licked his lips. "Downstairs, this way to that." He waved his arm in the same direction that I'd already walked. "First one, not going to answer since he never does. You only see him out when he's going back and forth to his car." He walked to the banister and peered over. "Not home. Second one shies away from human contact, only talks to her dogs. Next one has an outstanding warrant or several; he says that they're parking violations and he's trying to get them paid before he gets hauled off to jail. The one underneath me is a drug dealer." He whispered that part. "You can catch him out and about in the middle of the night."

"What about this floor?"

"Who's that?" He pointed to Fab, who was climbing the steps.

"She's my trainee, and she's not doing a very good job. I'll be interviewing for a replacement." I said it loud enough for her to hear and earned a snort.

"Far end—she died, hauled away but left a smell. Thought it could be aired out by leaving the windows open. Hasn't worked so far." He wrinkled his nose. "The next one, that woman was hanging out in the parking lot a couple of nights ago and got hauled off by the cops; haven't seen her since. Then another old guy who keeps his nose clean... and me." He grinned.

"I appreciate your help." I pulled out a business card. "Here's my number, in case there's any issue."

"Do you know what the new owner plans to do with the place?" he asked. "Raise the rent, I suppose."

"I know the owner sees the value in stable tenants." If not now, he soon would. "I'm going to suggest that, in his introductory letter, he give a preview of his plans." I waved and walked down the stairs. Fab had eavesdropped for a minute, then gone to the other end and was using those stairs.

We crossed the street and got in the SUV. Just then, a pickup truck squealed into the driveway, a guy rose up out of the bed and another hung out the passenger window, and both began shooting at the unit occupied by the drug dealer. The man I'd been talking to beat it inside his unit and slammed the door.

Fab and I drew our weapons and slid down in our seats, but as soon as the shooting started, it was over and the truck squealed down the street.

"What the heck?" Fab demanded.

"That's where the drug dealer lives, so I'm thinking he screwed someone," I said.

"To think that we almost made a clean getaway."

"Thanks for the job referral," I said.

"Sarcasm again." Fab tsked.

"You'll have to deal," I said. "In addition to the list of suggestions I already have, I'm moving dealer dude to the top. He needs to move out, and the faster he's gone, the better. Gunz needs to extend the same relocation services he does with his relatives. Strip the windows of coverings and let it be known to anyone driving by that he's long gone."

"Do you hear any sirens?" Fab pulled away from the curb. "So no one called the cops. None of the tenants or neighbors? That tells you it's not the first time it's happened and they're afraid that if they do, word will get out." She picked up her phone and called Gunz, reported what happened, and threw out my suggestion.

Fab handed me the phone.

"You in or out?" he grumbled.

"Maybe." I ignored his hiss of frustration. "You can muscle out the dealer and probably get away with it. The rest will have to be done legally. It's the kind of neighborhood where you're going to attract more of the same. My suggestion is if they're current on rent and the cops aren't beating on the door, make the best of it. Your scary mug shows up a time or two and they'll run for their lives, not knowing that you're a pussycat… which you aren't." I laughed and got silence. "I've got a suggestion for a manager, and it's not me."

"I'll be expecting that report of yours."

"Will do." I saluted the phone and handed it back to Fab.

The call ended in some kind of shorthand that I didn't understand and was only paying minimal attention to, too busy staring out the window.

Chapter Twenty

We were barely back on the main highway headed back to the Cove when my phone rang. I pulled it out of my pocket and saw Mac's face on the screen.

"We've got a few problems here," she said when I answered. "You might want to hop on by."

"Preview," I said.

"I'm thinking it should be a surprise, since I know how much you hate them," Mac said, overly pleased with herself. She somehow deciphered my grunting noise as "conversation over" and hung up.

"That was Mac, and she needs me to come to The Cottages. Sorry to renege on lunch." I pasted on a phony smile. "You've got choices. Take yourself home and drive your own car for a change to get a hamburger—oh, that's right, you hate them, which I might understand if you were a vegetabletarian—or drive me." It was thoughtful of me to give her choices, even though I knew what her answer would be.

Fab shook her head, as though summoning up patience, and hit the gas. Thanks to light traffic, it didn't take long to get to The Cottages. She rounded the corner and backed into Mac's driveway. "What does she want?"

"Let's hope it doesn't have to do with anyone shooting up either property," I said, not mentioning the "surprise," as I knew she hated them as much as I did and would've opted to go home.

We got out and walked across the street. The office door opened, and Alex Famosa waltzed out, a smirk on his face.

"Hi." I rushed over and enveloped him in a hug. "Good to see you." I noticed Mac shaking her head. "How did you get here?"

"I hired a car," he said smugly.

"You better be okay." I hugged him again.

"You're smothering me," he grouched, sounding exactly like his dad.

"I'm afraid to ask—does anyone know you're here?" I pulled him into the office and pointed to a chair while I sat on the couch.

Mac sat behind her desk, and Fab appeared to be guarding the door.

"Did you know that cat up there is dead?" Alex pointed to the top of the bookcase.

"Since I'm the one who's paid to have it restuffed on a few occasions, the answer is yes, and don't change the subject."

Alex wrinkled his nose. "I don't like it at my aunt's house. Maybe I'd feel differently if she didn't live there, but she does. I want to come back here, where my dad wanted us to be."

"I'd like the same thing, but Maya got a court order and it's illegal to ignore them."

"I heard Maya laughing with one of her friends that she put one over on you and you were too stupid to know it."

"Did she say what she did?" I asked.

"She caught me eavesdropping and sent me to check on my brothers."

"Everything going okay?"

"I may have called her a name or two and gotten sent to my room. She probably would've slapped me, but the first time she tried it, I grabbed her arm and told her I'd break it if she ever touched me or my brothers and sister."

I turned to Fab. "You're the only one that can talk to Brick—tell him to get his wife under control." I turned my attention back to Alex. "Does Maya know you're here?" He shook his head. "You're in a big pot of trouble, and I think you've dragged me into the deep end with you."

"You didn't know I was coming."

"Let's hope she hasn't called the police." I sighed. "I've missed you; it's been quiet around here. I know Crum feels the same, even though he doesn't announce his feelings. That said, here's why you have to go back." I held up my hand. "Hear me out. You're the oldest, and you need to look out for your siblings. They find out you took off, they'll be devastated." I continued before he could launch the argument he had ready to go. "What would your dad want you to do?" That deflated whatever he was about to say.

"He'd want me to go back. Does it have to be right now?"

"Not this minute. We're going to figure out a handoff plan, and not anything like the last time." I hoped I could keep that promise. "While we're figuring this out, go around and say hi to the residents; they'll be happy to see you. Don't go jumping in the pool by yourself."

"Got it." He hopped up and ran out the door.

I turned to Fab and said, "You need to make this happen. Get double assurances that they're not going to send Alex to reform school or some such. Offer to deliver him to the car lot, Brick's home, wherever is convenient. I know I should be all stern and take him back immediately, but the heck with that. After lunch. Gives me time to catch up on how everyone's doing."

Fab nodded, pulled out her phone, and went outside.

"You know that he had a car app installed on his phone?" Mac said with admiration.

"I thought Maya had banned electronics."

"She did. When she showed up with the cops, Alex had his phone in his pocket, and no one searched him or asked for it. Once he got to Brick's, he stashed it away. He said he had to be creative, as she continually searches their rooms."

Fab came back in, slamming the door. "Brick

has smoke coming out his ears. Didn't see it firsthand; let's just say it sounded like it. He's going to get with the wife and call back to arrange a time for the drop-off. It won't be the house, since the wife can't stand you or me or anyone else."

"I don't recall ever meeting Maya before, so I'm not sure why she's got a hate-on for me."

"Nothing personal. I met her once, and she has an abrasive personality. I did get it out of Brick that after Casio's wife died, Maya thought it would be better if the kids came to live at their house, and it was a unanimous thumbs down. When Brick gloated that Casio had left the kids here and they were having fun, let's just say it didn't sit well with the wifey."

"Casio needs to get his butt back here," I said. "I refuse to believe anything other than that he's going to stroll up one day, all cocky and arrogant, crowing 'I'm back.'"

"More news," Mac said.

"Good news?" I asked in a hopeful tone.

"No, but just for you, I can make some up." Mac grinned. "Last night, trouble cruised the street in a couple of sedans. The kind that sent the locals back into their houses, and most didn't even peer out. Then a gangster-mobile—SUV with tinted windows—pulled up and parked in the street in front of the apartment building, and a youngish woman and a man got out and went banging door to door, wanting to know anything about the new owner. Only a handful answered, and I'd guess those that did claimed ignorance, as so far, it's been a well-kept secret."

"And you know all of this how?" Fab demanded.

"I was sitting on the porch when they pulled up, and as you know, I've got an unobstructed view of the comings and goings from that property. When the SUV double-parked, I decided it was time to go back inside and watch on my security feed. They knocked at my door, and I answered. Little did they know I had a firearm hidden behind the door, ready to shoot." Mac pulled her imaginary six-shooters and shot up the office.

"That tells us Trigger doesn't know who it sold to," Fab said. "The duo that questioned everyone must have believed the people they spoke to, as no one got hurt. Right?"

Mac nodded. "Two men pulled up in another truck and walked the block, searching the perimeters of all the properties. Once they were done, they came back and walked the driveway of The Cottages from one end to the other."

"Don't you ever sleep?" I asked.

"I was about to come inside and go to bed when they pulled up. I knew right off they didn't live around here. As far as I could tell, they didn't find anything. Let's put it this way— neither man came back to the street with anything in his hands."

"What do you think they were looking for?" I didn't expect an answer. "I need to give Toady a heads up."

"We need to come up with a plan to make Trigger go away," Fab said.

"Trigger's probably one of those guys that doesn't lose often, and when he does, he's like a dog with a bone and chews on it until he finds out how it happened," Mac said. "One more thing, Karen was here yesterday afternoon."

"Can't wait to hear what she wanted," I said.

"She practically kicked a dent in the door of the pink house, and I'm happy to say the woman was smart enough not to answer, although I know she was home because I'd just talked to her. I haven't talked to her since, but I'm assuming she's scared; she's no match for Karen."

"I can tell by your gloaty smile that there's more," I said.

"As you know, there are times when my nosiness gets the better of me, so I walked down there, asked Karen what she wanted, and said I'd relay it to the woman. If looks could kill… She told me to mind my own f-ing business. I responded with, 'You're not very friendly,' and she stomped off."

"What did I tell you about being careful?" I said.

"I hang on your every word." Mac grinned.

"What a suck-up." Fab snorted.

"I don't go anywhere without a gun in my pocket," Mac said. "I wouldn't hesitate to use it if I thought my life was in danger. Hope it doesn't come to that, because I'd probably have to move. One of those good-bad situations—'yeah, I have to move, but I'm still alive.'"

"Let's go out by the pool," I said, and stood up. "Too nice of a day to be sitting in here."

The three of us walked over to the pool, and on the way, I checked all the porches for anyone passed out and was happy that all was clear. When we rounded the corner, Crum and Alex were sitting at a table, playing cards. They looked up and waved.

"You'd think Brick would've called back by now," I said to Fab.

"I'll give him another half hour, then call again. He wasn't happy," Fab whispered.

"I imagine not. He's used to telling people what to do, not having one give him the slip," I said. "Especially not a fourteen-year-old."

Mac suggested lunch and said she'd pick it up. She'd already decided on Jake's and took everyone's order and called it in. Fab got a call from Didier, or so I assumed, since she started speaking in French as she walked out of the pool area.

Now that I had a few minutes to myself, I pulled out my phone and crossed to the far side of the pool, out of anyone's hearing. I had a surprise for Creole and didn't want anyone to know, not even Fab. This deal wasn't open to anyone else's input. I called Toady, and when he answered, I said, "I've got another deal I want you to broker."

"I'm in. Same kind of deal as before?"

"Yes, and once again, secrecy is important. It's a surprise for my husband. I'll email the information. Same fee for you as before."

"You're good for my bank account." Toady laughed. "No worries, I keep my trap shut on everything."

We hung up, and I sent a message to Gunz that he'd get my recommendations later. I left the pool area and crossed the property back to the SUV, sliding inside. Grabbing my laptop out of my bag, I sent Toady all the information he'd need to make a deal on the warehouse. Once Creole and I owned the building, I'd work on getting the other buildings.

Mac pulled up and jumped out, reaching for a large shopping bag of food.

I got out and joined her. "I'll grab an assortment of cold drinks," I said and veered toward the office, where I filled a tote bag and went out to the pool.

The five of us grabbed stools at the tiki bar, and Mac passed out the containers of food. I used the opportunity to ask Alex about what he and his siblings had been doing and how school was going. Everything was just okay. Nothing stand-out.

When we finished and cleaned up, Crum offered to lend Alex a bathing suit. I suggested that they hold off while Fab called Brick again. She'd barely gotten her phone out of her pocket when two cops rounded the corner and came to stand at the pool gate, reminiscent of the last time the cops were called on me.

"Madison Westin," one of them barked.

I really didn't want to identify myself. But I hadn't done anything wrong. Had I? "That would be me." I slipped off the stool and walked over.

"You aided Alejandro Famosa in leaving his home, and since you don't have custody, that's a crime." He eyed Alex.

I reached up to open the gate, but before I did, I said, "I didn't do any such thing."

Both officers came in, and one motioned me off to the side. "What's your story again?" he barked.

The other cop walked over and spoke to Alex. To my surprise, he didn't tell Crum to scram.

This time, I started by telling the officer that Alex's father was Casio Famosa. Then I told him that Alex was here when I arrived, adding that we'd contacted Brick and offered to drive Alex back to Miami and had been waiting for him to return the call.

After the two officers were done questioning us, they met up for a short conversation.

The first one came back and said, "We'll be

taking Alejandro home."

I nodded. "Can I give him a hug?"

"Go ahead." The two of us walked over to where Alex stood with the other officer.

I hugged him hard.

"You're suffocating me again," Alex groaned.

I heard one of the officers laugh.

"I'm sorry this day has ended this way." I kissed his cheek.

"I get to ride in the back of a cop car. Maybe we can agree not to tell my dad about this." He grinned.

"Maybe." I served up my best "behave" stare and walked with him to the patrol car. One of the officers ushered him into the backseat, reminded him to buckle his seatbelt, and they left. I waved as they backed out to the street and roared off. "That kid is such a pain in the butt, but my heart is hurting again." Fab crossed the driveway and stood by my side. "You tell Brick that he's a giant dick. I realize that's repeating what he already knows, but this could've been handled with a lot less drama. I hope Casio serves up some serious payback for all this."

"I swear, I didn't have a clue that Brick would try to get you arrested," Fab said.

"It might have worked if the cops hadn't believed me when I said I didn't 'nap the kid and suggested they check with the car company that delivered Alex," I said. "The cop lightened up even more when I informed him that Alex's father was Casio. So, they must not have known."

"Now where to?" Fab asked.

"I know this great strip of private beach, and I'm thinking about pulling out a raft and enjoying a cold drink."

Chapter Twenty-One

It took some work and the help of friends to sneak behind Creole's back and plan a surprise getaway. I'd gotten up early and made coffee, bringing him a cup in bed. While he was drinking it, I hopped off the bed, went into the closet, and wheeled out a suitcase.

"You going somewhere?" He eyed me over the rim of his cup.

I tapped my forehead. "You're so smart." I disappeared back inside the closet and came out with clothes for him, which I threw on the chair, dropping the shoes on the floor.

"I don't know what you're up to, but I've got to get to the office."

"I got special permission and got you the day off. You're all mine."

"So, what you're saying is that my two partners are in cahoots with you and not a word to me."

"Pretty much." I winked at him.

We showered and dressed, then climbed in the Hummer, where I programmed the GPS.

"Do I get a clue where we're going?" Creole leaned over to get a look at the screen, and I turned it away.

"Nope." I gave him a big grin.

He was a little surprised when we headed north. I'd chosen a local resort that hadn't been open long to avoid spending a lot of time on the road, and booked a bungalow on the beach that had every amenity. We only had to pick up the phone to order anything we wanted.

We spent three days without our phones turned on, sleeping late, spending time on the beach, swimming in our own private pool, and booked a canoe once I was assured I wouldn't have to pull my weight.

On the way home, Creole said, "We need to do this more often."

"I wanted you to know that I appreciate you and don't take you for granted."

"Same here. I worked hard to get you, and I'm keeping you."

I laughed. "How long after we get home before the phone starts ringing?"

"I did ask Didier if they had a telescope; told him your theory that that's how his wife knows everything going on. He laughed without commenting. So, it wouldn't surprise me."

* * *

The next morning, Fab and I were sitting on the sidewalk at the Bakery Café sharing a pecan roll when my phone rang. I showed the screen with

Joseph's face on it to Fab.

"I didn't do it," Joseph said in a freaked-out tone when I answered.

I couldn't put the call on speaker or the other tables would eavesdrop. I leaned over so Fab could listen. "Take a breath and calm yourself, then tell me what you didn't do."

"He's dead. I'm pretty sure… He's bloated and smells. I need to get out of here," he babbled, his frantic tone becoming a screech.

I heard a door bang and grimaced. "Where are you?"

"The funeral home," he wheezed.

"You need to sit down and breathe. We're on our way." I turned to Fab. "This should be your problem."

"He's your tenant, not mine."

"Dead body. Funeral home. Screams you. You can thank me later." We crossed the sidewalk and got in the car. "Would you call one of the diggers and ask them to check on Joseph? I don't want him expiring."

Fab gave me a sidelong glance. "Stop calling them that. You're going to slip up and say it to their faces, and then what?"

"Easy. I'll say I got it from you. They'd forgive you for anything."

Fab picked up her phone, and when they answered, she put the phone on speaker. "Joseph just called and—"

"He's lying on the grass," Raul said. "Not sure

what happened and was about to go out and ask him. We hired him to clean the museum."

The owners of Tropical Slumber had tricked out what was once a drive-thru hot dog stand, where they offered every send-off service imaginable, and if one came up that they hadn't heard about, they added it to the menu. Hence the museum they'd built to display various vignettes showing the options.

"Dickie…" Raul yelled.

"We're on our way."

"I'm thankful for that," Raul said, and hung up.

"I'm quite certain Raul wouldn't have said that to me, so another reason why you're perfect," I said.

Fab tossed her phone in the cup holder and hit the gas, careening around the corner. "What do you suppose happened?"

"Here's what I know: Joseph didn't kill anyone."

Fab sped down the street, pulled into the parking lot of the funeral home, and parked next to the red carpet. "A tasteful touch," Dickie had said to me once.

The two men had Joseph on his feet and were leading him over to the patio.

We both got out, and before we reached the three men, I said, "You can tell me what to do, and I'll let you know if I'm going to do it."

Fab led the way. "What's going on?"

VANISHED IN PARADISE

The owners of the funeral home, Dickie and Raul, were opposites looks-wise—Dickie stick-skinny and pale, more like colorless, and Raul the brawny bodybuilder.

"Joseph says there's a dead body in the museum in one of the caskets," Dickie said. He trooped across the parking lot, Fab and Raul right behind him.

I sat in a chair next to Joseph. "Any clue who the dead guy is?"

Joseph shook his head. "He wasn't there last week when I was here. I only took this job because it's not stressful and I thought it would give me more beer money."

I looked up as the three went into the museum and came back out in less than a minute.

"It was gross." Joseph shuddered.

I patted his shoulder. "I suppose if you're going to die, what better place than a funeral home?"

"I'll need to call and report this," Raul said as the three approached. "Fab found the broken window right off." He smiled at her. "She thinks he was murdered. Dickie and I agreed that we'd never seen the man before."

"Any reason you can think of that someone would dump a body here, or was he killed on site?" I asked.

Rather than answering, Dickie lamented, "We'd hoped to have the museum open for tomorrow's funeral."

177

"The good news is that once law enforcement is done with their investigation, they usually release the crime scene fairly quickly," Fab told the duo. "The problem is the smell."

I refrained from making a retching noise, but thought it.

Raul walked away, taking out his phone. I assumed he was calling the cops and sat back in my chair. It didn't take long for two local sheriff's department cars to pull into the parking lot.

Kevin got out of the first car and an officer I didn't recognize out of the other. Kevin walked over and asked a couple of questions. "When you found the body, why didn't you call the cops instead of these two?" he asked Joseph.

Joseph put his head between his legs. Kevin growled at him and walked over to the museum, circling the exterior. Then he and his partner questioned us one at a time. As soon as he'd finished with Joseph, Kevin waved me over.

"I don't know anything. I didn't even go in for a peek," I said. "Please, be nice to Joseph; you know him, and you know he's not a killer." Since Kevin didn't look his usual grouchy self, I asked, "You got any clue what happened?"

"You know I don't talk about cases. I will tell you that I'm confident there's no reason to arrest anyone here."

"Can I leave now?" I asked in a whiney tone.

"If you take Joseph home," Kevin said.

"I'll assign Crum to watch him so he stays out

of trouble."

"Wait until you see what Crum's up to... unless you already know," Kevin said evasively.

I groaned. "I'm afraid to ask. What?"

"You think I'm going to ruin the surprise?" He held up his hands and grinned. "No way. Get your friend to snap a picture of your response."

"It can't be illegal, or you would've squashed the fun already."

Kevin laughed and walked away.

Chapter Twenty-Two

"I don't want to go," Fab whined when Joseph climbed into the backseat.

"Drop yourself at home then. This is my car, after all, and I'll be needing it." I said as we both got in, not bothering to disguise my exasperation.

My phone ringing cut off whatever comeback she had. "I'm afraid to ask what's up," I said when I answered, having checked the screen and seen Mac's face smiling back.

"We have a small issue or two that need your attention. I'd have called sooner, but I just found out about the one, and the other, well… I thought that could be a surprise."

"This is the second surprise lately, and I'm requesting no more," I said.

"It sounds a lot better than problem, don't you think?"

Not really. "Anyone die?"

Fab knocked me in the shoulder, wanting me to put the call on speaker. I ignored her and turned away.

"Thank you for that," Mac said. "I was looking for a happy spin, and it'd escaped me until just now… No one died."

"I'll wait for the details. Be there in a few... after I get rid of 'grumpy' behind the wheel." I shoved my phone in my pocket.

A loud snore came from the backseat. No wonder Joseph had been so quiet.

"You're going the wrong way," I told Fab when she turned in the opposite direction from home.

No response. The Cottages weren't that far from the funeral home, and it only took a couple of minutes to get there. Fab rounded the corner, and as she turned into the driveway and pulled up in front of Joseph's cottage, I noticed the police car parked in front of the apartment building.

I got out and opened the back door, nudged the man, and helped him out. I took the keys from his hand, unlocked his door, and helped him over to his easy chair. "Anything I can get you before I leave?" I asked.

"I'm going to take a nap. Later, I'll call the funeral guys and quit my job. I can't clean up that mess." His whole face wrinkled up.

"Don't worry about that. Fab suggested that they call out the crime scene cleaner dude so he can get rid of the smell." I reassured.

"I'd barf if I did that job. Almost did that today but managed to swallow it down."

On that yuck note, I waved and escaped to freedom, stopping before closing the door to say, "You need anything, call Mac." Once outside, I sucked in a much-needed breath of fresh air. Fab had disappeared; my guess, she was finding out why the cops were next door. I headed to the office and found Mac peeking out the blinds. "What's going on out there?"

"Saw the cop car pull up and wondered the same thing. I know you don't want anyone to make a connection between the two properties, so I circled the block and hung out with three people who'd gathered in the front and were pointing and taking pictures. Someone painted graffiti on the doors."

"In broad daylight?" I asked.

"No one saw a thing, and they're sticking to that story. I'm guessing it had everything to do with the two men who pulled up in a pickup truck in the early hours, grabbed a couple of bags out of the back, and disappeared out of sight of my camera."

"You were awake again?" I shook my head in disbelief.

"Not this time. After a couple of minutes, I realized that the little group I'd joined didn't know squat, so I hustled back and replayed the security footage from last night."

The door slammed open, and Fab came in, kicking it closed behind her, and threw herself down on the couch. "Someone's not very creative over there. One letter was painted on each door, spelling out 'bitch,' and smiley faces were spray-painted on the rest. Artwork stinks."

"Interesting choice of tag. Wonder if it was meant for Karen or if they know the buyer was a woman," I mused.

"The tenants think that Toady bought the building," Mac said. "And they're not the least bit happy, as he scares the devil out of them."

I flourished my hand towards Mac, and she caught Fab up, then continued: "Ten minutes later, the artists left. They didn't seem to be in any kind of hurry as they jumped in the truck and drove off. Not a single light went on in the building during that whole time."

"Forward me a copy of the footage," Fab said.

"FYI: The license plate was removed from the truck," Mac told her. "Did a close-up on the windshield and no sticker, so it wasn't a new purchase."

"That's not the first person we've seen do that. How do they get away with it?" I asked.

"They could've stopped around the corner and taken it off," Fab said. "I'm surprised they didn't just cover it up. We've seen that done, too."

"What you need over there, and pronto, is a manager," Mac said. "It's hard to get away with anything if you've got someone up in your business. Another good reason to have a manager living on site is that two of the tenants are running illegal side operations, and that would make it more difficult."

I leaned my head back and blew out a breath.

"Wonder if they're associates of Trigger."

"I'm sick of hearing that name," Fab grouched.

"You and me both," I agreed, then turned back to Mac. "If you're awake during one of these late-night visits, do not confront anyone. It's not worth getting hurt over." Or worse.

"If I'd seen them lurking, I'd have called the cops from one of my burner phones," Mac said. "There's one more thing."

Someone laying on a car horn interrupted her.

Mac stood and circled her desk, opening the door. "I'm going to let this situation speak for itself."

Fab beat me out the door, then skidded to a stop and laughed.

I groaned, knowing that whatever it was was going to be bad. I walked around Fab, who was still laughing, and stared at the convertible Cadillac parked in the middle of the driveway, top down and piled high with sh... well stuff, including a mattress poking out of the back. Crum was behind the wheel, a stupid grin on his face.

"You moving?" I asked, finding it hard to believe.

"Oh, heck no. This is my new moneymaker after you dropped my services." He waggled his brows and slapped the driver's door.

He was so full of it. The poor-mouth routine was an outright lie and an old excuse for whatever he was up to. This time, the "what" escaped me. "Hauling stuff to the dump?" Not giving him a chance to answer, I added, "You're not using the dumpster here just because you're too lazy to make the drive and too cheap to pay the fee."

"Don't get your shorts in a twist. This is my moving service. 'Move for Crums.' Catchy, don't you think?" He slid from behind the wheel and grinned.

Much to my own disgust, I burst out laughing.

Mac moved behind me and patted me on the back. "The reason I kept it a surprise is that it's hard to get the flavor in a retelling."

It took me a minute to catch my breath. Then I walked over and peered inside. The back seat had been removed, and assorted boxes were stacked inside. "Hate to be a killjoy..." I said with a grin.

Crum snorted. "No, you don't."

"I'm fairly certain that what you're doing isn't legal... more like dangerous. If a stiff wind blows that mattress into the next county, do you have insurance to cover the damages?" I asked, knowing the answer.

"How many takers for your hokey moving service have you had?" Fab asked, disdain dripping from her words.

I looked down at the ground, not wanting to hurt Crum's feelings by continuing to laugh.

Crum's nose shot into the air. "Mind your own damn business."

"So, one," Fab answered. "Just what I figured."

"You…" Whatever he'd been about to blurt out, he bit back when Fab growled at him. "It's more work than I like to do, so I'm going to turn the Caddie into a taxi cab." Crum turned and started to stomp down the driveway.

"Where are you going?" I yelled at him.

"Joseph's. If it's any of your business." He clearly thought it wasn't.

"Joseph is napping. He's had a bad day," I said to his back. "If you wake him, I'll have Fab shoot you."

Crum turned halfway.

Fab pointed her finger at him and made popping noises.

"If the gig pays, ask Rude; she'll do about anything," Mac said.

Crum stomped off, smoke blowing out his ears.

"That reminds me," Mac said. "Cootie and Rude would be perfect as managers next door. In no time, she'd know everyone's underwear size."

"That's useful information," Fab said.

"You know what the hell I'm talking about." Mac stepped toward Fab.

I grabbed the back of her shirt. "I'm the one you have to impress, not her, and I think it's a good idea."

"Another thing: we got money in the budget for me to buy that Caddy?" Mac asked. "I just came up with a harebrained idea that I need to run by Rude. Believe me, I'll get a good deal. If we double-team Crum, maybe he'll pay us to take it off his hands. Especially after I point out all the expenses he hasn't thought about for the taxi service he'll never get a license for."

"For what?" Fab demanded.

"Go ahead," I said. "As long as it doesn't become a problem for me."

"What am I here for," Fab grouched, "if you're not going to listen to anything I say?"

"Pretty the place up?" Mac smiled at her.

"Before we leave, the graffiti problem needs to be taken care of. Tomorrow would be good," I said. "You hear anything about anything, give me a call."

Chapter Twenty-Three

A whole day went by drama-free. Mid-morning the next day, Fab used her lockpick to open the door, a trick she only pulled when she was certain Creole wasn't home, as he'd threatened to kill her if she did it again and told her so in front of Didier. She wasn't amused when Didier shrugged and said, "I'll miss you." I bit back a laugh at the time.

"You're booked today," Fab announced, walking into the house. "I'm certain you don't have other plans or you'd have told me." She offered up a shifty smile.

"Can't you knock, like civilized people do?"

"At least, I'm not climbing in the window." She perused the refrigerator and decided on a bottle of water, then made her way over to the couch and sat in a chair across from me.

I laughed. "Good way to get shot. Now, what's so important? It better be good because I do have plans." I didn't, but why make it easy for her?

"What?" Fab's brows rose. When I didn't say anything, she continued. "I have a pro bono client that I've helped out in the past, and he needs my services again. You know Didier doesn't like it when I go out on a job without backup, even when I'm fairly certain that guns won't be involved."

"Freebie. So, that means it's not one of your crazy millionaire clients. And since it's a maybe on the use of guns, that means it'll probably happen. A few more details would be nice if you think I'm trading my flip-flops for tennis shoes." I held up my flop-clad foot.

"You remember Hank Roberts? Your old neighbor? Named his dog after your mother."

"I dare you to tell Mother about her namesake that isn't really. You think I forget everything like you do, but I do remember that Mother and Hank have never met. The dog go missing again? I suggest that he check the neighbor's house where we found it the last time."

"Hank called about his granddaughter. She was selling candy for a school fundraiser, and the boxes that hadn't been sold yet and a manila envelope filled with the money she'd collected were stolen. About two hundred, Hank said, and he wants us to recover it. She'd outsold everyone else in her class and was up for an award."

"And how are you supposed to do that? Please, tell me that we're not going to be scaring it back from another kid." I shook my head at her. "When you have wrinkles in your forehead, I'm going to remind you of all the times you rolled your eyes at me. Starting with now. You're going to find out that Mother's right about one of her pronouncements, and it'll be too late." The accompanying sound I made didn't come out right, but I went with it.

"If there was another kid involved, I'd have suggested that Hank take care of his own problem. In a nice way, of course." Fab flashed a sneaky smile. "His daughter and her husband have one of those security doorbells, and the same day as the money and candy went missing, they got a picture of the neighbor down the street casing their house."

"If they have him on camera, why not call the police?"

"They did call the cops, and they said that since the picture only showed him on the doorstep and not with the goods in hand, there was little they could do. Even with a rap sheet a mile long. They paid him a visit—a couple of times, in fact, because he didn't answer the door even though he was at home."

"You do know that the cash and candy are probably long gone," I said. "If he had any evidence hanging around, he got rid of it after the cops paid him a visit. Unless he's dumber than a stump."

"We need to think positive." Fab grinned.

"Oh, okay."

"The cops seem to think that after their visits, he'll lay low. At least, they're hoping he does. He does have a reputation for generally harassing folks just for the fun of it."

"You got a plan?" I asked. "Because I've got nothing. Except for knocking on the door, asking for everything to be returned, and getting the door slammed in our faces. Then I'll get arrested for harassing *him*."

"I'll come up with something before we get there."

"I'm coming along just to see what you come up with. Hopefully, it's something entertaining."

"You could sound more supportive."

"I'm giving up my do-nothing day for you. Now that's supportive." I got up, went into the closet, and ditched my cute skirt for crop sweats and a long-sleeve t-shirt. Tennis shoes and gun holster in hand, I went back and sat on the couch to finish dressing.

Fab leaned forward and thrust her phone at me. "This is who we're looking for."

He was a twenty-something with a sneer on his face—hard to tell if it was permanent or not— and unruly dark hair hanging in his eyes. "He's too old to be ripping off a kid. But I suppose when you're a thief, age isn't a consideration." I followed Fab outside and got into the passenger side of the SUV. "You better have a better plan than strong-arm robbery," I said as she slid behind the wheel.

We didn't have far to go; it was a short drive back to my old neighborhood. I'd rented house to Doodad, and he kept up the exterior, as evidenced by the pics he sent each month. "I want to prove I'm not a crap tenant," he'd told me.

"Have you even done a drive-by?" I asked as she turned onto my old street. "Scoped things out?"

"We're doing that now." Fab pulled up and parked across the street from an older cottage-style house. It was a little worn but had a large, welcoming porch. "Here's the plan — you're going up to the door, looking for your lost cat. You've used that story often enough; you must have it memorized."

"Once the door opens, then what?" I'd have liked her plan better if it was one where I could sit in the car. "And where will you be?"

"Right by your side, of course, and while you're mumbling about the cat you can't seem to keep track of, I'll flirt a little. Build rapport. Appeal to his sense of decency."

"Too late for that." I snorted. "I've got a better idea — we write a check to Hank."

"That was also one of my good ideas. I told Hank that we'd be happy to do just that, and he grouched back that he didn't want the 'little bastard' getting away with ripping off a kid."

We got out and stood on the sidewalk, surveying the street.

"Since there isn't a car in the driveway, our only option appears to be to skip the direct approach, snoop around the neighborhood, and then, depending on what we find out, hit up the house again." Fab pointed me toward an older woman in the yard next door.

I walked over and put on a friendly smile as she loaded the last of her gardening equipment in a small wagon. "Have you seen a large, longhaired black cat? He got out, and I've been looking everywhere. I knocked next door, but there's no answer."

"Haven't seen any stray cats around of late." The woman smiled back. "The Goods, who live in the front, are at work. Their son, Trent, lives in the guest house in the back. Doesn't look like much, but I think he likes it that way and he's lazy. I'd steer clear of him." She wrinkled her nose.

"Do you need any help?" I pointed to the wagon.

"I've got this. Handy little thing." She tugged on the handle and waved as she pulled it around the back.

Having thought Fab was behind me, I was surprised to turn around and find that she was nowhere in sight. If she'd heard about the guest house, then I knew where she was headed. I retraced my steps back to the Goods' driveway and inched my way towards the back. Sure enough, Fab was circling the small house, peering in the windows through the slits in the sheets that had been hung up in place of blinds.

The little cottage had a ton of cute potential,

but had been neglected for so long, it looked like a stiff breeze would blow it over. What had once been flower beds were now overflowing with weeds, which had inched up the sides of the small porch.

An older-model sedan squealed into the driveway and pulled up beside me. I barely had time to jump out of the way. The sullen face that Fab had showed me earlier stared at me over the steering wheel, and then the guy jumped out, closed the distance, and yelled in my face. "What the hell?"

"My cat got out of the house, and I've been looking all over. I saw him run back here," I said in a whiney voice, trotting out a childish tone that was beyond annoying.

"I don't give a damn about your cat. You're trespassing. So, git." He pointed to the street, his angry red face showing that he barely had control of his temper.

I didn't say a word, just turned and left. I could feel him burning a hole in my back. How the heck was I going to get Fab off the property? To do that, I had to know where she'd gone.

Instead of making a run for the car, I cut down the block a couple of houses and doubled back. Then I stood a couple of feet back and yelled, "Hello? Hello?"

Trent poked his head out the door, not looking quite as angry as before. "What do you want now?"

"Can I leave my phone number, and if you see my cat, could you call?" I asked.

"I hate animals. So, no. I'm not going to tell you again; do not come back."

I caught sight of Fab at the corner of the house, pointing to the neighbor's. I nodded and left. I'd planned to get into the SUV, then remembered I didn't have the keys and shooting the lock off wouldn't start the engine. I turned toward the neighbor's house, not spotting Fab anywhere. That was because she turned up one more house down. She came around the side with an older man, chatting it up, waved to me, and said something to the old guy that made him laugh. With a quick wave, she cut down the driveway and met me on the sidewalk.

"You do know that when you move to the old folks' home, the women are going to hate you."

"Put on a hat; you've been in the sun too long." Fab turned and waved to the man, a big smile on her face. "We've got a problem."

"We? You mean you. Your Plan A, the cat trick, was a bust. Can't wait to hear what's next."

"Trent's been a busy criminal. The two back bedrooms are filled with an assortment of electronics, none of it in boxes. I'm guessing that there are a lot of unhappy people."

I groaned. "I did read in the weekly that there was a burglar hitting up homes during the day, when no was home."

Fab nudged me.

I glanced over and saw that Trent, anger once again radiating off his body, was standing in the middle of the driveway, glaring, which made the hair on the back of my neck stand on end. Bad sign.

"He's got a handgun in the front of his waistband," Fab whispered.

"He draws on one of us, and he's a dead man." I moved my hand to my back and drew my Glock, keeping it out of sight.

"Love this new badass side of you."

"Just get us out of here without shots fired."

"Yell over, 'Did you find the cat?' and follow me; don't break stride."

I did, and he responded with an angry shake of his head.

Fab hustled to the SUV, we jumped in, and she pulled away from the curb like she had all day. "Now what?"

"We're turning this over to law enforcement, and with any luck, they'll find the candy box. In the meantime, we'll make a donation, and after you explain the facts to Hank, he better be gracious." I pulled out my phone and called Creole. When he answered, I said, "How's my favorite husband?"

"What are you up to?"

I told him about our good deed, as I couched it, and that Fab had most likely found the neighborhood burglar, as he'd been dubbed by the news media.

"You're supposed to call *before* the job."

"It's Fab's fault. You wouldn't believe the story she sold me."

Fab made the sound of squealing brakes, loud enough for Creole to hear. He laughed. "Tip Kevin off," Creole suggested. "It would be a big bust for him."

"We're headed to The Cottages." I punched Fab's arm. "See you at home." We hung up, and I repeated Creole's tip.

"My luck, Kevin will want to arrest me."

"You didn't do anything that was illegal except trespassing… but your poor kitty." I agreed with Fab that we couldn't be certain how Kevin would react. "Or we go to Jake's, tell Bouff, and let him put it in the right ear."

"I vote for the latter." Fab u-turned and headed to the bar.

"He works late shifts," I said and called Doodad. When he answered, I asked, "Do you have a number for Bouff?"

"He's right here; we're playing poker. He came in early and opened for me."

"Tell him not to go anywhere. Fab and I are minutes away and want to talk to him."

I wasn't far off; it was less than five minutes before we rolled into the parking lot and parked around the back. As we cut through the kitchen, I stopped and placed an order with one of Cook's kin for a sampler plate for two and told him we'd be out on the deck.

Fab passed me, going to the bar and placing a soda order with Kelpie, who waved like a crazy woman as soon as she spotted us.

I opened the door to the game room and poked my head inside. "Can we move this party out to the deck?" Both men nodded. They'd cleaned up their card game, as the table was empty.

The bar was quiet except for the jukebox playing. A few regulars lined the stools, hanging on Kelpie's antics, and two men played darts in the corner. The deck doors were open, and I went outside and claimed our usual table, tossing the "Don't sit here" sign.

Fab came out with a tray, served me a soda loaded up with cherries, and set down one with limes for herself.

"Am I invited to this tête?" Doodad asked from the doorway.

"Between you two, one of you will know how to handle this problem," I said.

Doodad and Bouff crossed the threshold and sat down.

Fab hit the highlights of the morning—a far more entertaining version than what had actually happened. I shook my head at her.

"Trent Good is his name, at least, according to the neighbor," I said.

"I've got a couple friends on the local force, and they'd be happy for this tip," Bouff said. "I'd say tip Kevin off, except he runs hot and cold.

Just so you know, unless there was a sign saying to keep off the property, you weren't technically trespassing. And when he asked, you left, so no crime."

"Could you ask your friend to be on the lookout for the candy box?" Fab asked.

"You're probably not going to get the money back. Sorry." Bouff frowned.

"I know the officers he's talking about, and they'll be all over this tip." Doodad nodded. "This Trent character will be in lockup soon."

Chapter Twenty-Four

For once, I rolled out of bed early and made the coffee. Creole, who was propped up on the pillows, watched me approach, cup in hand, with a suspicious eye.

"It's not poisoned." I gave him a deranged smile and crawled into bed beside him.

"I'm happy that Fab got law enforcement involved with the theft case and you two didn't decide to take the guy down yourselves."

"As you know, I wanted to replace the money and be done with it from the start. That's happening today. We're going to go to the bank and get a bunch of small bills. The story we're concocting for Hank is that we stole it back and the cops are investigating, so he won't go over and confront the man."

"I'm thinking that you should come to work with me; that way, I can keep you out of trouble."

"That sounds like so much fun, but I'm going to have to pass." I made a sad face.

Creole laughed. "Your excuse better be good."

"Gunz called." I ignored Creole's groan. "Well, not me, but Fab graciously passed on the message. He wants a sit-down about the apartment building he purchased. The report I sent apparently didn't answer all his questions."

"I know what he wants, and the answer is 'hell no.' And I'll tell him if you don't," Creole grouched.

"Are you going to enlighten me?"

"He wants you to manage that dump."

"I've got that angle covered and someone already picked out to do the job. And no, not Mac."

"That makes me happy." Creole leaned down and brushed my lips with his.

I snuggled up to his chest. "I'm doing my best to not give you an early heart attack."

Creole rolled out of bed, scooped me into his arms, and carried me into the bathroom.

* * *

When I went outside, it surprised me to see my SUV parked in the front, even though Fab had texted that we'd be meeting at her office. I cut across the Cove and was still late, which she loathed. First thing I noticed was that only Gunz's SUV was parked in the garage. I got out and trudged up the steps.

"*Bon* morning," I said when I threw open the door.

Fab smirked back from behind her desk.

Gunz swiveled his bulk, irritation sparking in

his eyes. "You're late." He tapped his wrist.

I wasn't going to be the one to tell him he'd left his watch wherever, since he wasn't wearing one. "A situation came up that needed my immediate attention, and it took a little longer than expected." Neither needed to know it was a little smoochy face in the shower. I followed that up with a contrite expression and decided from their mollified reactions that I'd done a decent job. I dropped my bag on the couch and dragged a chair to the side of the desk so I could keep an eye on both of them. "What's on the agenda, Big Dude?"

Fab raised her brows; she'd grill me later.

"I'd like you to manage the apartment building." Gunz's glare dared me to say no.

I'd have to tell Creole he was right, but I wouldn't phrase it that way. "I'm not going to list all the reasons why I'm not available. Why bore you? Knowing that you were going to need someone to ride herd over there—" I almost laughed at his forehead wrinkling; that's what he got for shaving off his eyebrows. "—I recommend the man who lives upstairs. He knows the players, and during the short talk we had, he didn't come off as anyone's fool. If he needs training, I can arrange that." Mac would love someone to boss around.

"I'd have to meet the guy," Gunz hedged. "Are you going to be overseeing the repairs and such, or you foisting that off on someone else?"

"I think that foisting is the best option." I smiled, which caused him to do a double-take, and that pleased me. "You need someone who has a construction background so the work is done right and you won't be taken to the cleaners." But he knew all that. "You could snap your fingers and have one of your guys trot over, and they could get back to you with a list of repairs."

Gunz grunted and opened his briefcase, handing me a sheet of paper. "I want these tenants gone, and the reasons are listed. You hire the manager. He gets free rent for a two-month trial period. He works out, we can renegotiate; if not, he packs up and I never see his face again. *Capisce*?"

"Got it." I scanned the sheet. "I'd be surprised if the drug dealer isn't already gone. These two non-payers, I'll serve notice on and let the lawyer handle the rest. The dead woman won't be a problem; I've got a cleaner dude that can take care of the smell."

"I know who you're talking about. He's weird."

"I'm sure folks think the same thing about us."

"You, maybe. Nobody's ever said that to my face." Gunz squinted, as though trying to recall.

I was certain only someone with a death wish would tell him that, but kept the sentiment to myself. "Anything we missed?" I certainly hoped not.

Gunz stood. "I figured it was a long shot that you'd take over as manager but had to try." He grabbed his briefcase. "We'll talk later." He lumbered out the door and slammed it behind him.

I waited until I heard his boots clunking down the stairs. "I need my memory refreshed; aren't we supposed to be co-whatever on this project?"

"You whistle, and I'll get back to you."

"Do you have any chocolate?"

Chapter Twenty-Five

"Now's a good time for an office meeting." Fab waved me to a chair in front of her desk.

I looked around to see if someone else had appeared and I hadn't noticed. No one. My eyes closed, head slumped to the side, and I let out a loud snore.

"I don't know why I tolerate you." Fab sniffed.

"Oh, hon, I can think of a few good reasons, the main one being you scare everyone else and don't have that effect on me." I fished my ringing phone out of my pocket and grinned at the screen, thankful for the interruption.

"Some woman just pranced up the street, pounded on Cootie's door, and getting no answer, started yelling as though that would make it open. When that didn't work she stomped off," Mac said when I answered. "You harp on calling at the first sign of s… stuff going awry."

"I'll be there in a few minutes. If the woman shows up again before I get there, call the cops." I hung up and looked at Fab. "I hate to break up this meeting, but something's come up." I flashed a pouty face. "You can use my beater truck to get home, or I can give you money for a cab."

I'd long ago purchased a truck for when an undistinguished ride was needed. It had come in handy more than a few times.

Fab reached down and grabbed her bag, pulling out a set of keys and jingling them at me. "You must've forgotten that I have my own keys to your ride, and no way can you beat me down the stairs."

"Oh, good, you're driving." I laughed at her back as I followed her out.

* * *

Fab and I pulled up to The Cottages and parked across the street in Mac's driveway. She started to get out, and I jerked on her arm. "The woman coming up the street has a shotgun in her hand."

"I'm not in the mood to go one-on-one with a shotgun." Fab hit the door locks.

"That's not going to protect us if we're in her sights. She'll just blow out the windshield and our brains along with it."

"Have you seen her before?" Fab asked.

"No, so hopefully that's good for us." I grabbed my phone out of the cup holder, called 911, and reported the shotgun-toting woman. The operator acted like she didn't believe me but took down the details and said a cop would be out to investigate. "Her tone suggested that maybe I'd been drinking and was seeing things," I said with a sniff after I'd hung up.

"They probably get those kinds of calls all day long."

We watched, eagle-eyed, as the woman turned into the driveway of the cottages and proceeded down to the end, where she banged on Cootie's door. I knew he was at work. He worked at The Boardwalk and did side jobs around the neighborhood on the weekends.

"This has to be the woman Mac called about, unless we lucked out and got two crazy women in one day." I got out of the car and slammed the door. The woman never looked over her shoulder.

Fab came up next to me. "You going to shoot her?"

"So far, she's just carrying it and not pointing it at anyone." And she better not because she'd be facing down two guns.

Rude answered the door in her yoga outfit. It was time for the class out by the pool to start, which meant more people would be spilling out of their cottages any second.

The two women exchanged a few overheated words. Then the rifle-toting woman took a swing at Rude's head with the butt end, which missed as Rude jumped back.

I broke into a run. "What's going on?" I yelled, skidding up behind the two women.

Not wanting to get involved, but also not

wanting to miss out on anything, Fab was right behind me.

Rude kicked the woman in the gut and she dropped the rifle, then hunched over and heaved. To my amazement, when she came back up, she jumped Rude and rode her like a pogo stick.

Fab grabbed the back of my shirt. "You don't want to get involved in that. You'll get your skirt dirty."

I pulled my Glock and contemplated firing a warning shot, then decided it was probably illegal and jail wasn't on my agenda for today. At that moment, a cop car screeched into the driveway and came to a halt. Kevin jumped out and ran over. I slid my Glock back into its holster.

"Break it up," Kevin barked in the loudest voice I'd heard him use to date. He reached out and pulled the two woman apart in one swift move, then attempted to hold off the unknown woman with his free hand. She came up with a closed fist that Kevin wrapped his hand around, then dumped her on the ground. She rolled over and dry heaved.

"Either of you moves, and I'll handcuff you." Kevin turned and asked me, "What happened?"

I told him what we'd both witnessed, and Fab nodded in agreement.

"Wait in the barbecue area in case I've got any questions," Kevin ordered.

I waited until his back was turned to salute. Fab and I walked back to the front of the property, where the barbecue area was prime seating for watching every corner of the property.

"I'd rather sit in the office." I knocked into Fab, and we veered off course. The door opened as we got to it. "I'm happy you took cover," I said to Mac.

"I heard you yell and came running, as far as the door anyway. I wasn't getting involved in that. Look at me." She twirled around in her short ruffled skirt and stuck out a spaghetti-covered high heel.

Fab stared at her shoes until I knocked into her and shot her a "you be nice" look.

"Cute," Fab said of Mac's heels, which someone had apparently glued cooked pasta on before slapping on a coat of varnish. She didn't mean it, but hopefully Mac wouldn't notice.

"What was the fight about?" I asked Mac.

"You always think I know everything." She tried for an innocent face, which turned into a grin, then wiggled back to her desk.

"Maybe because you're up in everyone's business and know what's going on around here." I took a seat opposite Mac, and Fab stretched out on the couch.

"You make it sound like I'm nosey." Mac crossed her arms, clearly pondering whether she was or not.

"It won't bother you if you don't think on it too long," I said.

"Seely, the other woman, says she's in a relationship with Cootie, who claims not to know who she is. Also, her description of Coots doesn't quite match up. Rude's already warned her to stay away from her man or she'd rearrange her fake boobs." Mac arranged hers and blew them a kiss.

"Ouch." I made a face.

"If it's the truth that Cootie doesn't know Seely, then I say we have a lineup and see if the woman picks him out," Fab said, clearly proud of her idea.

"You've lost your mind." I shook my head. "We fill up the car with men and haul their butts to the police station? Bet the cops will jump at that opportunity, as they have nothing better to do and it's probably illegal."

"Forget the cops; we'll do it by the pool," Fab said, ignoring my sarcasm. "Tell Madison it's a damn good idea." She pointed at Mac.

"It has merit." Mac reached for her phone and called someone. "Get your tail feathers back to The Cottages. We've got a sitch, and you're just the man to clear it up. Pronto. No dragging your work boots. Life and death, in case you didn't get that part." She threw her phone back on the desk.

The door opened, and Kevin crossed the threshold. "I need something cold to drink." He held out his hand. Mac turned in her chair, grabbed a soda out of the fridge, and handed it to him.

"Isn't this bribery or something, since you're on duty?" I asked.

Kevin ignored me with a snort, popped the top, and downed half. "Are you sticking to your story that it was self-defense?"

"Gun-toter showed up to pick a fight. So, what's Rude to do?" I asked. "It's not like she rearranged the woman's boobs; at least, not that I saw. I'm certain I wouldn't have missed that."

Fab, who'd pretended to be asleep as soon as the door opened, snickered, giving herself away. That was if anyone had believed her act to begin with.

"Seely's under arrest, since she was planning on using the shotgun, though not on Rude. She planned to fill Cootie's backside with buckshot." Kevin was clearly amused by that.

"Did she say why?" I asked.

"The two were in a relationship, which he refused to consummate, and she felt that she was entitled to recompense." Kevin did his best to hide his grin but ended up looking down.

"I find it difficult to believe that Cootie would two-time Rude, as she'd cut off his man goods and serve them as an appetizer at one of her yoga classes. You know how popular that would be?" I nodded, letting him know it would be a huge draw.

"I don't want to even hear about a pretend

version of that happening, you got it?" Kevin said.

"You need to turn your dark-eyed stare over there," I said, pointing to Mac. "She's the one that lets the train jump the track, then pleads, 'I didn't know.'"

"If you'd shuffle your feet for a few," Mac said to Kevin, "Cootie's on his way. We can clear up this situation so it doesn't happen again."

"That was my idea." Fab waved her hand. "Let's see if crazy broad even knows who Cootie is."

"She's still going to jail," Kevin said.

"If Seely can be convinced that Cootie isn't her man, then she won't come back. One less nutjob hanging around should make you happy." I bared my teeth in a smile.

Cootie's truck rumbled into the driveway and squealed to a stop.

"He's here," Mac announced.

"I'll handle this." Kevin tossed his empty can into the trash and banged out the door.

I was right behind him. "I'm not missing this."

The three of us filed out. "The barbecue area," I whispered, knowing that from that vantage point, we wouldn't miss a trick.

Kevin walked over and talked to Cootie, then crossed over to his police car, helped Seely out and asked her a couple of questions, and beckoned Cootie over. It was hard to see everything that went down, as Kevin stood in front of her. She looked at Cootie and shook her head, then squealed and banged her head on his arm. Kevin helped her back in the car, crossed over to talk to Cootie again for a moment, then got in his car and drove out.

Mac unleashed a shrill whistle and motioned for Cootie to join us.

The man lumbered over. His clumpy grey hair standing on end, Cootie looked tired. "Mistaken identity. I tried to tell a couple of people, but nobody listened. Kevin asked if she knew me, and she said no, must be a different Cootie. How many of us are there around?" he asked in disgust. "It's good for everyone that she had a picture of Cootie Two on her phone, which Kevin showed to me. He turned out to be Lyle Locke, who lives one block over and probably gave a phony name so he could play games and his wife wouldn't find out."

"Why did Seely think he lived here?" Fab asked.

"He told her," Cootie said, indicating that was a no-brainer. "My guess is that Lyle figured out she was unstable and thought, why not give her false information?"

"Someone needs to pay Cootie Two a visit and tell him he better not set foot on this property, make it the street, unless he wants his wife finding out about his catting around." I stared pointedly at Fab.

Fab saluted. "I always get the dirty jobs."

Chapter Twenty-Six

It had been a quiet couple of days, and heading into the weekend, I told Creole to come home early, that I planned for us to have dinner on the patio. We'd watch the sunset and afterwards go for a walk on the beach, and then fun and games. "No phones." I forewarned him that I'd be picking up a piece of fresh fish that would need to be barbecued, which would be his job, and I'd take care of the rest.

I'd cleaned the patio and set the table. Right before he was to arrive, I got out a bucket and filled it with ice, beer, and water, then set out the tequila and blender for a margarita. And then I waited.

Sometime later, I checked my watch again and wondered what was keeping him. It was long past the time he normally got home. I went in the house and picked up my phone, sitting on the couch and calling him.

Straight to voicemail. I made a face and tried again. Voicemail.

I called Didier's phone and the same thing.

It was unusual for Creole not to call. I called Brad. "I'm trying to get ahold of Creole, and his phone is turned off. Was there a meeting or something that ran over?"

"He and Didier left the office about three hours ago, headed home," Brad said. "Hang on while I try the office line." After a minute, he said, "No answer."

"He probably stopped for a beer at Fab's." Even as I said it, I knew it wasn't something he'd do without calling, especially when he knew I was expecting him to walk through the door. I got off the call in a hurry and hit Fab's number.

"I'm trying to track down my errant husband. Is he at your house, by chance?" I asked when she answered.

"I was just wondering where mine is. Didier's phone is turned off," Fab said in an irritated tone. "We need a new rule—if I can't turn my phone off, then neither can he."

I was in total agreement. "I called Brad, and he said they left the office hours ago, and no one's answering at the office. I'm going to call the hospital; not that I think anything happened, but just in case." I knew I was overreacting, but it wouldn't be the first time one of us ended up there.

I hung up and made that call, and they didn't have a record of either man.

I called Fab back, and she walked through the door as her phone was ringing. "I wish Creole was here to grumble at you about using your lockpick."

"Where the hell are they?" Fab grouched, worry lines etched on her face. "It's not like them to go off the radar and leave us to worry. Do we call the police?"

"I'm sure there's a reasonable explanation."

Both of our phones rang at the same time, which was a first. My screen said private caller. Fab glanced at hers and walked outside to the patio.

"Madison Westin?" a female voice asked as soon as I answered.

"Yes. And you are?"

She laughed. "We have your husband and his friend, and if you want them back in one piece, you're going to listen very carefully. Got it?" She didn't wait for an answer. "I'm sure you're smart enough to figure out not to involve the cops."

"What do you want?"

"Shut up," she snapped. "Remember what I said about listening? We'll be keeping an eye on your every move, and if you're keeping your mouth shut, then we'll be in touch with further instructions. You don't get another phone call, it's because you screwed up and didn't do what you were told. Your husband's body parts will be left on the side of the road." She hung up.

Fab came back inside, the color drained from her face. "That was some man threatening to kill Didier. Said he'd call back with terms."

"I just got the same call, only it was a woman. Did your screen say private caller?" I asked.

Fab nodded and paced the room. "Kidnapping?" We both had the same look of disbelief. "Didier's never done anything to anyone in his life, so why him?"

"I have no idea."

"I'm going home." Fab started to go back out the patio doors.

"Since it sounds to me like we're being watched, are we agreed that we don't do anything without telling each other, and I mean before doing it and not after?" I asked.

"Yeah, sure." She waved over her shoulder and jumped down the outside stairs to the beach.

I got up and watched as she ran down the sand. Fab wasn't a woman to sit around and wait for the next phone call; she'd rather stir things up. I went back inside and opened a drawer in the island that was nearly invisible because it didn't have a handle. It had been outfitted with plugs, and I picked up a charged burner phone and a phone card. I sat back on the couch, turned on the television, and switched the feed to the cameras that scanned the street. Fab had installed state-of-the-art security inside and out, which I rarely had any use for. It wasn't long before Fab's Porsche flew down the street. So much for keeping each other informed before the fact.

I loaded the minutes on the burner, scrolled through my phone, and punched in a number, hoping the other person would answer. Calls from unknown numbers could mean any number of people that one wasn't interested in talking to.

"Hello?" the deep, masculine voice grouched.

"I wasn't sure you'd answer, but I'm damned happy you did."

"What the hell number is this?" the Chief asked.

"Burner phone."

He groaned. "This can't be good. I'll help in any way I can."

I told him about Creole and Didier running late and the phone calls that Fab and I got.

"Do you have someone that can trace the number for you?" the Chief asked. "Most people don't know that it can be done."

"I've got a guy I can call anytime, and he always comes through," I said.

"Have him track the numbers from both calls. The next phone call you get, I want you to record it. Hit the start button before you answer so you get every word. You need to keep a low profile, since you don't know how closely you'll be watched, but we can easily get that figured out. Don't use your other phone unless you have to, since you don't know if they have a trace on that one. I'm assuming the next call is going to include a list of demands, and you have one of your own—proof of life."

I gasped. "I'll agree to their demands and do whatever they ask."

"Don't you worry; we're going to get the guys back," the Chief reassured me. "You're going to have to be patient in waiting for the next call. You, I'm not worried about, but your friend's another matter."

"Both of us will do what you tell us because we want our husbands back."

"Tomorrow morning, you're going get a pizza delivery. He'll check out the surrounding streets. If there's anyone doing a stakeout, they'll stick out on that busy highway and side street, and he'll go over your house for bugs."

"It's highly unlikely that whoever this is knows where we live, as we don't give out the address and don't receive mail here. Unless we were followed, and we're always on the lookout for a tail. We've tried to protect our privacy as much as possible."

"I'll give Bouff a call and have him on alert at Jake's, and if he hears anything, he'll get in touch," the Chief said. "You piss anyone off lately? Anyone stand out that would do this?"

The questions felt like a punch in the stomach. "I'm hoping this doesn't end up being all my fault." I told him about besting Trigger on the deal for the apartment building and the middle-of-the-night goings on that had happened since.

"Boy, am I sick of that name," the Chief barked. "I hope that any day now, Trigger will be behind bars, where he belongs."

"Is Casio involved in that case?" I asked.

"Why do you ask?"

I told the Chief about how Casio had wanted

me to look after his kids and was now out of touch, and that it had me worried. I also told him about Brick's wife snatching up the children and whisking them off.

"I'll put out some feelers. If Casio and Creole are in this together, they're going to put up a fight and bring everyone home. They were two of my best men, and that hasn't changed with Creole's time off the force."

"You're going to need to be prepared with more pep talks."

"You listen to me," he said gruffly. "We're going to get both men home. Creole's going to be happy that you called me. Call me from this number anytime of the day or night. I'll be in touch and keep you updated. I'm thinking it's time to call on a contact or two and get an update on the Trigger case. As soon as you get the next call, you call me, and call if anything else happens in the meantime."

We hung up. I continued to stare at the television and watched as Fab drove back in and headed toward her house. I called her, and when she answered and didn't say anything, I asked, "What did you find out?"

There was a long pause, and I almost thought she'd plead ignorance. "I drove the main route to The Boardwalk and then the back way, knowing it's the one that the guys almost always use, and nothing. No sign of Creole's truck anywhere. It's too big to easily stash away."

"It was smart of whoever's behind this not to ditch it in plain sight. That would bring in the cops. Tells us that whoever's orchestrating this knows how to cover their tracks."

"I'll talk to you in the morning." Fab hung up abruptly.

Chapter Twenty-Seven

The security gate buzzed early the next morning. I'd sat in the same chair facing the television all night, and maybe dozed off a couple of times. Fab had left again in the middle of the night and came back a couple of hours later. She must've cruised every street in town.

"Can I help you?" I asked in a snooty tone when I recognized the man's face. I wondered how the Chief had roped in Help, since he was also retired from the police force and, last I'd heard, had gone fishing.

Fab and I had given Help that moniker, since every time we called, he showed up. He'd adopted the nickname, which saved him from making up a different name every time we saw him. It didn't occur to him to reuse a name he'd previously used.

"Pizza delivery," the man growled back.

I buzzed him in and went outside to meet him. He rolled down the window and waved, pulling up and parking next to the Hummer.

"You could've at least brought pizza," I said when he got out empty-handed.

"I thought that was a stupid cover." Help

snorted and slid out of the small sedan in beach bum attire. First stop, my SUV. He got down on the ground and checked the underside, coming out with a tracker unit. "Anything you know about?"

I shook my head. "I'm surprised that Fab didn't find it. Can't have been there long."

"We're going to leave it right where it's at, get you another ride, park this one at The Cottages and only take it out to do something you'd regularly do." He finished putting it back, then got up and brushed off his knees.

"What did the Chief use to lure you out into public?" I asked as I linked my arm in his and walked him into the house.

"Retirement's a bore." He appeared annoyed at finding that out. "Kicked back and took it easy, felt like I got my common sense back, and then missed the excitement. I didn't make it as a commercial fisherman, which is only to be expected, since I had a bad attitude."

"Coffee, water, or beer?" I asked and crossed to the refrigerator.

Help slid onto a stool at the island. "Grab your purse and a hat and glasses. We're going to get you another ride, so you can come and go as you please. The Chief filled me in on the details. Anything new happen?"

"I'm afraid to leave the house. No calls, but I didn't expect one this soon." I told him about Fab's late-night adventures and that I assumed she hadn't made any discoveries, since I hadn't heard from her.

"You need to tell her to check her own car for a tracking device."

"I will, but it's unlikely, as she rarely drives her Porsche and the only way to put one on would be to sneak into the compound and then into her garage, and the security sensors would go off. Wouldn't surprise me if most people think my car belongs to her and that I don't know how to drive."

Help laughed.

I grabbed a hat, sunglasses, and my bag and followed him out, climbing into his car, which was hard to identify, as all the markings had been removed. "Did you actually hand over cash for this car?" I wiggled to get the spring out of my butt. I tucked my hair up inside the baseball hat and donned the sunglasses. I'd chosen the largest lenses that I had.

Help laughed. "Loaner. It's hard to believe it runs, but no problems so far. Told my friend that if it did break down, I'd leave it on the side of the road and not bother to text him the location."

"So mean."

Help drove out of the compound and stopped at the sign. "Keep your head turned toward me. I checked out the area before driving in, and there wasn't anyone staking out this section of the road. I'm going to head over to The Boardwalk, and you can show me the route that the guys take home."

I gave him directions. "I know that they take the back way because there's never any traffic to contend with; most of the people that have businesses back there use the same route."

"Don't worry. We're going to get them back," Help reassured me.

He cruised down to the dock area; you could only catch glimpses of the water due to one commercial building after another. As we passed the four warehouses, I pointed them out to Help and told him about the con one Michaels brother played on the other.

"There's some brotherly love." Help snorted. "I'd be tempted to dump him where he couldn't be found."

"Especially if you'd spent any time in jail."

Help cruised the street slowly, and neither of us spotted anything out of the ordinary. We didn't even pass another car. "Is it always this quiet back here?" he asked.

"Pretty much. I know the buildings look abandoned, but most have thriving businesses behind the electric fencing. Spoon's auto body shop is one of them."

"Spoon and I hit it off—kindred spirits, checkered pasts, made something of ourselves, and couldn't give a flip what people think." Help beat it back to the highway and turned south. On the outskirts of town, he made another turn, pulled up to a security fence that surrounded a house and two large warehouses, and pushed a button. After a pause, the gate opened, and he drove to the warehouse on the right. The roll-up doors were open, and he parked under them.

I looked around in awe. There were at least three dozen cars, from beaters to luxury autos, a couple of speed boats, and an assortment of motorcycles.

"You can have your pick of a ride." Help motioned to one wall.

I walked down the row of cars and chose an old sixties Falcon. A family friend had had one, and I remembered thinking it was cool. I wanted something that wouldn't stick out and thought it would fill the bill.

"If for any reason you think you're being followed, lose your tail, head back here, and trade it for another ride," Help said.

A sexy mountain of a man strode into the garage area. "Booker," he said to me, giving me an intimidating once-over that had me holding my breath.

"Madison," Help introduced. "I was just telling her what to do if she's made behind the wheel."

Booker nodded. "Don't be giving out my address. You've got to be vouched for to get in here. The Chief holds you in esteem and seems to think that your partner will try sneaking up on me. He asked that I not shoot her."

"I'd also appreciate that. I'm sure you know

the story. We're both trying not to overreact and stay calm until we figure out what to do next. I'm thinking one of our infamous plans isn't going to work." I pointed to the hunter green car. "I choose the Falcon."

"Good choice." Booker grunted and walked over to a cabinet on the wall, came back, and handed me a set of keys. "You got your phone with you?"

I pulled my burner out of my pocket and handed it to him. He looked it over and nodded, then inputted his contact information and handed it back. "You get into trouble, call. There's a tracker on the car, so we'll be able to find you."

I thanked him and got behind the wheel, and followed Help to the highway. He'd traded in the first car for another small, nondescript sedan. We hadn't talked about it, but it didn't surprise me when Help followed me back to my house.

Chapter Twenty-Eight

We barely got the door closed when Fab burst in. "What's going on?" she demanded. "We're supposed to keep each other updated."

"Like you did last night?" I turned on her, hands on my hips. "Cruising the streets at all hours…"

"Okay, ladies. You're both worried, and snapping at each other won't help." Help waved his hand for us to sit.

I slid onto a stool at the island, Fab next to me. "Since you're up, I'll take a cold water," I said to Help. Fab nodded when he raised his brows. He fetched them from the refrigerator and sat across from us.

"I'd like to know what you've been doing," Fab said in a more reasonable tone. "And where did the old cars come from?"

Help recapped our morning trip and the plans for the Hummer and told her the Falcon was to be used for any trips where we didn't want to attract attention. "Here's what you two are going to do. As hard as this will be, you're going to go about your day and be seen around town.

Whoever called says you're being watched; give them something to see. You don't have to stay out all day. Go a couple of places and come home. The Chief has a man on you, and he'll pick up any tails. I'll be around. I'm going to hit up all my old contacts and find out what's been happening in my absence."

"You're going to need a place to stay," Fab said. "Might as well be my house, as I have plenty of room. It won't seem so empty with you grunting around."

I shook my head and laughed. "Since I'm certain the invitation was forthcoming, I'd like to reclaim my bedroom at the manse." I winked at Fab.

"Bring the cats. They like my house better. It's bigger."

When Fab and Didier first bought the house, they'd wanted Creole and me to move in and renovated a bedroom suite for us. We declined, as we wanted to stay in our beach house, but we'd stayed over a couple of times and marveled at the double-king-size bed.

I told Fab about my conversation with the Chief. I reached over and pulled open the drawer for Help's benefit. "You need a phone, help yourself," I said to Help.

"You two are going to need to play it cool, even though you're not going to be feeling it," Help warned.

My burner phone rang, which surprised me, as it was a first. I answered with a subdued, "Hello?"

"It's Xander," he said.

"I forgot I called you. I apologize again for the middle-of-the-night call. Can I put you on speaker?" I motioned for Fab and Help to say hello, which they did. I wasn't sure that Xander knew who Help was, but I'd explain later.

"I've been working on tracking down addresses for the numbers that called last night," Xander said. "I got a name on one, Cherry Simms, and an address, but the girl doesn't live there anymore and didn't leave a forwarding. It's highly likely she's still in the area. Nothing on the other yet."

"Why would you make a phone call basically admitting to kidnapping using a phone registered in your name?" Fab asked. "Assuming they did."

"It works in our favor if they're not the brightest," Help said. "Hopefully, they'll make more mistakes that we can capitalize on."

"I asked for information on Trigger a while ago, no rush. Now it's top priority," I told Xander. "A home address would be ideal."

"I've been working on it since you expressed interest in the apartment building," Xander said. "I discovered by a fluke that his birth name is Seymour Houser—he's done a good job covering his tracks."

"No wonder he calls himself Trigger," I said, exchanging a chuckle with Fab.

"Xander, how about you set me up an appointment? We'll meet and discuss a little business," Help said.

Before Xander could answer, I said, "Hold on a sec. Xander doesn't do face-to-face."

"Maybe, since you and I are besties," Help said to me and I rolled my eyes, "he'd make an exception. I can be a useful connection." He gave me an innocent smile that had me blinking.

"As long as you agree that you won't connect Xander up with anything that will get his backside dragged through a swamp," I said.

"Yeah, yeah." Help grinned.

"You know I can hear every word?" Xander said, amusement in his tone.

"When you first meet Help," I said, "he comes off shifty as hell, but he's a straight-up guy and won't leave you hanging out to dry."

"I'm at the office if he's approved to come here," Xander said.

"Your feet better not be on the furniture," I said.

"Just a little." Xander laughed.

Fab spoke up. "Did you happen to notice anyone loitering around?"

"I'm always on the lookout for anything suspicious," Xander said. "If I'd noticed anyone hanging out within a block of the gate, I would have not opened it, passed up the place, and called you."

"Just be careful coming and going," I said.

"I'll get your number from Madison and give you a call," Help told Xander. "Feel free to tell me you're not interested."

"Anything else?" I looked at Fab and Help. Nothing. Okay then. "Keep me updated," I said before hanging up.

"When do you think the kidnappers will call back?" Fab asked.

"My guess? Sooner rather than later," Help said. "If it's money they're after, they'll want their payday ASAP. Maybe they know they've got two of the partners of The Boardwalk and you'll pay big to get them back."

"I can get whatever cash they demand," Fab said. "But I'm hoping they don't know that."

"Since you've never flaunted your relationship with your father, it's unlikely anyone knows of your connection," I said.

"Caspian wanted to keep it quiet in the hope that this kind of scenario would never play out." Fab had recently reconnected with her bio-father, billionaire Caspian Dumont.

"You two go put on a show of being distressed, and I'll see you back here later." Help stood. "I'm thinking we'll have a conference call with the Chief, and we can get updated all around." He banged out the door.

"How are we supposed to..." Fab started,

trailed off, then restarted with a jerk. "…go about our day? I'd rather stay here and wait for the next call."

"We're going to do what we have to. It's what the guys would expect," I said. "We're going to get them back."

"And in the process find out who's behind all this by whatever means necessary and make certain that they never do it to anyone else," Fab said.

I reached for Fab's burner phone and inputted the numbers of Help, the Chief, and Booker. "You're going to want these numbers. Wait until you meet Booker, and whatever you do, give him a heads up that you're about to invade his privacy—ring the bell, don't hop the fence. Any kind of surprise won't go well." I told her about meeting him. "I'd love to hear his backstory. I'd bet he's another detective who's now doing who knows what out on that big piece of land."

Fab stood. "Let's go be visible."

I grabbed my bag and told her about the tracking device. She gave the Hummer a once-over and, like Help, checked the underside before getting behind the wheel. "I didn't think about my cars, but I'll be inspecting them later." Fab drove down the street to her house, ran in, and grabbed her purse, and came back out.

"Do you have your recorder on you?" I asked. "In case the plan is to catch us out somewhere and make the ransom call…"

"Got it. I'm thinking it's going to be at least a day, so they can be somewhat certain the cops aren't involved. Except that we *have* involved the cops. But even if these people have a connection on the local force, they won't know that." Fab pulled out of the compound. "Where to?"

"The Cottages. I'll walk around like I own the place, and after a drunk check, we can leave."

Fab laughed. "I feel more confident with the Chief orchestrating everything than having to rely on Kevin."

"I don't know if you've given this any thought, but if one of your clients calls with an out-of-town job, I'm going to pass. I don't want to venture past the welcome sign," I said. "Another thing, if any ransom gets shelled out, I'll pay you back, no matter what it takes."

"Haven't given work a thought. It's not like my phone rings off the hook anyway. Whatever does come in, I can assign to Toady." Fab kept her eyes glued to the highway, driving slow by her standards. "What are you going to do about your family?"

"After the ransom call, I called Brad back and lied, sold him a story about a flat tire and said they were home. He must have believed me because he didn't show up this morning. He's not going to be happy when he finds out the truth." I blew out a long sigh. "I'm going to have to tell them and then keep my distance."

"Since Help was talking an update with the

Chief later, give him a call and suggest dinner at my house. That way, everyone gets updated at once and I don't have to cook." Fab flashed her sneaky smile.

"This is where Mother and Spoon come in — one shops, the other cooks?"

"Good plan, don't you think?" Fab said. "You can't not tell them, or it might unravel in a way you don't want."

"I'm hoping that we don't have any uninvited guests," I said.

"I'm keeping an eye out for anyone lurking around, and so far, I haven't seen anyone. Now, there was a guy in a truck staking out The Cottages, and a different truck parked overnight in the parking lot of Jake's. So, I think the tracker was placed on the SUV at The Cottages or when we were out somewhere. You'd think we would've noticed that kind of activity unless we were being distracted on purpose."

"You should've told Help — it could be useful information."

"I forgot but will do it tonight. Unfortunately, it wouldn't have been of any use, as one truck didn't have plates and the other's were covered."

"I'm thinking — I know that scares you," I teased Fab, " — what if the reason that the compound hasn't been discovered is because whoever it is thinks we live at The Cottages? I've been there a lot lately, with the kids and everything."

"Now, we're going to have whoever this is thinking we live there."

"Time to move the Falcon. Should we flip to see who drives?"

Fab grabbed the keys from my hand and drove back to the house, she jumped out. "I'll park a couple of blocks over and meet you at the property."

I got out and rounded the front and slid behind the wheel.

Chapter Twenty-Nine

I followed Fab to The Cottages, and turned into the driveway and she disappeared into the neighborhood. I parked in the space at the far end knowing the cottage was empty and got out and stared up.

Cootie was standing on the roof of Crum's cottage. I hoped he didn't fall off into my flowers. And that he didn't get hurt.

Mac joined me, saying, "That's nothing. You've got a lot on your plate right now, so I'm taking care of it. No need to worry."

Fab showed up at my side and we exchanged a "sure" look.

My phone rang, cutting off my demand to know what was going on. I saw that it was Toady and clicked it off. Heading for the barbecue area, I took out my burner and called him back as he walked into the driveway.

He shrugged as if to say, what the heck?

"My phone might have a tap on it. Until further notice, I'm using this phone."

"That's a good idea. When you get a name, I'll pay the person a call, and whoever it is won't be bothering you again." Toady made a noise that made my hair stand on end. "I've got some good news for you. That warehouse building you want is all yours. That cretin brother accepted the offer with no negotiation. I was surprised, since I figured he'd at least check me out and he didn't. He did say as-is, and I almost laughed in his face. He was focused on getting out of town and excited that, in the end, he put one over on his brother. I acted like I didn't know what he was talking about."

"How soon before I close the deal?"

"I told him ten days, as that's what the last deal took, and he was fine with it. I think he was surprised I could make it happen that fast."

"I really appreciate this. Creole encouraged me to go for it, and I'm going to surprise him."

"Anytime. I'm here to help. My lips are glued shut."

"There's something else. Well, maybe." I looked around to make sure no one was eavesdropping, then lowered my voice. "What do you know about Trigger?"

"He's someone you need to stay away from," Toady growled. "Keeps a low profile and has others do his criminal acts. I suppose somehow he thinks that keeps his hands clean."

"You got a home address? Somewhere that he hangs out?"

"You don't want to be flipping the top on that box," Toady said, his tone full of warning.

"I wouldn't if it wasn't really important."

"I don't have the answers you want, but I can make a few inquiries and get you what you need. As long as you promise that you and your friend won't go off half-cocked to help some client."

"I can promise you that won't happen."

I thanked him again for being the go-between in another deal. Maybe Trigger wasn't involved in the disappearance of our husbands, but the sooner we eliminated him from the list, the better. Either way, I'd turn the information over to the Chief and he could put it to good use.

I had attracted Fab's attention, and she started over and joined us where we stood in the middle of the driveway, Mac behind her, hustling to keep up.

"I've got an update on the car retrieval case." Toady eyed Mac. If he expected her to leave, there was no way that would happen.

"She's good. If it needs to be secret, she won't say a word," I said.

"Or I'll shoot her." Fab graced her with a deranged smile.

I shook my head, knowing that Mac saw that kind of talk as proof of girl bonding.

"The dead guy, Dodds, and his business partner didn't agree on how to handle business matters, so he paid to have him offed. I'd say he hired a killer without a lot of experience, because there was security footage of the man coming and going from the parking lot." Toady snorted, conveying that it wasn't a good time to cheap out.

"Oh! I just read about that case online. The shooter flapped to the cops about who hired him," Mac said. "Millionaire," she said in disbelief. "His money will get him a good lawyer, but he can't spend the rest in prison."

"Didn't take long for law enforcement to get the parties involved locked up," Toady said.

"You'd think people would be smart enough to weigh the consequences and move on. Beats a prison cell for life. Or worse. They don't," Fab said with a shake of her head.

Toady's phone rang, and he took it out of his pocket and checked the screen. "You need anything, call." He waved and walked out to the sidewalk. I turned and faced Fab and Mac. "What's going on?" I demanded.

They exchanged a look.

"I'm not telling her," Fab said. "I'm not the property manager. Thank goodness."

"Crum had a small issue that needed taking care of," Mac started evasively.

Fab snorted. "Just spit it out."

"I'm thinking the beginning is a good place to start." Mac gave me a sly smile. "Right after Crum moved in, a raccoon ate its way into the crawl space above his ceiling. So, doing the humane thing, he drilled holes in the ceiling and shot ammonia up there so it would relocate back to nature."

"This is the first we're hearing about it?" I demanded. Mac nodded. "The ceiling fell down?"

"The good news is that it's still intact," Mac said. "Mostly anyway."

"She's about to get to the part where Crum's on the commode," Fab said with a grin.

"Seriously, keep it vague but don't leave out the important parts," I said.

"The professor was sitting on the throne, doing his business, when water dripped on his head," Mac related.

"That's not possible because we don't have plumbing up there," I said.

"That's because it wasn't water; it was urine. The raccoon came back." Mac was enjoying the retelling way too much.

I wasn't sure if my mouth dropped open or not.

Mac hurried on. "I called out a racc catcher, and he relocated the preggo mom and told us to get the holes sealed or she'd be back, and she might put the word out to her friends. So, I've got Cootie on the job, fixing all the holes."

I covered my face with my hands and took a breath, noting that Fab was laughing. "Crum's evicted, and you need to kick him to the curb tomorrow." I turned and walked away.

"She didn't take that well," I heard Fab say behind me.

Mac ran after me and grabbed my arm to slow

me up. "You can't do that. I need him to drive the Love Caddie. I've already taken deposits on reservations." Her imploring look changed to a militant one.

"I need caffeine. Not coffee. Something cold and sugary, and then life will make sense again," I groaned.

Mac hooked her arm around me, led me over to the barbecue area, and shoved me down on one of the cement benches, hemming me in so I couldn't get away. "Listen up and keep an open mind."

This can't be good.

"Remember the caddie?" Mac asked, and I nodded. "I got a *great* deal, and you now own it. It's insured and everything."

Of course, you did. Who else would want it?

"Rude and I got together and came up with the idea of sunset drives for lovers—cruise around town, top down, little stop at the beach for a sip of champagne since they can't drink in the car. We spread the word and got a good response. I called Spoon and made a deal for him to get it running like a charm. Can't have it breaking down on the highway." Mac grimaced.

"That old piece of…" I stuttered.

"It's getting painted the original light pink, and the top is getting replaced. We've got to have that working—it's a selling point: the wind in your face." She fanned herself with her hand and smiled dreamily.

"Your hair blowing all over, sticking in your teeth," I said.

Mac sighed. "You need to get your romance on."

"You talked the most sought-after mechanic in the Keys, maybe all of Florida, to work on that piece of…?" I asked incredulously. "We're paying through the nose."

"There's the happy ending."

"I hate that phrase," I snapped. "Just tell me."

"Even with the repairs, it's a good deal, and the cost was kept down because I ponied up the golf cart. Course, I didn't tell Spoon that it was a blessing he was taking it because once the cops found out that it was Crum who dumped it in the empty field, they'd be all over him like a pack of June bugs."

I squeezed my eyes closed, warding off that image. "You're telling me that Spoon took a wrecked-out junk of a cart in exchange for repairs?" I asked, not believing her. I peeked out of the corner of my eye, expecting someone to jump out of the bushes, screaming, "Pranked."

"Isn't that great?" Mac smiled big.

"So, you've got paying customers for this idea of yours?" I asked.

"It's going to pay for itself in no time." Mac clapped her hands together.

"How does Crum fit into this arrangement?" I didn't want to know but felt compelled to ask.

"He's getting all decked out in tropical chic to

chauffeur the lovebirds," Mac said excitedly.

"New clothes?" I raised my brows. "Or he's been digging in the trash again?"

Fab finally showed up and sat across from us.

"You're going to be pleased," Mac said.

I doubted it, but stayed silent.

"I stressed the importance of running a classy operation, and he agreed." Mac sounded so sincere, I didn't have the energy to mutter, "Sounds great," and mean it.

"Did you know all this before me?" I demanded of Fab.

"Just got the details from the professor himself, and he's excited about being part of the new venture. He feels like he did his part to make it happen." Fab smirked, thoroughly enjoying the situation.

"What else did you talk about?" Mac asked Fab.

"What it's like to get peed on by a rodent."

"I'm going to let you run this new operation however you see fit. I'm certain it's going to be hugely successful," I said with fake enthusiasm.

Mac threw her arms around me in a crushing hug. "You're the best." She pushed me back and smoothed down my hair. "There's another thing," she whispered and motioned for us to put our heads together.

Not one to be left out, Fab plunked down next to me, giving me a hip shove.

"Another unwanted visitor last night," Mac

whispered. "Parked out at the curb all night." She pointed to the hedge that now only partially blocked the view to the street. Crum had gotten carried away on the trim job.

"If that happens again, could you forward the security tape to Fab?" I asked and then told her the Hummer would be parked on the property and if she saw anyone show the slightest interest, in no way was she to confront them. Call the cops.

"I kept the tape from last night. And she already asked me, and I told her I'd do it."

"I'm afraid to ask if there's anything else," I said.

Mac surveyed the driveway before answering. "The inmates are quiet for the most part."

"One more thing. If Crum has any repair issues in the future, he's to report them to you immediately, not take care of them himself."

"I drummed that into him already."

Chapter Thirty

We were about to walk back to the Falcon, but Fab stopped on the sidewalk and stared down the street for the longest time. She crossed the street to Mac's driveway and hunched down to check out the underside of her truck. Then she walked back down the driveway and moved the Hummer so that the bumper stuck out of the parking space and could be seen from the street.

Mac and I stood and watched.

"What's she doing?" Mac asked.

"Sending a message," I said as she marched towards us, her face conveying that whatever her idea was, she thought it was a good one.

"If anyone asks what unit Madison's staying in, tell them you don't give out that information," Fab told Mac.

"Please, be careful," I said to Mac. "Besides anyone snooping around, keep an eye out for anyone you don't know asking questions of the tenants."

"Let's hope that whoever we're dealing with isn't that smart and that they do post someone close by," Fab said.

"What about your car?" I asked.

"You want me to guess? Because that's all it would be," Fab said, and I nodded. "Everyone knows you don't know how to drive; so whoever this is thinks they have the right car." She ignored my snort. "Your earlier theory that whoever it is thinks you live here is probably correct. Either way, that's what we're going to let them think."

"I like the idea of steering the kidnappers away from where we live, but don't want any problems here."

"Agreed. But they probably already think you live here, so this changes nothing. If we want this to stop without anyone being hurt, we have to figure out who's behind it. I've made a list. Didier's not on it, as I'd be shocked if this had anything to do with him. Under Creole's name, I've got nothing… unless it's someone from his past. Don't know who that would be. That leaves you and me. You've pissed off a major criminal lately, and I have a host of so-called clients that I never know what they're going to do next."

"Can you get ahold of Dodger and see if he'd like to come back and resume his guard duties?" I asked Mac.

"About that…" Mac hedged. "Must have slipped my mind. My plate's always full these days, or so it seems."

"You want to hurry up before we forget what the subject is?" Fab said.

"He's still here." Mac pointed to the end

cottage. "Felonious activities kept popping up, so I extended his stay."

"Great idea. Let's keep him until we're certain everything's calmed down." It sounded ridiculous, as something was always coming up. Maybe it was time to think about a security guard.

"You need a ride somewhere?" Mac shook her keys.

"We've got a backup ride close by," I said. "Be alert. And don't get involved."

"You need to take your own advice," Mac said.

Fab nodded her head towards the corner. I waved as we set out on foot.

"Don't tell me you're taking me a direct way instead of cutting through people's properties."

Only the shaking of her head let me know that she'd heard me; otherwise, she ignored me.

"I like that Mac never says no and doesn't ask a bunch of stupid questions," Fab said, leading the way back to the car, veering off the sidewalk and across a vacant property overgrown with mile high weeds.

"You might want to add that she keeps her lips zipped." I grabbed the back of her top, bringing her to a halt. "Before we go any further, have you been this way before? I don't want any unpleasant surprises, like a bear or something."

"Bears?" Fab snorted. "Where's your sense of adventure?"

"Maybe next time." I turned around and, a foot or so later, was back on pavement. "You can pick me up on the corner, and regale me with how much fun you had."

Fab ran and caught up with me and tugged on my shirt. "You're weird." She turned me around. "Have a little faith."

"Guilty as charged. But then, you've known that about me from the start." I liked that I'd gotten her to smile a couple of times that morning, and over stupid stuff.

Only Fab would know that a run-down house would have a walkway along the far side that led to the next street over. At least, it was paved. I spotted the Falcon a half block away.

When Fab turned toward the main highway I said, "If you want another car, maybe something that doesn't stick out like your pricey sports car, I'll introduce you to Booker."

"Is Booker his real name?"

"Probably not. Not a single one of these ex-undercover detectives is using their real name, and I think that it's a good idea." I turned to her. "Dare you to ask."

"Since Booker isn't our contact, I'll get Help to take me. It might be weird, the two of us barging over. We should cultivate him. Being able to swap rides without a lot of hassle would be great."

"You've had a couple of good ideas today." I smiled at her. "When we find out who napped our husbands, I say we kill the abductors. And not leave a trace. Make sure they don't have the opportunity to come back. We don't need to learn that lesson a second time."

"I'll have to think on good ways of disposing of a body or two." Fab gave me a crazy-girl smile.

"We could fob the job off on someone we know who could turn the bodies into kibble, but what fun would that be?"

Fab put her hand on my forehead, and I smacked it away, laughed at her, and changed the subject. "You're going to have a full house—you, me, and Help, the three of us shacked up together. You better have plenty of food and drink."

"I object to your classification."

I wiped the non-existent tear from my eye and grinned. "I'll behave. Maybe."

Thanks to no traffic, it was a quick trip home. We got to the security gate, which Fab opened with her code. We waited for it to close.

"We'll hit your house first, pack up the Falcon, and go to my house," Fab said.

"Won't whoever's tracking us think it's weird when the Hummer doesn't move?" I asked.

"Or they'll think we're following instructions and lying low. Besides, we'll be moving it around every day."

We packed my suitcase and the cats into the car and drove down the street. Fab turned into her driveway and parked behind Spoon's car.

"I called your mother on one of the burner phones when you were otherwise busy and told her to hotfoot it over here and put together a family dinner," Fab said. "I requested that she request the Chief's presence. Before she could ask a dozen questions, I instructed her to write down the new code to get in, and that excited her and derailed her train of thought."

"I'm going to give Xander a call and see if he's got anything new. Hopefully, the Chief will also have something to go on."

"If Xander does have anything, pull me aside and share with me first," Fab said.

"I'm hoping for an address on Trigger so I can do my own snooping and cross him off the list."

"Anyone finds out that's your plan, and you'll find yourself cuffed to a chair."

Chapter Thirty-One

One thing about Mother—when she put out the call for a family dinner, everyone showed up, the Chief and Help were also included. The only one missing was Liam, who was studying for finals at the University of Miami.

When Help showed up with the Chief, Fab led him down one of the long halls to a guest bedroom. I caught Mother staring, a look of surprise on her face.

When Brad and his five-year-old daughter, Mila, showed up, the little girl ran into the house like a whirlwind. Fab was ready for her and had one of the couches filled with toys and books to keep her entertained after dinner.

"When are Creole and Didier getting here?" Spoon asked.

"About that…" I hedged.

"You lied to me, didn't you?" Brad demanded.

"I did. When you find out why, I'm hoping all will be forgiven." My voice trembled with sadness.

Brad set down his beer, closed the space between us, and enveloped me in a hug. "Nothing to forgive. You know I'm always here for you."

"We're going to need all of you to be discreet about this one," I announced to the room at large, then pointed to Fab. "You tell them."

"Let's have a seat at the table." Fab motioned to the patio, where earlier, the two of us had set the table.

Once all of us were seated, Fab, who'd taken the chair at the head of the table, stood and updated everyone on what had happened, or what we knew anyway, and that it was imperative that no one say a word to anyone not seated at the table and that they go about their lives as normal.

A silence descended on the table. It didn't happen often that everyone was at a loss for what to say at once.

"I've been called in to consult on this case since I know all the players and have dealt with them in the past," the Chief said. "We have a few ideas on who the culprits could be. But nothing definitive, and we won't until that second call comes in. With any luck, they'll get stupid and use a different phone that will give us a good lead."

Help spoke up. "Stopped by Fab's office. Xander and I had a conference call with the Chief. We were both impressed by the young man. He's better than some of the specialists we've used in the past, and the plan is to continue using him."

"If someone calls for Creole or Didier at the office?" Brad asked. "In fact, there was a call—the same woman called twice, asking for Creole. She refused to identify herself or leave a number. The second time, I stressed that if she wanted to be assured of speaking with Creole, she had to leave her number, and he'd call back when he returned to the office. She hung up."

"Is that how you typically handle calls?" the Chief asked.

"It was Creole's suggestion when we first started working together that we not give out information about our comings and goings to anyone, not even another business associate. 'None of their damn business' is what I recall him saying at the time." Brad chuckled.

"It will be easy to have Xander track the office calls," the Chief told Help.

"I have a tidbit to share," Help said. "Xander got me two dogs to take for a walk in the neighborhood where the guys went missing. I have to say, I was impressed that he could do it so fast. Ten minutes."

"That's where my Dobermans went?" Spoon laughed.

"You walked his trained killers?" I asked in dismay.

"If you're not crawling over my fence in the middle of the night, they're sweethearts," Spoon insisted.

"Sure they are." I rolled my eyes at him, and

he grinned. "Happy to see you're still in one piece," I said to Help.

"You want to hear what happened or not?" he grouched.

I flourished my hand.

"Me and my two pals were out foot-cruising the street and ran into a woman walking her giganto poodle." His eyes crinkled at the corners. "The dogs sniffed each other in a way that suggested they'd met before, and I knew I was in trouble, since I'd already forgotten their names and Dog One and Two sounded fishy."

"So, you charmed the woman," Fab drawled. "She lost her train of thought and didn't ask why you were stealing someone else's killers."

"Pretty much." Help grinned. "We got to talking, and I commented that I was new to the area and was happy that the street didn't attract a lot of traffic, which made it a good place to walk. That's when she told me about two trucks that got into a fender bender, and from the description she gave, one of them was Creole's. The men got out and examined the damage. She continued her walk, and when she came back, both trucks were gone."

"Spoon and I should check our security cameras," Fab said. "Too bad we don't know anyone else on the street we could ask."

"Did she tell you where along the road it happened?" I asked. "If we knew the exact location, or close anyway, Xander could hack into the neighboring business's system, if they have one."

The Chief cleared his throat. "That's illegal."

I didn't say anything, and I know it surprised him when I didn't back down from our staredown.

"Spoon and I are available anytime to do whatever you need," Mother offered.

Spoon nodded. "Anytime," he stressed.

"You can help perpetuate the charade that all is well and, more importantly, that law enforcement isn't involved," the Chief said. "You need to talk, call on one of the burners."

"Fab and I think that the kidnappers might be under the mistaken impression that I live at The Cottages. Her idea was to leave the Hummer parked there. I agreed. The last thing we want is to lead anyone back here."

"We'll use the Falcon for driving back and forth," Fab added and told them we borrowed the ride from a friend. "We can easily park on any of the streets around The Cottages; I know most of the shortcuts."

"That's so modest of you." I laughed. "Fab knows all the shortcuts. As we're creeping across the properties of old men, they'll be ecstatic to see their girl again and renew old acquaintances."

One would've had to be quick to catch Fab's smirk.

"I wasn't happy to be informed that I

wouldn't be getting Dodger back on the job anytime soon, and it amused him to tell me the reason was 'need to know,'" Spoon related. "He's having such a good time hanging with 'them weirdos' and flexing his muscle that I may never get him back on the job."

"I can't believe it, but I'm thinking about hiring a guard. Maybe not full-time, but definitely nights," I said.

"You could probably work a deal with Dodger. He'd happily give up that studio apartment he's stuffed up in," Spoon said.

"I invited Help and Madison to stay here until the guys come home," Fab said. "So we can all be found in one convenient location."

"I like that idea... a lot," Mother said.

"Does that mean we can count on you to bring pink boxes for breakfast?" I asked. That was code for yummy food from the bakery.

"Free breakfast? I'm in," Brad said.

"Chief, you're invited anytime," Fab said. "I'll give you the code."

"Are you two bonding?" I asked.

Fab rolled her eyes. The Chief glared.

Spoon stood. "If we're done here, time for dinner. I've got everything ready to toss on the barbecue."

Chapter Thirty-Two

The next morning, Help got the coffee brewing, and the three of us gathered around the island in Fab's mammoth kitchen.

"I called Xander last night and asked if he could hack into security cameras along the road, and he said he'd get on it today," Fab informed us.

"Did you not hear the part about it being illegal?" I asked.

Help watched our interaction with an eagle eye.

"I gave Xander a heads up about that and said that if he wanted, we'd find someone else. He insisted he was in."

"I have mixed feelings. I don't want to corrupt the hell out of Xander. But I trust him. I think that when we have requests that border on or flat out are illegal, we should have a backup to call."

"He's a great kid and smart as they come," Help said. "When we talked yesterday, he told me he had other options, including an app he's designed, which pretty much impressed me. But he admitted to liking the spy game, and he loves working for the two of you."

"We can't repay that by getting him a criminal record," I said.

"That's where your backup comes in," Help said.

Fab broke the silence that settled while we finished our coffee. "Another stop on the agenda: we're going to work up disguises."

"You already have hats and glasses," Help reminded us. "In a different car, no one's going to notice you."

I bit my lip to keep from laughing, knowing that she wanted something Help hadn't seen, but would she fess up? She'd find out that it wasn't so easy sneaking around under the nose of a detective. I'd stopped, since Creole caught me every time.

"It doesn't hurt to have a change of hats and glasses," Fab said. Typical of her when she didn't want a follow-up question, she changed the subject: "I searched under both my and Didier's cars early this morning, and no tracking devices. Before you got out here this morning, I shared my suspect list with Help, who wasn't helpful." She made a face at him, which he returned.

"Not so fast. It's only been an hour or so. I emailed the list to the Chief, who didn't have a comment, but I did get permission to share that Casio's also been listed as missing. He hasn't checked in, and no one has heard from him."

"His kids," I said sadly.

"Missing means just that. He's a tough bastard

and has been in impossible situations before and walked away. He's going to this time. As a betting man, I say we'll be dealing with his smug self again."

"This big case that was so all-fired important, does it have to do with Trigger?" I asked.

"I can't tell you that."

"I'm hoping that I'm not partially to blame." I banged my head on the counter. "My husband and my best friend's husband getting kidnapped over besting Trigger on a real estate deal. Just flippin' great." I turned to Fab. "I'm sorry."

Fab patted my arm. "Even if... who could predict a business deal would go that badly?"

"Not so fast," Help said. "Until we know for sure, all suspects are on the table."

* * *

Fab and I got in the Falcon, baseball hats and glasses in place, and cruised over to The Cottages.

"We should cruise through the coffee drive-thru and see if we're recognized." I scooted down in my seat just enough to keep an eye on the road.

"That's as good an excuse as any for more coffee."

"I'm excited that, by the time we're done slinking through the neighborhood, I should know the shortcuts as well as you do."

Fab shot me an unsupportive "sure you will" glance.

Fab went through the drive-thru, placing our usual order. The attendant barely paid us any attention, as she was busy talking. Fab exited out the back and wound around the neighborhood, cut over to The Cottages, and cruised past the property. All was quiet there, as was the rest of the block. She parked a couple of streets over. We ditched our accessories, throwing them in the trunk; then I followed her as she maneuvered her way to The Cottages. We came up on the side street and cut through the pool area, not crossing paths with a single person the whole time, then got in the Hummer and drove out.

Fab jumped back on the highway and headed south out of town. "I asked Xander if he wanted to come and work out of my house temporarily. He hemmed and hawed for so long that I felt bad and changed the subject. Mostly, it was because I didn't know what to say."

"That was nice of you." One of the burner phones rang, and I answered. "Xander. You got something for me?" I hit the speaker button.

"Got addresses. For the guy who called, on what I'm guessing is a burner—it's registered to John Smith, and the account had an address. Also, found a couple of addresses for Trigger. One is a commercial office building and the other residential. From the picture I was able to pull, the latter looks like a drug house that no one would want to live in. I'm thinking both are a waste of time. When I do find something, I'm hoping you're going to be careful."

"That feels like all we've been doing, but I get it, so the answer is we will." If I had a good address, I'd be tempted to kick Trigger's door in and use him for target practice, except that probably wouldn't get me my husband back.

"How are things at the office?" Fab asked.

"Quiet, which is always good. I did check before I opened the gate, and no lurkers. Toady's going to be here in a few; says he needs a place to spread his paperwork out for a couple of hours."

"I talked to him the other day about an address for Trigger, and he thought maybe he could get one. Would you follow up for me and run a check?" I asked.

"Either way, I'll get back to you." Xander hung up.

"Like you, I'm thinking that my property could use a few more bodies hanging around at odd hours to discourage trouble," Fab said as she cruised into the grocery store lot and back out again. "I'm going to rent the other office building out to Toady and Xander, and I'm fine with Toady living there."

"I think it's a great idea." I was keeping an eye on the side mirror, and what I thought might be a tail turned off and no other car took its place. "Once we get our hands on those addresses, are we going to skulk by at night?"

"We'll take the Falcon and cruise by in broad daylight so we can get a good idea of the layout of the properties. Then we can make a plan from there." Fab u-turned, and we drove back to The Cottages and parked. She grabbed my hand, and we ran across the street and went in the opposite direction from the way we came, back to the car.

"I'm open to any plan that leads to getting our husbands back," I said.

The first text was the address for the man who'd called Fab's phone. We headed south and, at the outskirts of town, turned off the highway. Turning the corner, we saw that the first part of the street was commercial, and then it turned residential. The address we wanted was near the end of the block, and it turned out to be a run-down apartment building. The owner hadn't lifted a finger to improve its condition, including regular trash pickup—the dumpster had overflowed and broken furniture had been tossed in a pile.

"If we call out 'John Smith,' I wonder how many heads would poke out the doors? Even if we had a unit number, I don't like our chances of asking questions without inviting trouble." I stared out the window as Fab drove slowly by.

"Agreed." Fab turned and, with one last drive-by, headed back to the highway and turned south once again. She drove a few miles and turned off. The commercial address for Trigger turned out to be a pair of warehouses with no signage, which appeared to have been vacant for a long time, except for the two cars parked in front, which looked out of place in front of the large building. She passed it up and continued to the end of the street, a dead end. The block held one other commercial property, a large boat storage business that took up one whole side of the street.

"You see a sign of any kind?" I asked.

Fab pulled over to the side of the road. "This is risky, but what the hell. I'll get in the back, and you're going to drive through the parking lot so I can grab pictures of the license tags and the building. If we attract attention, you'll have to channel your inner race car driver."

"I should probably be the one taking the pictures," I said.

"You've got this." Fab climbed over the seat, and I scooted behind the wheel. "There are no windows on the front of building, so we won't attract immediate attention unless it comes walking around the side. Drive in about halfway up, and I'll get the shots."

"If we attract any attention, we're going to need to turn this car in, hopefully in one piece." I winced, wondering what kind of story I'd come up with and whether my insurance covered an unofficial loaner.

"Ready," Fab said.

I followed her instructions and drove through the parking lot while she snapped pictures, then out again and headed back to the highway.

Fab climbed back into the front. "Love to know what's going on there. Maybe something we can have Xander check out."

"I'm surprised that you didn't hop out and knock on the roll-up doors. Or, at the very least, run around the building a couple of times." I was surprised she hadn't demanded to drive.

"I thought about it." She half-laughed. "Also thought about asking questions at the boat storage lot across the street and decided against both."

"You'd think that if the owner of those warehouses was running a straight-up business, they wouldn't look abandoned and would have a sign. Even if you were running an illegal operation, you'd do the same things to avoid attracting attention."

When Fab had no comment, I turned and stared hard at her. "If you come back here at night, I'm coming along. It'll be interesting seeing how you're going to sneak past Help."

Fab turned and looked out the window.

"Now what?" I asked as we got back to the Cove.

"We go home, wait for the damn phone to ring, and find out what their demands are."

Chapter Thirty-Three

Another long, nerve-wracking day went by before we got the call we were waiting for. We were sitting in Fab's living room, reading the reports that Xander had sent over. The warehouse was in foreclosure and owned by a bank. The cars belonged to lowlifes, who had them registered to addresses that didn't exist.

Both our phones rang at the same time. My screen read "unknown caller." I hit the record button on the small recorder that I carried everywhere, then got up and walked into the kitchen. Fab strode out to the pool area. Help waited with a contrived look of patience.

"You've been a good girl," the man boomed through the phone. "It's going to take a couple of days to set up this transaction, and in that time, no cops, or else you won't even get a body back."

"Before I agree to anything, I'll need proof of life," I cut in.

"You'll agree," he barked. "Remember this: you're not in charge. You want proof of life, how about a finger or some other body part?"

"I'm not ponying up anything for damaged goods, you remember that," I said with more

266

bravado than I felt.

"Whatever." He seemed surprised that I hadn't backed down. "There'll be another call. Be ready to follow directions. No cops. If you try to pull one over on us, we'll know. Their deaths will be on you." He hung up.

I slumped over, my head on the island, and squeezed my eyes closed. "Will this ever end?" I asked myself.

Help came up behind me and rubbed my back. "Hang in there." He picked up the recorder and listened to the call.

Fab handed over her recorder. "I got the squeaky-sounding woman this time, and she basically said the same thing as the guy that called you. I got the impression she's new to this game, and when I made the proof-of-life demand, she stuttered a response that she didn't seem certain of."

"Why the delay?" I asked. "Kidnappers want money. Name an amount, and let's get this over with."

"You're right about that, and they generally want it as quickly as possible," Help said. "I agree with Fab's assessment that these people aren't that organized, and that works in our favor. Based on how long you two have waited already, I'm thinking you'll be getting another call sooner rather than later."

"Do kidnappers release their victims once they get what they want?" I asked Help.

"Not always," Fab answered. "I did some research, and it all depends on if they ever planned on releasing them. We have to be prepared for the possibility that the guys might be dead already and there's nothing we can do to change the outcome."

I couldn't even wrap my head around the idea that we'd agree to all the demands and I still wouldn't see Creole again.

Help pulled out his phone. "I'm calling Xander and having him run down these calls." He got up and moved outside.

"I think we should be more visible around town," Fab said. "Change things up. If someone's following us, we'll spot them."

"Why do you suppose they need more time?" I asked.

"My research says that it's always about money. If they're new to the kidnapping game, maybe they don't know how much to demand." Fab tapped her fingers on the island. "Or maybe this has something to do with the Boardwalk… but no attempts to contact Brad have been made."

"On my list, I have me, Creole, and The Boardwalk as being the possible focus of this stupid scheme," I said. "Didier got napped because he was in the wrong place at the wrong time."

"We can make endless lists and still not be certain until we get the call, and not even then, as we'll know the demands but not the reason."

Help came back and sat down. "Xander's on it."

Fab had told Help about our tracking down the addresses that Xander gave us, and he wasn't happy. He ordered us to stay away from the warehouse and said he'd check it out himself. He came back after a night out and told us it was used to run drugs and there was a surveillance team already in place on the outside of the building and an officer planted inside.

"Why would a drug dealer link his phone to an address where his illegal business was going down?" I'd asked.

"They often think they're smarter than everyone else, and they're not. It's these little screw-ups that get them caught," Help had said.

My phone rang, and Jake's popped up on the screen. "I'm afraid to ask," I said when I answered and hit the speaker button; I wasn't in the mood to repeat every word.

"Had to close early," Doodad said. "A fight, more like a brawl, broke out, a few things got broken, and I'm in cleanup mode now. We'll be ready to open for the beer-for-breakfast crowd."

"Anyone get hurt?" I asked.

"A couple of the brawlers left here bellyaching about their aches and pains. The employees left unscathed, as we stood back and didn't mix it up until it looked like the fighters had run out of gas."

"A well-placed bullet couldn't put a stop to the fight before it got started?" I asked in annoyance.

"Did I leave that part out?" Doodad continued before I could respond: "I came in on the middle of the action, and since you don't pay me enough to get my ass kicked, I did put a slug in the ceiling. And then another. Slow bunch. I hadn't fired my Smith & Wesson lately, so it was good practice."

"I'll be by first thing in the morning to assess the damage. Do I need to get my insurance agent out there?"

"No need. Just some broken tables and chairs. I'll get with Junker and see what he's got in the back room, and maybe we can do a swap. I told him he should keep a couple in inventory."

Although Junker usually dealt in garden things that he hawked to out-of-state dealers, he occasionally stockpiled things we could use at Jake's.

"See you tomorrow." I hung up.

"Doodad didn't mention the cops; maybe you caught a break," Fab said.

"That would be a first, but I'll take it."

Help's phone rang, and he answered. After a few grunts and indecipherable words, he hung up. "The phones are burners, and Xander's going to trace them back to where they were bought. If they were recent purchases, we might be able to get a photo from the security cameras."

"We get pictures, I've got street sources that can ID them," I said.

Chapter Thirty-Four

Fab and I decided to hit up the Bakery Café, and after ditching the Falcon, we retrieved the Hummer and headed over there to claim our favorite table on the sidewalk.

"Is this day one of being seen all over town?" I asked Fab.

"I'm thinking we should make a scene wherever we go." Fab laughed.

"That's a terrible idea." I made a face.

Fab continued to laugh.

"I can't believe my luck," a young woman said, sliding onto a chair across from us and plunking a large bag in her lap. "I didn't have any clue how to hook up with you, and then I see you sitting here. I'm so excited."

I squinted at her, remembering her as a wannabe client of Fab's but not remembering her name. That was Fab's fault; her bad habit had rubbed off on me. Fab stared also, and I was wondering if she was thinking the same thing.

"Miss… what's your name again?" I asked. Okay, that was rude-ish. I'd try harder the next time.

"Asha Webster," she said. Her eyes skittered around. I'd already been rude once, so asking for a drug test might not raise an eyebrow.

"I'm not taking on any clients at this time," Fab said in a tone sweeter than the sugar substitute on the table.

"You know how I had you track down an old family friend? I just need his address." She tittered.

"As I recall, I forwarded you the last-known address for the man," Fab said evenly. "Alaska, I believe."

"Yeah, but I think you lied. So, if we could straighten this out, which should only take a minute or two, I'd be on my way." Asha bared her teeth in a smile and wiggled around in her chair. She opened her bag and reached inside, and before Fab or I could react, Mother turned up out of nowhere and booted her out of her chair, screaming "gun," then gave it a kick as it tumbled out of her purse, hitting the ground.

"You go, Mother." I beamed at her.

A couple sitting at a nearby table jumped up, ran full bore to their car, about a half-block down, and squealed off down the road.

Fab wound her hand in the woman's hair and gritted, "What the hell's the matter with you?"

"Just give me what I want," Asha mewled and jerked out of Fab's hold, screeching at the top of her lungs.

A siren screamed up the street.

I looked around, and there were phones out at nearby tables, catching the action on video.

Asha reached out and grabbed her purse.

Mother jerked it back. "You're not going anywhere."

Asha shook her head and hopped to her feet, breaking into a run as a cop car pulled up in front.

"Isn't one of you going to stop her?" Mother demanded of me and Fab. "She shouldn't be running around."

"I like this skirt, and I'm not getting dirty." I smoothed my hands down my front.

"Thumbs up on my outfit, and I'm not getting hurt." Fab smiled down at her skinny jeans.

Kevin got out of his car and strode up. "If it isn't my favorite felon wannabes." He grinned.

"You're not funny, young man." Mother used her lecturing tone and followed it up with a "behave" stare.

He just grinned bigger. Another officer joined him.

"Since I'm the normal one…" I waved my hand. At Kevin's snort, I added, "Of the three of us." I told him what happened. What a star Mother was. She beamed at him. Fab pointed to the gun.

The other officer nodded, poker-faced, and took the gun into evidence. He removed the wallet from Asha's purse, took out the driver's license, and went back to his car. When he came back, he exchanged words with Kevin that we couldn't hear.

"What will Miss Webster's version be?" Kevin asked.

Fab's "who cares" expression echoed all our sentiments.

"You'll have to ask her, and she'll probably lie through her teeth," I said.

"Let me tell you about the case she hired me to investigate," Fab said. She gave him the details and how, when she contacted the man in question, the last thing he wanted was his personal information released to "that woman." "Apparently, she's had stability issues for quite a long time."

"I read somewhere that it's all the sun we get down here," Kevin said. "Don't go anywhere in case I have more questions." He turned to his partner, and they walked to the curb.

Another cop car raced past in the direction that Asha went.

I leaned over and kissed Mother. "Hungry?"

"Oh, good, you haven't eaten." Mother turned and waved to a waiter. "I saw your car and knew right where you'd be."

The waiter came over and took our order. We'd eaten there enough that we didn't need a menu.

"Does your husband know you're out cruising the streets this early?" Fab shook her finger at Mother.

Mother leaned over to bite it and laughed. "Wait until he hears that I was a 'badass.'" She grinned. "That will lead to a serious discussion." She faux-pouted.

"This better not be your way of sneaking something about s-e-x into the conversation," I said.

Mother leaned over and whispered, "Sex. You're a prude, daughter."

I scooted closer to Mother and quickly updated her on the latest about Creole and Didier, though it was sparse, and added that she needed to call Brad.

"Brad's working out of his house, which makes me happy," Mother said. "He's not anticipating any problems on the job, but thinks it's better to keep a low profile."

The food arrived, along with coffee refills.

"What are you two up to today?" Mother asked.

"Looking for some excitement?" I asked her. "We're headed to Jake's." I told her about the bar fight and that I wanted to get a look at the damage. "And before you start, I'm not selling."

"Spoon tells me I need to stop harping on that." Mother sighed. "To tell the truth, I'd miss the place. I don't play poker very often anymore, but when I do, it's a fun place to go."

The waiter came and took our plates. I was thankful that no one noticed I'd run my food around the plate as though it was in a road race to disguise that I hadn't eaten anything. Fab had at least eaten something.

"You're welcome to come with us," I said to Mother. "Just for you, we'll make a stop at the funeral home, check out the dead, and see if the guys have come up with any new tricks for splashy send-offs."

"Thankfully, I've got an appointment," Mother said. "This was fun, and we need to do it again as soon as the guys get home."

"Kevin and the other cop left, so I assume we're free to go anytime," Fab said. "If not, he knows where to find us."

Mother pointed. "There goes Asha in the back of a cop car."

"They probably found a warrant or something," Fab said.

Chapter Thirty-Five

When Fab pulled into the parking lot of Jake's, there was, as usual, no sign of life at Junker's, but it was clear a new shipment had been unloaded. Out of the corner of my eye, I caught sight of the backside of a human disappearing into the lighthouse.

I twisted in my seat as Fab parked in the front.

"What already?" she demanded.

"I don't see Gunz's car."

"Gunz is looking for a more professional office space, although that's not the way he worded it. Also, one of the reasons I was happy to rent the other warehouse to Toady and Xander. Didier tolerates Gunz but wouldn't want him next door."

"Someone just went into the lighthouse, and we need to check it out." I flipped the visor down and stared out the back window. "If someone's using the building, we need to know who they are and run background checks unless someone reputable is vouching for them."

We got out and walked over to the lighthouse. Fab tried the knob and, finding it locked, used her key. Kicked back on the couch was a thirty-something with his feet up. He rolled over and faced us, a deer-in-the-headlights look on his face.

"We're closed," he snapped.

Fab stared, and I stepped around her. "Who are you, and what are you doing in here?"

He sat up and flipped his dirty feet on the floor. "Whoa. I haven't had my coffee."

I was already on edge, and his beady appraising stare set me off. I drew my Glock and had to bite back a smile when he squealed. "Get out." I looked around. "Take your backpack, and don't set foot on this property again. If you're so stupid that there's a next time, I'll shoot you."

The man scrambled to his feet and started for the door, then skidded to a stop and grabbed a dirty jacket that matched the rest of his rumpled attire. "You won't get away with this." He raced outside as I took aim.

"You need to calm down," Fab said.

I walked over to the couch, grabbed the beach towel and pillow, and threw them out the door. "I need to disinfect my hand."

"I'll find out what's going on, and in the meantime, I'll have the locks changed."

"If Gunz is subletting, he's banned from the property." I stomped outside and back down the parking lot, cutting around the back of Jake's.

Fab caught up with me as I was about to enter through the kitchen. "Gunz didn't know what I was talking about, and since we didn't get a name, I couldn't be of any help. Next time, wait until after you ID someone before pulling your weapon."

"Next time?" I did my best not to shriek. "There better not be one. Tell Gunz to have the place fumigated." I waved to Cook, who was on the phone.

We walked down the hallway and up to the bar, where Doodad was finishing stocking. On the opposite side in the area in front of the jukebox, two tables and chairs were missing. Two other chairs had been pushed up against the wall.

"It doesn't look as bad in here as I thought it would." I mentally inventoried the rest of the room, and there was no more missing furniture.

"You have that ass-kisser Bouff to thank for that." Doodad grinned. "Wanted to make a good impression on the boss and cleaned it up himself. Threw the pieces in the back of his truck, said you look like a recycler, and hauled it off to a friend who makes decent stuff out of crap."

I slid onto a stool as Bouff slid out from under the sink. "What the heck are you doing down there?" I asked, shooting Doodad a glare.

"You had a leak, but not anymore." Bouff flashed a megawatt smile. "I object to being classified as an ass-kisser, in case anyone cares."

"You'll find that a lot of name-calling goes on around here, especially hyphenated 'ass' words, and as the boss, I've done zero to put a stop to it because sometimes it makes me laugh." I spun towards Fab as she slid onto a stool next to me. "Where have you been?"

"I stopped to say hello to Cook and see how he's been doing, inquire after the family. It's the friendly thing, you know," Fab said, so sweetly my teeth ached.

"When you find out what Fab was really doing back in the kitchen, let me know." I pointed at Doodad. "In the meantime, keeping to my resolution not to start my day off with tequila, I'll have my other regular and extra cherries."

"Where's pink hair?" Fab asked.

"That's not nice," I said.

Bouff and Doodad laughed.

The front door blew open, and pink hair stomped inside. "Cops are here," Kelpie roared. "One, anyway. Tried to keep him out, but he threatened me with a triple felony." She turned and threw out her arm to usher said cop into the room, bending at the waist to give him a prime view down to her navel.

Kevin stepped inside, soaked in the view, turned, and grinned. "It's been requested that I arrest the owner on assorted felonies. In the meantime, I'll take a soda and hear your side of the story before I haul you out of here."

"I suppose it's too late for me to make a run for it." I frowned and scoped out the exits, knowing that the kitchen was the ideal getaway.

Kevin slid onto a stool. "Chuck or Tuck." At my raised brow, he said, "Now that was funny. It's hard to keep names straight."

"What already?" Kelpie slapped her hand on the bar. "Bet it has to do with that cretin outside."

"Chuck claims that he rented the lighthouse and has a wadded up receipt as proof." Kevin slurped his soda and squashed the can with the heel of his hand, handing it to Bouff, who exchanged it for a new can. "Then you came along, roughed him up, and threatened to spread his guts to Miami."

I held up my hands in a defensive posture, then threw one arm around Fab's shoulders. "In my defense—ours, actually—I was defending our lives from an intruder. We were terrified."

"I'm sure you were trembling in your sandals," Kevin said. "Him being unarmed and all."

"Chuck moved so suddenly. You just never know." I feigned shock.

"I don't know what kind of con Chucky is running and don't care," Fab said. "The lighthouse is rented to Gunz, and if this guy wants to play games, he can take it up with the big man himself. Everyone sitting here knows that Chucky doesn't have a winning hand."

"So, I can tell Chuck no problem with him moving back in," Kevin said, and I nodded. "He turns up dead, and I'll be back."

"You should be more worried if he disappears without a trace," I said.

"There's a rumor that there was a brawl here last night." Kevin looked around. "I told them that there couldn't be any truth to that, as there was no 911 call."

"I don't know why you don't think this is a respectable joint," Kelpie said.

"Maybe because it isn't." Kevin looked up at the ceiling. "You got yourself some new holes. You should get those patched before another storm rolls through."

"Am I free to roam the streets?" I asked.

"Try not to shoot anyone," Kevin admonished.

"What happened with Asha Webster?" Fab asked. "Saw that you hauled her away."

"Outstanding warrant," Kevin said. "She'll be on her way to Tallahassee when they send someone to escort her."

I sent Fab an "I told you so" stare that she ignored with a glare.

"Let's hope that's the last we hear of her," she said.

"What about the body at the funeral home?" I asked Kevin.

Several sets of eyes swiveled in my direction.

"Surprised you two don't know, since it made the news," Kevin said. "Heart attack. Clear as we can figure, he couldn't afford a motel and the next best option was breaking into the funeral museum."

"Thanks for not making me drag the information out of you. We both know how tight-lipped you can be." I smiled at him.

"Here's one for the road." Kelpie handed Kevin a soda. He waved and left.

I slid off the stool and waved Bouff over to the patio. I opened the doors, flipping on the fans and the overhead string lights, and waved him to a chair, where he sat across from me. "Any word on Casio?"

Bouff stared at me for so long, I didn't think he was going to answer, then said, "Nothing so far."

"You know about my situation?" I asked, and he nodded. "If you hear *anything,* I want to know." He gave me a hard stare. I noticed that he didn't commit one way or the other. "How's it going? Been challenged to a fight yet?"

Not sure what it was about fighting that made him laugh, but it softened his features and made him even hotter. Who knew?

"A couple of drunks came in and wanted to start something. They copped an attitude when I refused to serve them. Jerked their heads toward the door and told me, 'Out in the parking lot.' I told them, 'Meet you out there in five minutes.' I never went out, and they didn't come back in. It might have had something to do with the fact that most of the customers clapped as they exited."

"Anything else?"

"Well, I had a couple of men come in and inquire about buying the place. I told them I didn't know if you were interested, but I did know that you were never here at closing."

"If you get any more inquiries like that, do what Kelpie does—take a message and never give it to me."

Bouff laughed.

Fab moved out to the deck, Doodad behind her.

"Your manager wants to know if we're staying for band auditions," Fab said.

I squeezed my eyes closed. "Sorry, we're really busy."

"As the owner—" Doodad started.

I cut him off. "As such, no thanks. I shouldn't have to make up an excuse, but the last time I stayed to give my inexpert opinion, that one group gave me a headache and it was a doozy." I looked at Fab. "Did you call Gunz?"

"I did, and he promises that Chucky's on his way out and won't be a bother in the future. He's also going to check out his story and see if we've got someone renting out places they think are empty… again."

Great. When that happened to me, I had to take it to court. Then the squatter turned up dead. If that happened to Chucky, I'd have Gunz's head.

Chapter Thirty-Six

The days ticked by, and no phone call. In the meantime, Xander was able to get pictures of the girl who bought the burner phones and IDed her. The address turned out to be a two-to-three-hundred-square-foot house elevated a foot off the ground. I imagined the land was worth more than the so-called improvement. The plan had been to stake the house out in the early morning hours, but the driveway was empty.

Fab spotted an old man sitting on his porch drinking his morning coffee, his dog asleep on his feet. "Wait here." She opened the car door.

I grabbed her arm. "Call me, so I can listen in."

We'd found out that our earpieces could pick up the sound of a pin dropping and had used them to eavesdrop on several occasions.

I watched as she crossed the street and approached the man, waving.

He gave her a once-over and a toothy smile. "Have a sit, hon." He waved to one of the rickety beach chairs.

"I haven't seen my friend, Josie Gant, in a couple of years." She waved her hand to the house across the street. "I'd like to surprise her."

"Years, huh?" The man grunted. "Not to be saying mean stuff about your friend, but you need to watch your back with her. She's not a favorite on this block. Had her boyfriend come over and kick a couple of asses over nothing."

"Good to know." Fab pulled cash out of her pocket. "What's a good time to catch her at home?"

He took it and shoved it in his shirt pocket. "Josie shows up around midday and leaves again around dinner time. Claims she has a job but never said what exactly."

"We never had this conversation," Fab told the man. "If what you say about her is true, anyone else shows up asking questions, you don't know anything."

"That's a good reminder that I talk too much."

Fab waved and crossed the street, getting back behind the wheel. "We'll come back later."

"Then what?" I stayed crouched down in the front seat of the Falcon.

"We're going to go to the bank and withdraw plenty of cash to bribe Josie with and hope its incentive enough to the tell the truth, then get out of town."

"Not to nitpick your idea, but we don't know if she's a peon or one of the architects of this kidnapping. And even if it's the former, that's no assurance that she won't double-cross us and tell whoever she works for that we paid her a visit." I sat back up as Fab turned the corner. "After your chat with the neighbor, that plan sounds like it might backfire on us."

"Okay new plan. We come back tonight and find out if this is the woman who bought the burner phone, and if so, we'll follow her to her job. Then what, you ask? You better come up with something."

* * *

We were back several hours later. This time, a small sedan was parked in the driveway. Fab rolled down the window and snapped a picture of the tag before parking up the block.

The neighbor had given us good information about the woman's comings and goings. We didn't have long to wait before the door opened. The woman who bounced out of the house in a pair of black skinny jeans and a button-down shirt and high heels was the same one from the surveillance footage.

"I'm thinking that wherever she works, she's not standing on her feet," I said.

Fab let her get to the end of the street, then followed her. "Since we don't know if she can spot a tail, I'm not going to be brazen. Instead, I'll hang back." We followed her to the outskirts of town, where she turned on a side street.

"We've been here before," I said.

Josie turned into the driveway of the warehouses, which still looked rundown and abandoned. No cars were parked in the front. She pulled around the back and out of sight.

"Missed the parking behind the building the last time we were here," Fab said.

"There's no way to check out what's going on back there unless you get out and walk, and then you don't know what you're going to run into and if you'll be a sitting duck."

"There's nowhere to park. The boat place is locked up, and if we hang out much longer in the middle of the street, we're sure to attract attention." Fab drove slowly to the corner, checking out both sides of the street. "Without knowing what the setup is, there's no way to sneak closer for a look." She pulled into the gas station at the corner and over to the air hose. "We're going to sit here until someone runs us off. We'll be able to check out any cars that go that way."

"This is Josie's job? I'm thinking attempting to buy her off is a bad idea," I said. "I'm telling you, I wouldn't set foot inside there in broad daylight, let alone at night."

Over the next hour, six cars drove past, pulling into the parking lot and around the back. A few minutes later, a beater truck rolled up next to us and the window rolled down.

I looked over Fab's shoulder. "We were

wondering what Help was doing tonight—guess we know."

Fab rolled down her window.

"What the hell?" Help yelled.

"What's going on?" Fab pointed to the warehouse.

"You two going to sit here until someone sees you?" Help snapped. "Before you insist you're keeping a low profile, you're not. I made you in a second."

It appeared that those two were going to play answer a question with another question and we'd be there all night. I laid my head against the seat. "Tell him we're headed home and we'll see him there, and you two can continue playing twenty questions then."

Fab turned and repeated what I said, then without waiting for a response, rolled up the window and drove out to the highway. Help followed us back to the house. We filed inside and congregated in the kitchen, where all the intense conversations seemed to take place.

"In the spirit of being upfront, we'll go first." I pointed to Fab. "You're up."

Fab told Help what we'd been doing, starting from when we left the house in the morning, and didn't leave anything out.

"Those warehouses were in foreclosure and bought for pennies on the dollar by a sham corporation," Help confided. "It's the place that Casio was reporting on, and it's possible that he might be being held there."

"Or he's dead, and we'll never see him again," I said.

"If whoever it was had any idea that he's undercover, we'd have the body; they'd dump it as a deterrent."

"Casio. Sham corporation. That means it's likely that Trigger is involved, since that's who he was investigating." Fab shut Help up with a wave of her hand. "Don't bother denying it. Makes too much sense."

"What else?" Help demanded of Fab.

"We've got a possible home address for Trigger. Gated beach mansion. No, we haven't driven by. What are we going to learn from that? About as much as we did tonight. Nothing."

It surprised me that she'd disclosed Xander's latest find re: Trigger. "It's been a few days now, and no calls. What's up with that?" I asked.

"The Chief's wondering the same thing," Help said.

"Do you think it's some kind of cruel game, and they're not going to call again?" If that were the case, then the outcome would be grim. I grabbed my burner phone and called the Chief, and when he answered, I said, "I'd like to meet."

"Tomorrow night, I'll meet you at Jake's, and we can have the deck to ourselves."

It surprised me that he didn't want details. Must have been something more going on. "I'll make it happen. And I'll put a bug in Cook's ear to whip you up something special." I hung up and relayed the short conversation.

"We're all invited," Fab said.

"Of course."

Chapter Thirty-Seven

Fab and I arrived at Jake's early the next evening.

"You go inside. I'm going to hang out here. See if we're followed." Fab parked in the front and stared out the side mirror. We'd swapped out the Falcon for the Hummer. "Don't worry, I have no intention of confronting anyone. Just to be on the safe side, though, I'll call you, and if I scream, come running." She called me, and when I answered, blew in my ear.

"Not funny," I complained. "Let's hope that doesn't happen."

"I've turned over a new, cautious leaf, and once this mess is over, I'll have to decide how I feel about it."

"You be careful," I admonished and went inside.

I'd already booked the deck and was happy to see the doors closed. I'd also talked to Cook earlier in the day. I waved to Bouff, who'd taken a shift for Kelpie. The Chief was going to be disappointed that he wouldn't be getting a quick flash of cleavage. I crossed the room, opened the doors, and tied the "Keep Out" sign on the knob. It'd been suggested that "Private Party" sounded friendlier, but I turned my nose up at that. My sign was more direct.

After checking to make sure that everything was set, I went back inside. "How's tricks?" I asked Bouff.

"I got me a fan club." He turned and winked at the two women on the far end of the bar.

"Taking off your shirt might be too obvious, but unbutton it and the women will be pushing and shoving to get at you."

He laughed. "Your alcoholic usual?"

"You bet, and I'm impressed that you know." I smiled at him. "Easy on the tequila. The Chief wouldn't appreciate me getting sloshed. I do that, and there's no telling what I'll say or do. I'm not averse to creating a scene when I've tipped a few." I grabbed my glass. "I'm going to forgo a pitcher tonight, but I'll have another one, half-strength, and then I'm done." I crossed to the deck and left the doors open so I could see when everyone arrived.

"I'm on my way back inside," Fab said in my ear. "Bringing the Chief with me."

Before I could answer, a man towered in the doorway. Well over six feet, dressed in jeans and a dress shirt, he peered down at me, a smirk on his face.

"I'm sorry, but this space is reserved for a private party." Now that was friendly, or so I thought. The man didn't move.

"I've heard this is your own private domain

out here." He scanned the deck, and it was clear it wasn't up to his standards, but he chose to slide into a seat across from me anyway.

I knew who he was but decided to pretend ignorance. "If you're selling something, my manager is the one to speak to."

His brown eyes narrowed to a beady stare. "I hate you," he seethed. "Let's not play games. I've got you in my web, and I'm enjoying watching you twist."

"Since you know what you're talking about and I don't have a clue, how about you start?"

He extended his hand, which I ignored. "Mr. Trigger."

"Your underlings didn't do their homework; I don't swap sweat." I smiled. "I think I prefer Seymour Houser. Not many Seymours running around."

If looks could kill… The upside was, it would've been fast. "If you want to keep your teeth, it's Mr. Trigger."

"Got it." My stomach churned into a knot. I caught sight of Fab out of the corner of my eye, and the Chief walked up next to her. I knew they were talking but couldn't hear anything they said, so I didn't know if the line had been disconnected.

"You cost me a good deal, and you're going to be making it up to me," Trigger snarled. "The way I see it, we each have something the other wants."

"You'll have to be more specific."

"I'm making you an offer on the apartment building that you recently acquired, one I'm certain you'll accept." He pulled a dollar bill out of his shirt pocket and flicked it at me.

"Your offer is woefully under market, and unless you have something to sweeten the pot immeasurably, I'm not interested."

Trigger stood. "You'll be getting a call in a day or two, and it's imperative that you follow directions. As for your friend, she's not invited to this meeting."

"I'm not going anywhere unless I know there's something in it for me."

"My guess is that there's a bit of gambler in you, and you'll do as you're told. Otherwise, you'll never know if there could've been a different outcome."

Fab burst through the door and knocked into him, which almost took both of them down. Trigger managed to keep them upright.

"Sorry, Seymour. Good to see you, though," Fab cooed, then bent down and handed him his phone, which had fallen on the deck. To me, she said, "When are you going to get that board fixed?"

He leveled a glare at both of us, turned, and left the bar.

Fab reached out and closed the door, then whistled.

Farther down the deck, the Chief and Help

came through the doors of the game room, closed the distance, and sat down. Behind them was one of Cook's relatives, who'd been backing up at the bar, with a tray of drinks in hand.

"That was an intense conversation," I said to the Chief. "Seymour's attitude is that he's untouchable."

"Heard every word." The Chief filled Help in. "Trigger's been running his criminal enterprise without a lot of scrutiny, and he's gotten sloppy these last few months. He's in for a rude awakening."

"I suppose you heard about last night's adventure," I said to the Chief. "Frankly, it was boring."

"You need to stay away from there," the Chief said gruffly. "The last thing law enforcement wants is for the occupants of that warehouse to get wind they're under surveillance and disappear. You get caught again, and if you're lucky, you'll get locked up until the investigation is over, and if not, you'll be killed."

"Are the warehouse operation, our missing husbands, and Trigger all intertwined?" I asked.

"I can tell you that your husbands are still alive and we want to keep them that way. So let law enforcement do what they're trained to do." The Chief's intense stare bored into me until I squirmed.

"So Fab and I are supposed to sit around and wait for the phone to ring?" I asked.

"That's exactly what you're supposed to do. Tomorrow, you're both going to be given trackers so I can keep tabs on you. When this meeting with Trigger goes down, you'll be mic'd. Since we're not certain what the man is up to, we need to plan for contingencies, and it would be helpful if you didn't go off the rails. Help and I have already figured your friend into the equation, as both of us know she never does what she's told and can't imagine her waiting patiently at home. We'll utilize her bodyguarding skills."

"If the next meeting is going to be last-minute, like Trigger suggested," Fab said. "It can't be about cash."

"Even he knows that banks can't accommodate a large withdrawal without notice," Help said.

"He made it clear in his uncommunicative way that he wants the apartment building. I'm thinking his plan is for me to sign it over to him. That might fly if it didn't have a mortgage, but it does because I immediately refinanced and my lender will want their money."

"If it's his game to strong-arm you into signing over the property, he's got to have a title company in his pocket to pull that off," the Chief said.

"Maybe he plans on paying off the loan," I said. The look on the Chief's face said Trigger probably had something illegal planned.

Fab's phone rang, and she answered, "Uh-huh?"

I stared at her. She obviously didn't want us to know who was on the other end. So much for her putting the call on speaker. The conversation was short, and she ended with, "Good job." She made eye contact with all of us. "Seymour has a second set of digs just off the Overseas in the middle of town. There are a couple of problems. One is that the manse sits on the water and it's not easily seen from the highway; you have to know where to turn, and it isn't marked. Second: good luck getting past the security gate." Fab's phone pinged.

"We've got a list of addresses for the man but missed that one," the Chief said. "Send it to me."

"The title to the property is held in a corporate name, but my source says he lives there and said source has never let me down," Fab told him. "Same source told me that Trigger doesn't own zip in his own name."

Cook rolled a cart through the game room doors. The men exchanged hellos and engaged in conversation.

I leaned forward and asked Fab, "How did you get that?"

"When I knocked his phone out of his hand, I planted a tracking device smaller than a pea on the bottom."

"Nice job." I smiled at her. "Xander doing all this?"

Fab shook her head. "I contacted an old acquaintance of ours and reminded him that he owed me a favor. He said he hadn't had an interesting job in a while and was all in."

"I'm thinking the food is safe to eat, since Cook and the Chief are friends." I eyed the plate as Cook set it in front of me, and he laughed.

Chapter Thirty-Eight

My phone rang the very next day, and my unknown caller was on the line.

It was Fab's idea to move to The Cottages and not have the lag time of getting to the Hummer, especially if there were eyes on the property. Thus far, we'd spotted plenty of late-night traffic in the neighborhood and didn't know what to make of that, since the cars drove the block slowly a couple of times and didn't come back.

When we began parking the SUV in the space out front, I told Mac that the unit was not to be rented, in case we needed it. So we had a place to hang out while we waited. I was dressed and ready to leave on a moment's notice, and that included being outfitted with two tracking devices. Fab had downloaded the tracking app on her phone and amused herself testing it out, ordering me to walk this way and that.

"I'm not going to be sitting here in this cottage like a crappy friend while you have all the fun," she'd grouched.

"You'd never allow that to happen." I laughed. "I'm telling you now that I'm not agreeing to anything until there's a swap arranged. They don't need to know that I'd do anything to get the guys back. I'm going to try to get some kind of assurance from whoever calls. We still don't have proof of life from the kidnappers — only from the Chief, and I take him at his word. It would be nice if he didn't have to be so tight-lipped."

"I'm surprised he's told us anything. I got the impression that everything's tied into Trigger. I hope there's not something else going on that we're totally out of the loop on."

Help approached the cottage from the beach and peered in the window, waving like a crazy man. He jiggled the handle before opening the door and barging in. "Got anything new?"

"The only reason you didn't get shot is because I watched your approach." Fab made a trigger finger. "Not a very smooth entrance."

I ignored the two of them smirking at one another. "I'm ready to go." I'd chosen workout pants that had a pocket along the side of my thigh the right size for a small Beretta. The first time I wore them, Fab deemed them ugly, but when she found out about the pocket, she ordered herself a couple pairs. "We were just talking, and I feel like I'm reacting instead of acting from a position of strength."

"You know I can't disclose everything I know, but I can tell you that Seymour's definitely your man," Help said.

"He hates that name, which is why it's fun to

call him that just to see his face get all blotchy and red," I said.

"Hold on, more opinion coming." Help gave me a cheesy grin, which I knew was to lighten the tension. "In regards to the property, Trigger has to know that for him to enforce any kind of claim, whatever he's planning has to be legal."

"We're talking a lot of cash for him to make that happen," I said.

"Not sure why he thinks you're a pushover and will do what you're told," Help said.

"That's because I haven't put up a bit of resistance so far. But then, I haven't been given the opportunity," I said.

"Madison goes to this meeting and no husbands, then what?" Fab asked.

"If that's Trigger's game, then I expect he'll kill me," I said. "He can't leave me alive. Any of us. We're all witnesses to his crime." I turned to Fab. "If something goes awry, watch your back."

"I can tell you that Trigger is going down," Help said. "Right now, there's a dozen pair of eyes on him, watching his every move. He's going to be stopped. Also know that there will be eyes on your every move, and nothing is going to happen to you."

"You're acting shifty." Fab eyed Help. "Cough up what you know that we don't."

"This information is to ease your mind, not for you to act on. A big bust is going down. There's a big meeting of all the dealers in the area, and all the shakers will be in attendance. So, what better time?"

"That sounds like a really bad idea to me." I managed to stop myself from rolling my eyes. "Send out invites to your criminal associates to socialize in one place. Aren't they sitting ducks for not only law enforcement but anyone who wants to remove the competition? If I were a criminal, I'd pass. Give me a call on a burner phone that I'll toss once I disconnect."

"If the cops get lucky, it'll be a who's who of criminals," Help said.

My phone rang. I glanced at the screen and started the recorder before answering.

"Get in your car, pull into the convenience store around the corner, and wait for the next call," a male voice barked and hung up.

Fab grabbed the recorder and hit replay a couple of times. "It wasn't the same man as before."

"It's clear I'm being watched," I said. "Kind of surprised they didn't ambush me like they did our husbands."

Help picked up his phone, made a call, and was out the door before either of us could say, "Just put it on speaker." He left the door open, and Fab took that as an invitation to stand in the doorway and eavesdrop.

It heartened me to know that there were numerous officers involved in this case. I just wished that more details had been shared with

Fab and me.

I hugged Fab before she could get away. "You better keep up."

"If I had my choice, we'd be walking into this with our own plan in place. Because we know how to wing it, and this is one of those situations. Whatever happens, do not get hurt. The guys would agree."

I didn't give voice to, *There might not be any way to avoid it.* I grabbed my purse and walked out to the SUV, got behind the wheel, and cruised to the end of the driveway. It would have been hard not to notice the big pickup truck in the middle of the street, blocking traffic if there'd been any. Instead of attempting to pull around it, which would have taken the paint off the side of the Hummer, I turned in the opposite direction and wasn't surprised when it followed me. I described the truck into my mic.

"I'm here," I said, pulling into the parking lot and stopping beside the store. Minutes later, my phone rang. I answered and pressed the record button. "Texting you the address. You have five minutes to show up." The call disconnected. I checked my messages and read the address out loud as I entered it into the GPS. Looking at the overview map, I knew the next location was on the outskirts of town. "I'm feeling less brave."

A minute later, Fab said in my ear, "It's a small strip mall. I count three doors and no signage."

"Last time we were at one of those places, wasn't there a shootout?" I asked.

Fab laughed. "I don't know how we get so lucky with all the hair-raising jobs."

I pulled up to the dilapidated building and parked. "I'm guessing it's not the liquor store. Thinking it's the title company."

"You listen to me," Fab ordered. "If it comes down to you or whoever—shoot. If I have to sneak you out of the country, I can do that."

"I'm glad you're here." I got out and walked to the door, found it locked, and knocked.

A forty-something woman poked her head out. "Madison Westin?"

I nodded, and she pushed the door open, ushering me inside. The office was more upscale than the exterior would have led you to believe. The two offices and reception area were small and painted all white, with splashes of turquoise used sparingly. A quick glance around told me that we were the only two in the office, unless Trigger was hiding in the bathroom.

My first tip that the woman knew this wasn't a straight-up deal was that she hadn't introduced herself. She tugged on her ill-fitting suit, stray hairs coming loose from her blond bun, and her beady eyes danced. She led the way through the closest door and waved me over to the small conference table in the corner of the office.

"Will Seymour be joining us?" I asked once we were both seated.

Her eyes jumped at my use of his birth name. "I'll be calling him as soon as we've concluded the transaction."

"I'm not signing flip until you produce my husband and his best friend." I heard, "Take a breath," in my ear.

"I don't know what you're talking about," the woman lied through her teeth.

I had plenty of experience with liars, and she wasn't even very good, squirming in her chair, unable to make eye contact.

"Then you need to get Seymour on the phone," I said.

She fiddled with the file she'd placed in front of her and flicked through the pages while she came to a decision. Then she handed me the sales contract for the apartment building and, at the same time, picked up her phone and made a call, I assumed to Seymour.

"Ms. Westin is expecting her husband." After a pause, she handed me the phone.

"Do you want them back alive?" a man barked and didn't wait for an answer. "Sign the damn paperwork." He hung up.

I ran my finger down the front of the contract; it appeared to be in order. "Are you aware that there's a loan on the property that needs to be satisfied for this transaction to be legal? A signed contract without the payoff doesn't mean anything." What it did mean was a lawsuit by the bank and ensuing court battle, which Trigger would lose.

"That's not your problem."

I signed the contract, initialed where indicated, and pushed it back at her. My eyes widened when she pushed another contract at me. After one quick glance, I blurted, "Trigger wants The Cottages?" I jumped up, catching her off guard, and grabbed the other folder back, shoving it under the one I already had. "This isn't going according to plan," I said for Fab's benefit, getting a confused look from the woman across the table. I pulled my Berretta and pointed it at the middle of her forehead. "I might feel bad about using such a high-handed tactic, pointing a gun at an unarmed woman, but since I'm fairly certain that you're up to your eyeballs in this crime, it doesn't bother me a bit to tell you it's your turn to do what I say or risk having your brains blown all over the wall behind you." I don't know whose hiss was louder, hers or Fab's. "This may not look all that powerful, but it packs the same punch as its bigger sibling." I waved my gun.

"I didn't have any choice," the woman stuttered.

"Get on the phone and tell Trigger that the paperwork is signed and it's a done deal. Now."

"He'll kill me."

"I hate to be the bearer of not-so-great news," I said, my tone telling her I felt just the opposite, "but he was going to kill you anyway. Old Trig can't have you alive and blabbing. You were only going to stay alive as long as you were useful. My way, you get a head start on running for your life." I made a popping sound that had her jerking in her chair. "Your choice." I motioned toward her phone. "Make the call. Tip him off, and you're dead."

She picked up her phone and stared at my gun as she made the call. "Mr. Trigger, the papers have been signed."

I motioned for her to hand me the phone.

"It's official," she continued. "Both properties are now yours. Ms. Westin would like to speak to you." She thrust the phone at me.

"Where can I pick up the two men you kidnapped?" I knew before I asked that I wasn't getting what I wanted. If Creole and Didier didn't come back alive, how I could've handled this differently would haunt me.

The woman showed no response, which reinforced my certainty that she knew from the start what was going down.

"You really are a dumb bitch. First you steal from me, and now you think you're getting what you want? Think again." The line went dead.

I dropped the phone on the floor and crushed it under my foot. "I can't have you calling him and boo-hooing that you're a victim."

"You're dead," the woman threatened.

"That's not news. I already know that. But I'm

not the only one." I trotted out my creepiest smile and opened both folders, ripping the sales contracts to pieces as the woman hissed and clawed to get them back. I shoved them back in the folder, stood, and opened the back door. Four plainclothes law enforcement officers, bulked up in body armor with badges clipped to their belts, crowded inside. "What now?" I asked.

One of the officers motioned me outside.

"The Chief isn't happy that you went off script," Fab said in my ear.

"That's too bad." My voice dripped with sarcasm. I backed up to the wall and waited.

An officer walked over and asked for my version of what went down.

I hit the highlights. "Don't you know all this, or weren't you the one listening in?"

He ignored my question. "It's a crime to threaten someone with a gun." A slight smirk twisted at the side of his mouth.

"It's also a crime to aid and abet a kidnapping." My voice caught, and I struggled not to let the tears that threatened at the back of my eyes spill down my cheeks.

"Hang in there." He patted my shoulder. "We know what we're doing, and this ain't over yet."

I nodded.

Pop, pop, pop echoed nearby. A spray of bullets ricocheted off the front of the building, sounding like a machine gun, and it went on for what seemed like ever. Then silence.

At the first pop, the cop pushed me to the ground.

Moments later, a loud boom rocked the parking lot. I managed to scramble to my knees and leap behind the nearby dumpster, throwing myself to the ground.

"You better be okay," Fab shouted in my ear.

"Get me out of here," I whispered.

"Whoever set the explosion didn't know what they were doing if they planned on blowing up the entire building." Fab appeared to have a perfect view of the action. "The front caved in, and the side of the building looks ready to crumble."

The cop got to his feet and came to stand over me. "You hurt?" I shook my head. He extended his hand and helped me to my feet, then ushered me to an unmarked car and into the backseat.

I was driven to the station by a different officer, who confided that they'd sent a decoy to my car, and that's when the shooting started.

"The officer?" I asked.

"Not a scratch," he said proudly. "She's tougher than I am."

I let out a long sigh of relief.

At the station, they hit me with minimal questions, and I was released. When I walked out of the station, Fab was waiting in the parking lot. I slid into the front seat of the Falcon.

"It's been suggested in the strongest terms that we keep a low profile," Fab said. "As in stay home until all parties involved in this case are in custody."

"One of those parties better be Trigger. When he finds out that not only didn't he get the property but I got away, it's going to be war."

Chapter Thirty-Nine

Fab drove us back to her house and hid the Falcon in the garage.

I hit the shower and stayed for so long, I was surprised that I didn't drain all the hot water. Not having a clue how what was left of the day and night would go, I put on another workout outfit and slid my Berretta into the side pocket. I ventured down the hall and found Fab and Help sitting at the kitchen island. "Please, tell me you have news."

"I didn't tell you this," Help said, "but the bust is going down tonight. I've got the two of you under surveillance, which means you won't be doing anything impulsive. Agreed?"

"You know we can take you," I told him, feeling certain it was true, but only if we hit him from behind.

Fab laughed and got up, pulling a drink cup with a straw out of the refrigerator and setting it in front of me.

I licked my lips and sucked down half of the strawberry lemonade. "So yum. Not sure how you made this happen, but thank you."

"It was our guard here. He asked for a couple

of hints, and then produced."

"And you got a triple espresso with extra caffeine?"

Fab turned her nose up, and I laughed.

"*Merci bon jour.*" I smiled at Help. "So swell of you."

"That's a new one for butchering the French language," Fab said.

"We all have our talents," I said. "Now would be a good time to pool any information we have on Trigger, such as addresses, in case he ends up eluding the cops like he's done in the past."

"Trust me on this one; it's not happening this time," Help said. "More information I didn't share: Trigger got the call from the title office and drove straight to the warehouse. That's where he's at, and the perimeter is surrounded."

"The warehouse," I mused. "Is that where the guys have been all this time? Do you even know if they're alive? If so, for how much longer? How do I live with their deaths on my conscience?"

"They're alive, and we've got men in place to make sure they stay that way," Help reassured me.

"I'm surprised you know so much when you're no longer on the force," I said.

"When's the bust going down?" Fab asked.

"Soon," Help said.

"Could you be more vague?" I snapped.

"Actually, yes, and it's all I'm going to say on the subject. You're lucky I said anything at all, and I only did it to keep you from worrying. When it's over, we'll get a call, and anyone held will be transported to the hospital to be checked out."

The afternoon dragged on. None of us were hungry. We sat in the living room as Help took his job of not taking his eyes off either of us seriously.

It was early evening when Help's phone rang, breaking the silence. He answered and, after a few cryptic words, hung up. "Creole and Didier are alive and were taken to Tarpon Cove Hospital." He stood up. "You want me to drive?"

Fab and I grabbed our bags and raced out of the house, Help hot on our heels. She'd opened the garage from inside, and we piled into the Mercedes. She flew out of the driveway, tires squealing against the pavement, and when we got to the main highway, she slowed only slightly and took the direct route. She parked at the emergency entrance.

The hospital had become a familiar place of late. The emergency room must have been having a slow night, as there were only two other people sitting in the chairs, and they looked bored. The backside of a nurse disappearing around the corner was the only action in the long corridor that led to the cubicles.

The woman sitting at the reception desk handled us with calm efficiency. She directed Fab to Didier's room, and she took off in a run.

I gave myself a stern shake, warding off the panic that threatened to suck me in. I took a deep breath, closed my eyes, and counted to three, knowing that I needed to get myself under control to face Creole. The nurse gave me the room number, and I hustled in the same direction as Fab. "I'm about to crack under the guilt; I know this is my fault," I told Help, who'd followed me.

"You're being too hard on yourself. I'm going to go check in with the Chief. You need anything, I'm not going anywhere."

I gave him a quick hug. "Thank you." I entered Creole's room and skidded to a stop. The bed was gone.

I almost missed seeing the nurse on the computer in the corner as panic set in. I approached her, and she turned. "I'm Creole's wife."

"He's been taken for x-rays. You can stay in here or in the waiting room, and I'll come find you when he gets back."

"I'll stay." I sat in an uncomfortable chair in front of the window. "Can you tell me how he's doing?"

"You'll have to wait for the doctor," she said and left.

The room was dark, with only one light shining in the corner. I texted Help that I was waiting for Creole to be wheeled back from x-ray, and if he needed to find me, I'd be in

Creole's room. On a whim, I walked back to the reception desk. "Do you have a Casio Famosa here?"

The woman checked her computer and rattled off the room number.

"Thank goodness," I sighed, thinking about Casio's kids and how happy they were going to be. I retraced my steps back down the hall and realized I'd passed his room a couple of times, not knowing he was inside. Before going in, I told Creole's nurse where I'd be when he came back. I pushed the door open.

Casio was sitting up in bed. He turned, a big grin on his face. "Damn, it's good to see you, Red. Had my doubts a couple of times that… Never mind… didn't happen. My kids driving you crazy?"

I walked over to the bed and hugged him. "It's really good to see you, you big oaf."

"Loving the sweet talk."

I backed up and grabbed a chair, pulling it over next to the bed. "You don't look like you're on death's door. So, that's good."

"It would take a lot to kill my big ass. If the tests check out, and the doc thinks they will, then I'm blowing out of here." Casio continued to grin. "Can't wait to hug my kids."

"You've got great kids, Casio. I fell for them, and every day was nerve-wracking and fun."

"But…?"

I knew I was going to wipe the smile off his

face, but it couldn't be helped. I told him what had gone down, including the details about my trip to Brick's office, which had him smirking. I told him about Alex's housebreak and how that ended. I didn't leave out a detail.

"That bitch," Casio barked. "I know Maya thought I was the worst excuse for a father, because she was quite vocal about it, ready to rant on and on to me and anyone else who would listen. But I never thought she'd stoop so low as to steal my kids, or that my fat-ass brother would let her get away with it."

"I told Brick I had your power of attorney, but that barely registered… or it did and he didn't care. I swear, had I known about the court hearing, I'd have shown up. It still might have turned out the same, but I'd have been able to prepare the kids."

Casio stared at the ceiling, growling his frustration.

"The kids are going to be ecstatic to see you. They think you hung the moon, and I'm sure it's because you've told them so often enough."

"I'm retiring. Not sure what I'm going to do, but for a while, I'm going to be a full-time dad and make this cluster-f— up to my kids."

"Your kids knew you were on a quest to save the world and why you had to leave. I'm thinking camping at Disney World is a great way to make it up to them." I raised my eyebrows.

"I'm not going to confess that their dad is full

of it about the camping. I'll book a fun theme hotel room, and hopefully, they won't remember."

"They're going to love every minute they spend with you, no matter what you do." I smiled. "I'm certain that this is official business for official folks, but what the heck happened?"

"Before Creole and Didier showed up, Trigger was already paranoid, not sure who was watching him and about to rat him out. Someone close to him fingered two men as snitches, and they were dead before they could defend themselves. He pulled a gun and dropped them where they stood. Surprised me. I thought he had others do all his dirty work."

"That must have been unnerving," I said.

"Situation got even more tense when Trigger's boys showed up with Creole and Didier. The two were locked in a room for a day, and then separated. Not sure what that was all about. Trigger left specific orders. He was adamant that no one except a couple of handpicked men have any contact with them." Casio drifted off for a moment. "It was like there was something more in it for him, but I never found out what it was. Kept his cards held tight."

"What do you know about Creole's condition?"

"Head injury of some sort, and it's unclear how he got it. We'll have to get the details from him."

I told him about the real estate deal and that I'd thought, based on the last phone call, that they were already dead.

"Trigger stepped into the warehouse, and a minute later, the bust went down. Most of the men put their hands in the air and went peacefully, but there were a handful that tried to make a run for it. Trigger pulled his weapon and was dropped where he stood."

"I should have at least a scintilla of sympathy, since he was a human being and all, but I don't. I'm damn happy to know I won't have to be looking over my shoulder while he barks orders from behind bars. Worse yet, be forced to move away from my family to parts unknown."

The nurse stuck her head in the door. "Your husband has been moved to a room on the ninth floor."

I didn't ask any questions, knowing that she'd only refer me to the doctor. I said to Casio, "How are you getting home?"

"Car's probably in impound."

"Alongside mine." I hadn't had a chance to check on its condition after the explosion and hoped it fared well. "One of your comrades, Help, is here. I'd give you a more legit name, but I don't know what it is." I did, but I'd promised not to divulge it.

"I know who you're talking about. Crazy ass loves that moniker. If he could figure out a way not to come off weirder than he is, he'd be saying: 'Help's here.'" Casio punctuated that with an exaggerated wave.

"I'll ferret him out, and he'll give you a ride wherever you want to go. If you want to stay overnight here in the Cove, I can arrange that."

"I never regretted the day we became besties." Casio grinned.

"Except that never happened."

"Oh, come on." He held out his pinkie.

I looped mine around his. "You tell anyone, and I'll deny it."

"Go check on your husband and send Helper my way."

"I'd dare you to call him that, except he'd punch you." I hugged him again. "Anything I can do with regards to the kids—help you drag Maya's body to the Gulf or whatever—let me know."

Chapter Forty

I slowed and looked in the window of Didier's room as I passed. He appeared to be asleep, Fab's head resting on his chest. I wasn't going to bother them. I got directions from the nurse and had to hike down a long, creepy hallway with minimal lighting. There wasn't a single person around, and the hall seemed to go on forever, linking one building to another. Thankfully, when I turned the corner, the bank of elevators I was told to be on the lookout for were just up ahead. I rode one to the ninth floor. Stepping out, I stopped at the nurse's station and, in addition to asking for the room number, asked, "How's he doing?"

"Your husband has a head injury. The good news is that all of his tests came back normal." The nurse smiled reassuringly. "He's currently unconscious, and we're waiting for him to wake up."

I nodded. "Thank you." His room was directly across from the nurse's station. I peeked in the window before pushing the door open. Creole was hooked up to machines, which were humming softly in the background. I took that as a good sign.

I crossed to his bedside and brushed his hair out of his face, kissing his cheek. Then I dragged a chair over and sat as close as I could get. The television on the opposite wall was tuned to a tourist channel for the local area. I hit the mute button.

"You need to wake up so we can get you out of here," I whispered in his ear. "I'm so happy to see you and can't wait until your eyes are open and I can tell you so." I intertwined my fingers with his and laid my head on the mattress.

The nurse came in sometime later to check his vitals, and I jerked awake.

More time went by—I wasn't certain how long, but sitting in the stiff plastic chair made it feel like an eternity—and the doctor finally appeared. He reached for the chart at the end of the bed, acknowledging me in a flat tone, which was a bit unnerving.

I stood and moved out of the way, consciously telling myself to let go of the death grip on my pants. "How's my husband?"

The doctor perused the chart, finally looking up. "We're waiting for him to wake up. He sustained a nasty blow to the head and a few minor scrapes. Your husband is very lucky. The good news is that I don't anticipate any problems." He put the chart back. "You're welcome to stay the night. You can stretch out on one of the couches over there." He pointed towards the window. "You'll find it a lot more comfortable than a chair."

I nodded and thanked him. "I'm going to sit here for a little while longer. I'd like to be by his side when he wakes up." I stretched my neck and walked over to the window. I couldn't make out much in the dark, except several floors of the office building next door that were lit up.

The doctor left, and a nurse came in and took Creole's vitals again. As soon as she left, I retook my seat.

It was another day before Creole woke up. Fab had texted me the night before that Didier had been released, and Help tracked me down to tell me that he was driving Casio back to Miami. I wondered briefly if Brick knew his brother was about to descend on him. I doubted that would go well.

I kept my vigil at Creole's bedside, staring at him, willing him to wake up. Midday, I snuck away and ran home, showered, and grabbed a sandwich on the way back to the hospital. I'd called Mother with the news, and she and Spoon stopped by. He'd delivered a loaner ride and dropped off the keys, and they left right after.

Finally, Creole's fingers twitched in mine, and his eyes popped open. He didn't appear to recognize me. "Madison?" he asked tentatively.

I leapt up and gently kissed his cheek. "So happy you're awake. I'm going to take such good care of you." I hit the nurse's button.

"How are you feeling?" the nurse asked as she walked in and smiled at him.

I moved to the opposite side of the bed, so I could watch as she checked Creole over.

"Everything looks good," she said. "I'll let the doctor know he's awake."

"Anything you want, I'm here. I'm not going anywhere until you're released," I told Creole once the nurse left, running my hand down his cheek.

"I'm feeling out of it. Not sure how I got here," Creole said slowly, looking around.

"You have a head injury. The doctor predicts that there'll be no lasting effects." I kissed his cheek. "Forget about all that and concentrate on getting better so I can take you home."

It was two days later when Creole was released. He was a quieter, more subdued and withdrawn version of his old self, and the doctor passed it off as a result of the head trauma. Creole didn't remember how it happened or any of the events that surrounded it. He knew who I was but little about our relationship. The doctor said that temporary amnesia wasn't uncommon, and it might only be a matter of days before he regained his full memory.

Didier and Brad stopped by every day, and the trio walked on the beach. Within days, Creole went back to the office.

I did my best to suck it up and not hover, to wear my all-is-normal face and try to mean it, since it was clear that he was missing memories of me and our relationship, as well as the rest of his life.

Chapter Forty-One

A month later, it was clear that a different version of Creole had come home from the hospital, and it was as though we were getting to know one another all over again. He still hadn't remembered the events leading up to his kidnapping, being held against his will, or the rescue. He saw the doctor regularly, and after each visit, told me not to worry, that the memories could come back anytime and the doctor was certain it wouldn't be permanent. I missed our easy-going relationship, where I could say anything, and now I caught myself thinking before blurting some inanity or bringing up something that he struggled to remember.

Sitting out on the patio, I looked up from my laptop and caught sight of Didier finishing up a run and pushing an inflatable chair into the water. Creole had gone into the office for an hour or two and promised to bring home pizza for dinner. I tied a gauze skirt around my waist and took off down the steps to the sand. I'd seen Didier several times but hadn't had a moment to talk to him alone.

Didier waved as I approached and got out of the water. He held out his arms, I walked into them, and he enveloped me in a hug.

"I want to apologize for what happened. I accept responsibility for everything that went down. It seems paltry, but I truly am sorry." I struggled to hold back tears.

"*Cherie*, stop with the guilt." Didier stared down at me and tightened his hold. "You were not to blame. There was only one person responsible, and he's dead."

Relief flooded through me like a tidal wave. I didn't realize how badly I needed someone to hold my hand and tell me I didn't suck as a human being. "If I had a do-over…" But sometimes I wondered, if I could do it again, would I make the same choice? If I hadn't bought the building, ignored the potential criminal consequences, what kind of person would that make me?

"Choosing to ignore a drug dealer moving into your quiet neighborhood would've been untenable. Your only other choice would've been to turn a blind eye to what was going on right under your nose. How would you keep all those tenants that you've taken responsibility for safe?" Didier untied another chair and pulled it into the water and helped on to the one, he sat on the other.

"You're amazingly sweet about all this."

"I'll share something with you that I haven't

even told Fab. I tried to talk to Creole, but he doesn't want to talk about the kidnapping."

"I don't bring it up for the very same reason. I think he's frustrated, trying to remember, and it's eluding him." I kicked at the water, which had a calming effect.

"I overheard a conversation between two of the kidnappers, and they were talking about how long they'd had the plans for the kidnapping in place. They didn't know what the holdup was and were beginning to think it wasn't going to happen. It was planned long before you negotiated the deal for the apartment building."

"I don't know if Fab told you, but Trigger also wanted The Cottages signed over. It surprised me that he wanted both properties and was cocky enough to think he'd get them." I was relieved to know that there was nothing I could have done to prevent the kidnapping from happening; it had all been about Trigger expanding his base of operations. "Any clue how he figured out I was the buyer?"

"Bought off a clerk in the recorder's office."

"I'm happy he's dead."

"Don't feel guilty about expressing that sentiment. Fab and I feel the same. As, I'm sure, does Creole."

"Creole and I are lucky to have you and Fab as friends. Your wife stood by my side when most would've passed blame and ended the friendship. I couldn't have gotten through it without her support." I paddled over and hugged him.

Didier jumped into the water and swam over to the floating dock, opening a storage box and dragging out a small basketball hoop, throwing it on the water. He tossed me the beach ball. I got the first shot. I laughed, swam after it, and tossed it to him.

* * *

A week later, I got a frantic phone call from Mac. One of the guests had fallen in his unit and was demanding to speak to the owner. I drove straight over and knocked on the door. A short, weasel-faced, thirty-something stuck his head out the opening. "Ms. Westin?" I nodded, and he threw the door open and shoved papers at me, which fell to the ground. "You're served." He hoofed it down the driveway and out of sight. I bent down and picked up the documents, knowing it was legal, however inelegantly done.

Mac had walked up on my heels, head hanging over my shoulder as we scanned the documents. Casio Famosa, plaintiff. Brick and Maya Famosa, defendants. The latter had me smiling. Casio was suing to get back custody of his children. I'd wondered how the kids were doing, now that they were back with their dad, but hadn't had time to call. It hadn't occurred to me that it would take a court order to get Maya to relinquish the children.

After I was served, Casio paid me an unannounced visit, managing to arrive just as Creole was leaving. I wondered if he'd been watching the house but didn't ask. Creole, who'd tolerated him in the past because they'd worked together, ignored him. When Casio stopped by after he'd left the hospital, Creole told the man that I'd done enough for him and to take care of his own problems. Casio couldn't care less what people thought of him and told me not to give my husband's "a-hole-ish-ness" a thought. It saddened me to hear that his little family hadn't been reunited… yet. I was certain that one of the strikes that would be used against Casio was that he left the children in my care. I was certain to need my wits about me.

Creole wasn't happy that I was involved in the case and suggested that I ignore the subpoena.

"I don't want to go to jail," I said testily.

Since we both knew that not showing up wasn't an option, we agreed not to talk about the case.

I got up early on the morning of my court appearance and dressed in a conservative, knee-length long-sleeved black knit dress, paired it with low heels, and chose a watch as my only accessory. I'd hoped that Creole would wake up and offer to go with me. Instead, he rolled on his side and went back to sleep. I got ready to leave and kissed him. "I'll call on the way home," I told him.

By the time I got the call to show up, the trial had been going on for a day and a half, and I hoped to get in and out in one day and not have to make the long drive to Miami by myself again. I was spoiled, always having someone to ride along.

I found a parking space in front of the courthouse, raced up the steps, and easily found the courtroom. Knowing I wouldn't be able to sit inside the courtroom until I was done with my testimony, I hurried inside and checked in with Casio's attorney, then left to cool my heels in the corridor.

It was late morning when I got called to testify.

I raised my right hand and swore to tell the truth, then sat in the box, making eye contact with Maya Famosa, who shot hate darts from her eyes. I wondered if that was a trick I could learn. Brick never looked up from whatever held his attention. Casio sent me an encouraging smile.

The attorney for Maya's side stood and asked the judge to declare me a hostile witness.

"Why don't you ask a couple of questions first, and we'll see how it goes?" the judge told him in a tone that announced to everyone he was out of patience.

"Did you shoot at Brick Famosa?" the lawyer asked.

The fun stuff right out of the gate. It would have put me off my game if I hadn't gotten a heads up from Casio that the office incident would probably come up.

"You mean the time I saved Brick's life? A man was holding Brick at gunpoint, attempting to rob him of cash and a car. The bullet might have whizzed by Brick as I shot the man in the shoulder. I'm pretty sure I saved Brick's life, as the man intended to leave him for dead." Okay, I'd had to dig back in history for that one, but everything I said was true.

The lawyer held up Brick's Businessman of the Year Award. "Isn't this your handiwork?" He pointed to the hole in the middle.

"There was another time in Brick's office and my partner was with me—I believe that we saved his life then, too. Was it then?" I asked Brick. Lucky me, I'd shot at the thing twice.

"I ask the questions," the lawyer snapped.

"Yes, sir." I struggled to keep my emotions under control and refrain from telling him what I thought of him. It was hard to figure out from Casio's grin how I did.

"How about we skip to your most recent visit—the one right after the kids had to be taken from your custody?"

"It's hard to remember the exact events. I was distraught that the kids were removed, crying at the top of their lungs, screaming to stay. I thought our chat went well, all things considered. Don't you?" I glared at Brick. "Sorry, I forgot about the question thing. I promise not to do that again." It surprised me that the lawyer hadn't asked more specific questions; he must have skipped that class in lawyer-wannabe school. It also wouldn't surprise me if Brick had been less than forthcoming with any information he coughed up.

"How many guns do you own?"

"Half a dozen, and every single one of them is licensed and locked up. I also have a carry permit."

"Just answer the question."

"I personally own six," I said.

"What makes you qualified to take care of four kids?"

"I've been a family friend for a number of years. Casio confided that his wife thought, if there were ever a need, that I'd be the perfect person to ask. I do love kids," I threw in, and the lawyer's brows went up, so he wasn't impressed.

"Do you have kids of your own?"

"Not yet. My husband and I talk about having eleven."

The lawyer rolled his eyes and sat down.

The judge coughed.

Casio's attorney stood, a woman with a sly look on her face. "How many times have you been shot at while working for Brick Famosa?"

"Dozens of times," I said. "Between the strip joint, pawn shop, and used car lot, it's dangerous not to strap on a gun when he calls about one problem or another."

The opposing side shot up. "I object."

The judge called them up, and after a short discussion, Casio's attorney walked up and smiled. It made me want to look over my shoulder.

"When the kids stayed with you, how did they spend their days?"

"They were home-schooled in the mornings by a retired college professor from a prestigious California college. Afternoons, I had activities planned. They went to an alligator farm, joined a reading group at the library, took a cooking class, and learned dog walking, in case they need a side job sometime. In addition to swimming, we played sports on the beach and shot hoops."

"Sounds like a good time."

"Me and my husband, a retired Miami police detective, enjoyed every minute with them."

She questioned me about their leaving.

"I was never notified of the court date, and had I known, I'd have shown up. The court might very well have ruled the same way, but it would have given me time to arrange to turn them over in a less traumatic way. Having the kids dragged off like they were common criminals was a little much. They'd also have gotten to take their personal belongings, which their aunt and uncle refused to let me send with them."

Finally, I was dismissed. As I got off the witness stand, Casio shot me a thumbs up. I managed to walk sedately out of the courtroom. Once in the corridor, I power-walked back to the car, called Creole, and told him I was on my way home.

Chapter Forty-Two

It surprised me that Creole wanted to go to the big party Fab was throwing at her house. He'd admonished me to stop hovering and reminded me that sometimes it took more time than expected to recover from a head injury. I decided to look on the bright side and see it as a good thing that he wanted to spend time with family and friends when the unexpected was known to happen at our gatherings.

Fab had organized the gathering so we could be updated on the case, and had also invited the Chief and Help. Though they'd both retired from the force, their old connections had continued to keep them informed and in the middle of everything.

I'd called Fab a few days before the party. "Do you mind if I invite more people?"

"How many?"

"Six." Fab wasn't often caught by surprise, and I was pleased with myself. "You have that extra table in the garage that could be set up by the pool."

"You do remember this is my house?"

"The perfect place to host this bash. Anything I can do to make this shindig even better than we already know it will be, snap those fingers of yours."

"Don't forget that you offered," she grouched.

"That went well," I said to myself when I hung up. I made two more calls to issue the invites and got enthusiastic responses. I told Creole about my phone calls, and he made it clear he thought I was nuts but chuckled.

Creole and I arrived early, so we could be of help in the preparations.

"You going to get your drunk on and put on a show?" Creole asked.

"I'm going to behave." I winked at him.

He drifted into the kitchen and gave good-natured advice to Didier, who was getting the food prepped for the grill. I went out to the patio, happy that the day had cooperated by dawning sunny and the baby blue sky was dotted with the occasional fluffy cloud.

"The tables are too far apart," Fab said, appearing at my side. I was happy to see that the extra table and chairs had been set up. "Didier informed me that they were where *you* wanted them placed and then laughed."

"How are you enjoying a taste of the high-handedness that I have to put up with from you?" I asked.

"Are you going to tell me who you invited?"

"And ruin the surprise?" I smirked.

Fab let out a long sigh. "Didier and I have a bet about who you invited. I better not lose."

"Something tells me you won't mind so much." I laughed. "I'm basing that on the fact that I haven't had any emergency calls from you."

Fab scanned the patio before answering, spotting Didier and Creole at the barbecue. "I've gotten a couple of business calls and was able to shuffle them off on Toady. Didier's made it clear that he likes that I haven't been working. I did warn him that it was only a short break and not permanent. I'm worried that he's not going to want me to go back to work at all. I only took the break because I wanted to nurse him back to health. Since I stayed home, so did he, and we set up office space at the kitchen island."

"I've been playing nurse as much as Creole will let me. I think my husband would like me to go back to work, as I've had a tendency to anticipate what he might want next and he's over it," I said. "I've been working from home and checking in on my businesses by phone, and there hasn't been any major drama."

Fab once again looked over her shoulder before saying, "I'm ready to go back to work."

"Me, too."

The short bus rolled into the driveway, little faces pressed against the glass, plus a few extras. Spoon pulled in next to the bus. He'd arranged for anyone that wanted a ride to meet at his and

Mother's condo and loaded up his Escalade with family, which included Caspian, and a couple of stragglers.

"How many kids did you invite?" Fab hissed in my ear. "And him?" Her eyebrows disappeared into her hairline.

"Calm your shorts. There's five kids and a wrangler. You know…" I made a roping motion over my head.

"You've got bugs in your head."

"Crum was the perfect choice. The kids adore him. Look at him—he made an effort to fit in and aced it."

Fab looked him over from head to toe as he climbed down from the bus. "If he were a complete stranger and I were into grandfathers, he'd be hot. Maybe."

I got minimal resistance when I'd informed him that Mac would be taking him shopping for an outfit and he'd better wear it—shoes and all. Mac had called, excited that she'd taken him to an upscale men's store and gotten him into tropical wear—shorts and shirt and boat shoes.

Casio came next, swinging his daughter to the ground and leaving his sons to jump down on their own. Liam was next, with Mila on his shoulders. She was eager to get down and play with the other kids. Help was behind him.

Caspian and the Chief were in a hot discussion about something as they climbed out of the Escalade, and Brad helped Mother out.

I went around and scooped all the kids into a hug.

"You hug too hard," Alex grouched.

"Please, you can take it; you're a growing boy. You're going to overtake your old man one of these days," I said.

Alex puffed out his chest. "We were all happy to be invited. Not a complainer among us."

"Super happy you're all here."

Casio yelled and indicated he was passing out drinks. The kids ran around until Fab produced the bullhorn and yelled for everyone to take a seat. I'd wondered where it went. She also decreed that there'd be no serious discussion about anything until after we ate.

Help and Liam decided to eat at the kids' table and said they'd be back afterwards. Crum sat at the head of the table, and from the sounds of it, they were having a good time.

Once the dishes were cleared away and the drinks refilled, the kids ran out to the beach and splashed along the shore, Alex in the middle of the fun and Crum keeping an eagle eye out.

"Welcome, everyone," Fab said, and she and Didier toasted the rest of us.

"You ever need a seat-filler at one of your soirees, I'm in." I waved my hand.

"Sorry, I was out of town." Caspian kissed the back of Fab's hand. "I would've flown home had I known about the kidnapping." He clapped Didier on the back.

Fab held up her glass again. "Another toast. To family, and friends that are as close as family. That includes you stragglers." She pointed at Help and the Chief. "That's what Madison calls you."

"Rerr," I said loudly as I mimicked being rolled over by something heavy.

Everyone laughed.

"Time for updates, new news, and anything shocking." Fab pointed at the Chief with a smirk.

"Good news—Trigger's dead. All of you knew that, but I wanted to say it again." The Chief had transformed from an easygoing guy into someone to be reckoned with in a second. "Turns out he was a paranoid fellow and didn't groom anyone to take his place, and that works in law enforcement's favor. His crew was arrested and is behind bars, and they haven't been able to make bail, which is hefty, so they'll be there until they serve their sentences. Trigger's organization was dismantled, his assets confiscated. The house he owned locally held a stash of cash. Quite an impressive haul." He nodded at Casio. "Good job."

"It was a good case to retire on," Casio said. "For those that don't know, I'm going to be a stay-at-home dad until I figure out what I want to do next."

"The kids must be ecstatic," I said.

"They are. I plan to keep my promise to my wife to raise them right."

The Chief turned to me. "Knowing you, you think this is your fault. You can knock that off. Now."

I smiled lamely, but warmed at hearing his words.

"A showdown was inevitable," the Chief continued. "Trigger wanted those cottages, and I'm certain that you wouldn't have been willing to part with them, even if he'd approached you with a legitimate offer. We also found a list of other properties on the street that he was interested in. He chose that block for some reason and wanted to buy it up."

"The property was left to me by my Aunt Elizabeth, and I don't see a day when I'll entertain the idea of selling it," I said. "I know that most of you don't agree, but it's something I need to do, for her and myself. I know she'd approve."

"Elizabeth would also understand your selling when we're talking about your personal safety," Mother said.

"Trigger's dead, so nothing to worry about there." My tone told everyone "case closed." I felt more than a few sets of eyes flicker my way, but no one said anything.

"You could transfer it into a corporation to hide your identity," Caspian said. "Hire someone to manage it, and you'd be free of day-to-day operations."

"That's a thought," I said noncommittally.

The talk moved to the Boardwalk and how it had, thus far, been highly successful and profitable. The guys bandied around ideas for expansion. It was when the talk turned to the eyesore of the empty warehouses nearby that I tuned back into the conversation.

"I approached Ted Michaels," Brad said. He went on to tell everyone who didn't know it that he was the man who'd wanted me to take the rap for the murder of his brother, who I didn't kill and, oh yeah, was still alive. "One look at me," Brad laughed, "and he knew I was Madison's brother and told me to get lost."

No one knew yet that I'd managed to buy the other building. I'd meant for it to be a surprise for Creole, as it had been his suggestion, but now wasn't the time to make that announcement.

"I've got good news," Casio said. "Got custody of my kids back. My lawyer insists that Madison testifying was good for me, and she held her own."

"I'm very happy for the kids," I said. "They love you, and it shows. I know they're happy."

"There's other news, and it could be bad or good, depending on your perspective," Casio said. "Brick is in the hospital." All eyes shot to him where he sat with a benign look on his face. "Someone beat the stuffing out of him, worked him over pretty good. Sadly, he wasn't able to be of any help to the investigating detectives. Amnesia and all."

Fab and I traded a smirk.

"I never liked the man." Mother looked at Casio, embarrassed, and added, "But that's too bad."

"What she said." Spoon hooked his arm around Mother's shoulders.

"I agree." Casio winked at Mother, which elicited a growl from Spoon.

"Good news all around." Liam smiled cheekily. "I've been accepted to law school and am joining the military in conjunction, with the hopes of serving in the JAG corps."

I started the clapping, and everyone joined in.

"That's impressive," Help said.

"I majored in International Law and had plans all along to join the military. After my service, I'd like to work for the government, if they'll hire me," Liam said.

"You're way too smart for this crowd," Brad said proudly.

I lifted my glass. "Congrats," I said to Liam. Everyone raised their glasses.

"To Creole and Didier," Fab toasted. "Just because."

I turned to Creole and mouthed, *Love you*.

Fab and Didier kissed.

Creole leaned forward and brushed my lips with his.

~*~

PARADISE SERIES NOVELS

Crazy in Paradise
Deception in Paradise
Trouble in Paradise
Murder in Paradise
Greed in Paradise
Revenge in Paradise
Kidnapped in Paradise
Swindled in Paradise
Executed in Paradise
Hurricane in Paradise
Lottery in Paradise
Ambushed in Paradise
Christmas in Paradise
Blownup in Paradise
Psycho in Paradise
Overdose in Paradise
Initiation in Paradise
Jealous in Paradise
Wronged in Paradise
Vanished in Paradise
Fraud in Paradise
Naive in Paradise

Deborah's books are available on Amazon
amazon.com/Deborah-Brown/e/B0059MAIKQ

About the Author

Deborah Brown is an Amazon bestselling author of the Paradise series. She lives on the Gulf of Mexico, with her ungrateful animals, where Mother Nature takes out her bad attitude in the form of hurricanes.

Sign up for my newsletter and get the latest on new book releases. Contests and special promotion information. And special offers that are only available to subscribers.
www.deborahbrownbooks.com

Follow on FaceBook:
facebook.com/DeborahBrownAuthor

You can contact her at Wildcurls@hotmail.com

Deborah's books are available on Amazon
amazon.com/Deborah-Brown/e/B0059MAIKQ

Made in the USA
Las Vegas, NV
21 August 2024